GOD HAS NO GRANDCHILDREN

Kim Kyung-uk

God Has No Grandchildren

STORIES

TRANSLATED BY KANG SUNOK
AND MELISSA THOMSON

 DALKEY ARCHIVE PRESS

Originally published in Korean
by Changbi Publishers, Paju, 2011.

Copyright © 2011 by Kim Kyung-uk
Translation copyright © 2015 by Kang Sunok,
Melissa Thomson
Afterword copyright © 2015, Gwon Hee-cheol

First edition, 2015
All rights reserved.

Library of Congress Cataloging-in-Publication Data

Kim, Kyong-uk, 1971- author.
[Short stories. Selections. English]
God has no grandchildren : stories / by Kim Gyeong-uk ; translated
by Kang Sunok and Melissa Thomson. -- First edition.
    pages cm
    ISBN 978-1-62897-117-0 (pbk. : alk. paper)
    1. Kim, Kyong-uk, 1971---Translations into English. I. Kang, Sunok,
1971- translator. II. Thomson, Melissa, translator. III. Title.

PL992.415.K896A2 2015
895.73'5--dc23

                                        2015030143

LIBRARY OF KOREAN LITERATURE

Partially funded by the Illinois Arts Council, a state agency
Published in collaboration with the Literature Translation Institute of Korea

Dalkey Archive Press publications are, in part, made possible through the
support of the University of Houston-Victoria and its program in creative
writing, publishing, and translation.

Dalkey Archive Press
Victoria, TX / Dublin / London
www.dalkeyarchive.com

Cover: design and composition by Mikhail Iliatov
Printed on permanent / durable acid-free paper

Contents

God Has No Grandchildren

One Monday morning—when, just in the city alone, hundreds of water pipes had frozen and burst—Kim Hyeong-tae stopped in his tracks as he was about to open the door to his real-estate office. There was a hole beside the doorknob and the deadbolt had been unlocked. There were visible burn marks around the hole. He stepped back and looked up at the sign: Silver Star Real Estate. The furrows between his eyebrows deepened. He pushed open the door and hurried inside. His hands reached out anxiously to open the desk drawer. Seven 100,000-won cashier's checks were there, in a neat pile. They were fees for the contract he had signed the previous Friday. He had put them in the drawer because the bank had already closed for the day. He let out a sigh of relief and looked around the office. The gold-plated hole-in-one trophy and the brand new LCD television were still there.

Kim Hyeong-tae flopped down on the sofa and stared straight ahead. The wall in front of him had been stripped bare. Where the land registration map of the neighborhood and plan of the nearby apartment complex used to hang, there was now nothing. He took the telephone directory from under the table, opened it and ran his finger down the page before dialing a number. Not the police, but a locksmith. He scheduled a service call, and then peeled the security company sticker off the door; he had swiped it from a nearby house.

One Monday morning—when, just in the city alone, hundreds of water pipes had frozen and burst—Seo Gap-seon arrived at school early. Only one person was there before her. It was the principal. He arrived first and left last every day. As soon as he got there he would open the door of his office wide. He did this every morning without fail, even in winter. Anyone going to the teachers' workroom had to pass the principal's office. He knew exactly who got to work first and who was last to arrive. Ever since "the incident," Seo Gap-seon made sure she got to work before all the other teachers, but not before the principal. Otherwise, the principal wouldn't know what time she arrived.

She smoothed out her clothes and took a deep breath before passing the principal's office. She turned and greeted him. He was sitting bolt upright behind his desk, holding a newspaper with his arms outstretched, white cotton gloves on his hands. He briefly glanced up over his reading glasses and then immediately turned his attention back to the newspaper.

Seo Gap-seon left the teachers' workroom. Before stepping into the empty classroom, she took a few more deep breaths. It was more bearable now than when it was packed with children. She often caught a glimpse of hell in their vacant eyes. To her, the thirty-two children were thirty-two versions of torment. She had never wished so hard for a year to end, although she would be thrown into the inferno once again when the new school year began. She firmly believed that time heals even the worst wounds, despite what people say about how their merciful God uses time, rather than a cane, to punish mankind.

Being a short-term substitute teacher, Seo Gap-seon didn't even have a cane. She had been taken on only until the regular teacher returned from maternity leave. The students knew this. There was nothing they didn't know. "Children are so simple and naive, aren't they?" Only parents—the root of all sins—say that kind of thing. The children knew what they were doing. They might not be able to explain what they knew, but they knew. The children called Seo Gap-seon "Miss Gap." She was puzzled as to why they were using only part of her given name. Then she realized that behind her back they called her "Miss Stopgap."

Seo Gap-seon's eyes widened as she noticed that the lock had been torn off the classroom door. She walked straight to her desk and checked her drawer, though she never kept anything valuable in it. The student profile cards were missing. She clenched her jaw, sensing that another misfortune had just struck her. Who had stolen them? And why? She didn't want to know; all she cared about was how to keep this from reaching the principal's ears.

One Monday morning—when, just in the city alone, hundreds of water pipes had frozen and burst—Go Man-seok's eyes opened wide as he stood in front of the apartment complex administration office and reached for his key. The keyhole had been reamed out and was now so big you could put a finger into it. The edge of the hole was scorched in places. He flung the door open and went inside. The desk drawer had been pulled out, but the safe was untouched. He turned the dial back and forth and opened the safe. Three bottles of whisky, the golden turtle figurine, three gift packages of red ginseng, and a box of cigars; they were all there. These were gifts he had been given by the construction and interior design companies. The apartment account books, and his private account book—which would be a problem if it were made public—were all there.

The apartments had been brand new two years ago when people had started to move in. Since then, however, one resident after another had filed complaints and requested repairs. Cracks had run up the walls of the underground parking garage, and a number of apartments had leaks in the bathrooms. Eventually, they organized a residents' association and, after a month of haggling with the construction company, persuaded them to provide free repairs for a year. During this one-year period the noise of renovation work never stopped, and it even continued beyond that date because there was such a backlog of repairs. The management company was forced to add a special repair charge to the monthly condo fee. The residents grumbled about it, but Go Man-seok was very pleased with the kickbacks he got for turning a blind eye to the way the construction company was padding out the bills.

Shutting the safe, Go Man-seok took a lottery ticket from the inside pocket of his coat. He had bought it at a convenience store in a neighboring suburb. He had gone there specifically to buy it. That particular store had already sold three winning lottery tickets. He changed the combination of the safe to the numbers of the lottery ticket. Then he started to tidy the desk drawers. The book where he had recorded the residents' parking permits was missing. He looked again, searching every corner of the desk. Knowing that the missing book was of no real value to anyone, he searched all the harder. To no avail. He was more curious to know why it had been taken than who had taken it.

One Monday morning—when, just in the city alone, hundreds of water pipes had frozen and burst—a man made two phone calls. The first was to the courier service he worked for. He said he needed to take the day off because he wasn't feeling well. That was a lie. Strictly speaking, though, it wasn't really a lie, because he never felt well. By late afternoon his legs would swell and his eyes wouldn't focus. Recently, his vision had been blurry even at mid-day. A few days ago when he was crossing the Mapo Bridge everything suddenly went dark. He had stopped his scooter and was immediately assailed by honking and cursing. If the traffic hadn't been so slow, he wouldn't have survived. Taking everything into account, it wasn't a downright lie to say that he didn't feel well. Nonetheless, he had to listen to the manager complain that the office was already shorthanded because of the holiday season and now he was making the situation worse. The manager asked if he could at least come in for the afternoon. He said he was afraid not. That was not a lie. He had something else to do and he had no idea when he would be finished. Does anything that a human starts ever get finished? The man didn't believe people who spoke of having "finished" something. Only the Supreme Being who had created everything could speak in those terms.

The second phone call was to the school. He told them that the girl couldn't go to school because she was sick. That was a lie too. Strictly speaking, however, it was not, because she was always ill. She suffered from asthma and she had a cold that never cleared up. They asked him what the symptoms were exactly. He hadn't prepared himself for the question. He stared at the girl, as if looking for an answer.

The girl had rolled herself into a ball and was lying with her eyes closed, gripping a Barbie doll in her hand. It was a Christmas present that her father had given her the year before last. The man couldn't tell whether the girl was awake or asleep. She would often close her eyes when she was awake, other times she would doze off with her eyes open. The doctor said it was "post-traumatic stress disorder." The man found that name difficult. The doctor said it was also called "PTSD." That was hard too. People in scrubs spoke a complicated language, as if they were afraid they'd lose their authority if ordinary people could understand them easily.

The day before the grocery store owner had stopped him and demanded to know when he would settle his account. The man had protested that they'd never bought things on credit. That was simply not true, the store owner responded. The girl had bought things from the grocery store whenever she felt like it. He didn't know what she was talking about, he said, and then she thrust a thick account book at him. It showed everything the girl had taken; there had been something almost every day. It was all the same type of thing, all sweet snack foods. Chocolate milk, honey-flavored cookies, Canaan chocolate bars, strawberry-flavored caramels, Alps candies ... To him, these words were evocative of something carnal that had permeated an ancient land and destroyed it. The man was incredulous. His granddaughter had never badgered him to buy her anything. He yelled at the woman, saying that she should never have allowed the girl to buy anything on credit. Raising her voice, the woman replied that the girl had said her mother would pay for everything. He was lost for words. His daughter-in-law was dead. After giving birth to the girl, she had been ill for a long time and then finally died. She had been frail even before she got pregnant. She had seemed to him destined for illness.

That night, the man drank—something he hadn't done for a long while—and muttered, "Father, I need to get drunk today. It's like the girl's possessed by demons."

The man hung up the phone and shook the girl by the shoulder. It took him a while to rouse her. Her eyelids fluttered, heavy with sleep.

"You don't have to go to school today," said the man. The girl's blank expression didn't change.

"Let's eat," he said, carrying in the tray table. Rubbing her eyes, the girl moved closer to the table and picked up her chopsticks.

"Aren't you forgetting something?"

The girl closed her eyes and, still holding the chopsticks, put her hands together. The man closed his eyes. "Thank you, Father, for our daily bread," he muttered. They began to eat. Neither of them said a word. The girl had been mute since "the incident" had happened.

She picked at the food and put down her chopsticks.

"When you're taking medicine, you should eat."

The man ladled some soup into the girl's rice bowl, and added an egg that had been cooking in the soup. He burst the yolk with a spoon and the yellow ran down between the grains of rice. The girl stared blankly at it. Then she yawned. Ever since she had started taking the medicine for post-traumatic stress disorder, she would often doze off at a moment's notice, and when she was awake her eyes were always blank.

"You want something yummy on that?"

The girl nodded. He left the tiny room and went to the kitchen where he took a packet from the shelf; he shook it, sprinkling scraps of roasted seaweed and sesame seeds over her bowl. This was a rare treat. He had to get her to eat. She had a difficult task ahead of her. When she had eaten all her rice, the man peeled a banana for her. This was a rare treat too. The girl nibbled away at the banana holding it in both her hands, her eyes darting about anxiously, as if she worried that this unexpected windfall would be snatched from her. She was like a baby monkey that had been abandoned by its troop.

The banana seemed to have made her happy, and she swallowed her pills without the usual protest. She took two blue pills, one red pill and one yellow pill. The blue ones were for asthma, and the other two were for what the man just called "trauma or something." When the man had asked the doctor if the medicine was, in other words, for healing the damaged soul, the doctor took a moment and said, "I suppose one could put it that way." So-called highly educated people would always speak in their snakelike way. Their words were as slippery as eels.

The man took a pill too. It was to lower his blood sugar.

The man showed the girl a series of cards, holding them up one by one. At the top of each 8.5-by-11-inch student profile card was a child's photo. The man watched the girl's eyes carefully. He opened his own eyes wide so that he would be certain to notice when her pupils dilated. He had never looked at the girl's eyes so closely before. He'd always thought they were black, but they were brown. They were the color of terracotta, just like her mother's. One of those pitiable beings whose eyes were not the same color as their hair. The man let out a heavy sigh. He remembered the color of death which he had seen again and again in the tropical country where the French army had been stationed. It was the color of dried blood.

The sight of some of the photos made her pupils dilate and her eyelids quiver. A nightmare played out in broad daylight. A terracotta-colored nightmare. The man set those cards down carefully on his right, as if his right hand wanted to hide them from his left. When she had looked at all fifteen cards the girl began to cry. The man held her in his arms and rubbed her back, singing under his breath.

"You better watch out, you better not cry, better not pout, I'm telling you why, Santa Claus is coming—to town; He's making a list, and checking it twice, gonna find out who's naughty and nice."

He suddenly noticed a sour smell. The girl had thrown up her breakfast: the egg, the seaweed, and the banana. And when she had vomited up everything she had eaten, she went on retching as if she were trying to bring up something more, but nothing came.

The man looked down at the girl. She had fallen asleep again. Wheezing, her body curled up tightly, her thumb in her mouth, she had escaped into sleep. That was how the doctor had explained it when the man told him that the girl did nothing but sleep like a sick animal. The man couldn't understand. He knew people could escape into a jungle or into a foxhole, but he had never heard of anyone escaping into sleep. He asked the doctor what was scaring her and making her want to run away.

"We'll find out what it is," the doctor replied.

When the man went back again a few days later, the doctor showed him a picture. It was a pencil drawing of a cylindrical object lying on its side. Something like the tines of a rake jutted out from each end of the black cylinder. There was a line drawn across the cylinder near one end. The doctor asked the man what the drawing looked like to him. He thought it looked like an electric wire with the insulation peeled back, but he was not sure and hesitated to answer. Then the doctor turned the drawing on its side and said, "This is what the girl drew when I asked her to draw a tree." Was it a tree from another planet? The man had never seen one like it.

The army staff sergeant, who had been to college, said that trees were created to reveal the Holy Spirit to humans. They had seen a tree standing alone, radiant with green, in a forest devastated by heavy artillery fire; the tree remained completely intact like the apparition of a prophet. It was a miracle, and a revelation. The man had knelt down on the ground in front of it. He had taken off his helmet and laid down his flamethrower too. Then he had wept. His tears had been just the beginning of a series of events. Clouds of ash billowing like ghosts; the popcorn-like sound of gunfire; explosions and waves of heat; sharp pain cutting through his spine; red leaves bursting out from his back; and the army surgeon's words: "You're very lucky. You would have been scorched from head to toe if you had been holding the flamethrower."

The tree was a miracle, and a revelation. No, a miracle had taken the form of a tree, and so had a revelation. When he came to after three days in a coma, the man, lying immobile, began to believe what the staff sergeant had said. He had asked the staff sergeant why a tree had one leg and a man had two. "A tree can take root because it has only one leg," the staff sergeant had replied. "A man roams because he has two legs. He wanders about until he dies, and then he is buried beneath a tree, to become a handful of dust." The staff sergeant's words were always puzzling, and he scribbled in a notebook every chance he got. He lost his leg when he was hit by a piece of shrapnel from a grenade, and he was shipped home.

The man stared blankly at the drawing. A black tree. A black tree without a single leaf. Perhaps the child's nightmare had been black, not brown.

"This tree is ill. Maybe long dead. Black signifies death or sadness. She drew roots too, which is unusual. She suffers from anxiety. She didn't draw any leaves, not even one. Barrenness. That means she's been severely damaged. The branches and roots look alike. If you look at the drawing upside down, the black branches look like roots in the ground. It could be interpreted to mean that she is frightened by a phallus."

"A phallus?"

"A penis."

"Are you saying my granddaughter is afraid of a dick?"

"I suppose one could put it that way."

"Why?"

The man had separated three profile cards to the right. Three out of fifteen. He scrutinized them closely, one by one. Each time he stared at one of the photos, the furrows between his eyes deepened. The boys were all smiling the same broad smile, as if they had agreed to it. It was the smile of someone who had never even thought of harming anyone. The most innocent look a ten-year-old could present to an adult. The man became confused. Had the girl reacted to these boys because she liked them, maybe? She moaned, her thumb in her mouth.

"There, there, everything's all right now," the man said quietly, patting her on the back.

On the doctor's instructions, the girl was led into a room where a two-way mirror on one wall meant he and the man could observe from outside. The floor was covered in brightly colored mats, and an entire wall of shelves was filled with boxes of toys.

Standing outside, the man watched as the girl and a woman in scrubs played with dolls. The woman held a Ken doll and started a conversation with the girl's Barbie. The girl made the Barbie's head turn from side to side. The Barbie was pointing at something. It was a plastic basket overflowing with dolls. Each time the woman picked a doll out of the basket, the girl's Barbie shook its head. Then, when the woman held up a doll that looked like a young boy, the Barbie nodded. Now the boy doll started a conversation with the Barbie. The girl grabbed the boy doll, her face growing rigid. The boy doll was lifting the Barbie's skirt and putting his hand up it. This time it was the woman's face that grew rigid. The girl took two more boy dolls out of the basket.

The student information cards listed every detail about the child whose photo appeared in the top corner: address, phone numbers, parents' names and occupations, siblings, friends, and the child's dream job. The boys all lived in the same apartment complex. The man jotted down the numbers of their apartments on a scrap of paper. It was the new apartment complex that people had started to move into two years ago, called Something-or-other Palace. A new development built where an old, but fairly acceptable community had been demolished to make way for the new.

The one-room houses where the man lived were going to be replaced by a new planned community soon. Two weeks had passed since the eviction date that had been posted by the local authority. The gas had been cut off two days ago. A rumor that they would soon cut off the electricity had reached his steep narrow alley. If the man still refused to leave after that, they would cut off the water. So as to build another So-and-So Palace. His son was working on the construction of another palace somewhere. His son phoned only when he was drunk. His son didn't have a mobile phone, so the man had to wait for him to call. Each time, it was from somewhere different. Once it was Yongin, another time Dongtan, then Sintanjin and Uijeongbu. The man would ask his son if everything was all right with him, and the girl would ask her father when he was coming home. His son would say "Forgive me" to him and "Sorry" to the girl. He was always remorseful no matter where he was calling from: Yongin, Dongtan, Sintanjin, or Uijeongbu.

The parents of the three boys from the girl's school didn't say "Forgive us" or "Sorry" when the principal had called them all in for a meeting. One of the parents said boys just sometimes behaved like that out of pure curiosity, and another said it was all the girl's fault because she was the one who hadn't behaved properly. And, they added, it wouldn't do the girl any good for the man to keep talking about it. They were so sure of themselves that the man felt as if he had been the one who had committed a sin and had been summoned to appear in front of them to answer for it. The father of one of the boys held out a white envelope. He said it was from all of them, and they had prepared it in good faith. Outside in the parking lot, each of the three cars that belonged to the parents had the same sticker on the windshield: the parking permit for the new apartment complex.

The man stayed awake all night. In the white envelope there were six one-million-won cashier's checks. That was enough for him to move into a new home. One where he would be certain not to have any worries about the water and electricity being cut off. The man sat with the envelope in front of him and drank his way through two bottles of *soju*.

"What do you want me to do, Father? You came up with the test, so you must know the answer. I'm going to roll the dice. If my lucky number comes up, I'll keep the money."

The man took the dice out of his pocket. There were two of them; their edges were worn and shiny. One die had one dot on each of the six sides, and the other had six dots on all six sides. The dice had been a parting gift from the staff sergeant.

"To those who don't know the truth about these dice, rolling a seven means good luck. But to anyone who does know, it's all about the die maker's plan. You see, the die maker's plan is realized when anyone who knows the truth rolls the dice. There are three types of people in the world: those who simply rely on luck, those who are fanatical about a cause, and those who realize they're instruments of a higher purpose. This war is a struggle between those who trust entirely to luck and those who are completely fanatical about a cause. Those who rely on luck are the first to lose their lives. Who do you think survives to the very end? The ones who are totally fanatical about their cause? No. It's the ones who realize they're instruments of the supreme purpose. Because they are free from responsibility. Those who shirk all responsibility will break up a family, but those who take on too much will destroy the world. I have come to believe something: that God took my leg in order to show how meaningless this war is."

The staff sergeant's leg had been blown off when a terrified new recruit had dropped a grenade.

The man tossed the dice high into the air. They rolled over and over on the floor before coming to rest. He frowned as he looked at the dice. One die was a six, but the other nothing; the dot had worn off. The man picked up the die and checked it. Each of the other sides had a distinct dot.

The man knelt and whispered, his voice shaking, "Father, have mercy on this little lamb. Satan tempted me. I'll do your bidding."

The next morning, at the crack of dawn, the man went to the school. Early though it was, the door of the principal's office was already wide open. The principal was sitting up straight at his desk holding a newspaper with his arms outstretched. And wearing white gloves. The man put the white envelope down on the principal's desk. The principal's eyes narrowed as he peered over his reading glasses. He asked if the money hadn't been enough. He seemed to know exactly how much money was in the envelope. The man said this was not the kind of problem you could throw money at, and the principal responded that refusing the money wouldn't solve the problem either. When the man asked the principal to tell him the names of the boys, the principal was startled.

"Brother, remember what our Lord Jesus says: love your enemy. Isn't it true that the little boys did what they did without really knowing what they were doing? What did Jesus say when he was nailed to the cross and died? Father, forgive them; they know not what they do. Brother, please forgive them all, and let the glorious will of God shine brightly on this world. Hallelujah."

The principal even knew that the man was a Christian. How thoroughly had they investigated him? The principal seemed to know everything about him. He had the look of a man who was surveying the chess pieces of a weak opponent — an opponent he could annihilate in a single move. The man sensed it, and the principal seemed to realize that the man had sensed it.

As he turned away from the principal, the man prayed inwardly, "Father, forgive the Pharisee who blasphemes your name, but never forgive that filthy mouth. The man speaks with a forked tongue."

"Professional gamer," "backup dancer," and "cosmetic surgeon." These were the dream jobs of the three boys, as shown on their student profile cards. The man picked up the girl's from the other pile of cards. It said "figure skater."

No punishment, no sin. The notion nagged at the man's mind as he left the principal's office. It was still nagging at him when he walked out of the police station having achieved nothing. The police had said that offenders under age thirteen were not criminally liable for assault and their parents could not be held responsible either. How could there possibly be a sin but no punishment? This world was no place for Good Samaritans. Far from feeling any sense of forgiveness, the man felt an impulse to blow something up, and his heart raced just as it used to race when he came upon a foxhole that had lain hidden like a camouflaged trap in the tropical jungle. As soon as they spotted a hole they would toss a grenade toward it. The staff sergeant, who liked to give everything a nickname, called the grenade a "roast walnut." When a "roast walnut" exploded in the hole, then it was a time for the "tiger moths" to fly into it. When the flamethrower shot flames into the black darkness, an overwhelming smell came from deep within: the smell of the tropical murky darkness and what had been hiding in it, burning. One time the man was sure he had smelled a heart on fire. A burnt body, blackened all over. The skinny little guy was barefoot. And he was missing one big toe. There was a gap where it had been. The flames that had burned everything up weren't able to burn away the look on the dead man's face. The hopeless and doleful expression of a man who must have witnessed many deaths in his time, and which seemed to say that there is nothing but death, and pre-death, and post-death, and anything like life or love is just a daydream.

The man couldn't forget the mutilated foot for a long time. To lose a toe, that guy must have disgraced his parents, stabbed his friends in the back, or preyed on women. That fucking Red son of a bitch. The guy probably had his toe cut off when he was caught cheating at poker. He must have cried and begged them to cut off a toe instead of a finger. That crippled son of a bitch. Every night, the man would imagine a series of evil deeds the guy with the missing toe might have committed, just to try to dispel the image of the maimed foot, which haunted him even in his dreams. Until he finally came to believe that the guy had died because of his missing big toe. The guy with the missing toe was the first enemy the man had killed. The war he believed he had left far behind, as distant as the underworld, had pursued him and was at his heels. Or maybe he himself had been caught in the distant underworld. Either way, one thing was clear: The war wasn't over.

Some people let chance dictate the course of their lives, while others are driven by a specific cause. People who believe in chance pay no attention to plans and strategies. But a man who is fanatical about a cause and convinced that every sin must be punished will pore over a map and draw up battle plans. To him, a map is essential to war, just as punishment is essential in the face of sin. The man felt God's fury burning in his heart. Now he had no doubt that he was an instrument of the supreme will. He had obtained two maps. He looked first at the land registration map of the neighborhood. He verified the location of the driveway leading into the So-and-So Palace apartment complex. He marked the police station and the fire station with a red X. He felt his vision grow blurry. It was as if a gigantic X had been drawn just in front of his eyes.

"Please, Father. Not yet," he groaned.

The man opened a drawer and took out something that looked like a fountain pen. It was a blood sampling device. Then he took out a plastic pouch that contained a disposable lancet. He tore open the pouch, took out the lancet and inserted it into the end of the sampling tube. When he put the cap onto the sampling device, the plastic cover came off the tip of the lancet. He set the depth to which the lancet would go in. He found he had to go deeper every time. This was because his blood had thickened and his circulation had become weak. The problem with his eyes was also caused by poor circulation. He touched the lancet to the tip of his finger and pressed down on the end of the sampling device. He felt a sharp pain like a bee sting. Then he reached into the drawer and took out something that looked like a stopwatch. It was a blood glucose meter. The man took a test strip and inserted it into the glucose meter, dabbing blood onto the end of the strip. When the blood soaked all the way up the test strip, the meter made a beeping sound and a number appeared on the screen: 345. The man's face darkened.

He took a disposable syringe and a vial of insulin—the last one he had left—out of the drawer. He also took out a piece of yellow elastic. He rolled up his left sleeve and wound the elastic around his arm, using his right hand and his teeth to tighten it. Breaking open the vial, he drew the insulin into the syringe. He clenched his hand into a fist and watched as his veins stood out slightly from his skin. Sticking the needle deep into his arm, he injected himself with the insulin. Drugs had given him so much, and taken away still more. They had given him drowsy relaxation, and taken away fear and guilt. Just as they had in the battle in the jungle.

Pulling himself together, the man looked at the plan of the apartment complex. He marked the enemy bases with a big X. His quarrel lay with people, not places, but the battle would occur in the area shown on the map. The purpose of the battle was simple: to alter the map. It could only take place within the specified zone. Elsewhere, there existed only the misfortunes of those who were hoping for good luck to come their way, and the misfortunes of those who had grown accustomed to their unhappy lot. On those few occasions when they encountered good fortune, it came in the form of death either physical or spiritual. There were no exceptions.

The man took the girl to a restaurant where pork was cooked on charcoal grills set into the tables. He couldn't remember the last time he had been to a restaurant. He ate nothing and just drank *soju*, while the girl just ate meat. The man took a handful of cold charcoal and put it in a plastic bag. He slipped the empty *soju* bottles into his backpack. Then he took the girl home and went off by himself to reconnoiter the area. To avoid attracting attention, he left his scooter at home. This was the first time that he had ventured inside the So-and-So Palace apartment complex.

There were two security checkpoints: one at the main entrance and the other at the back gate. The guards were all slouching at their desks, their heads slumped between their shoulders as if their only responsibility was to protect their own necks. There were two underground parking garages, but there was no security booth at the entrance to either one. The man went down into the parking garages. They felt like huge foxholes. The cold, dark air, the concrete columns standing at intervals, the security cameras in almost every corner of the ceiling. He checked the location and direction of all the cameras and made a note of them on a piece of paper. He also checked the location of two of his targets. One was parked in front of the apartment building, and the other was in the underground parking garage. The third hadn't returned to its base yet.

Finally, judgment day dawned. That night, the man put the girl to sleep early. In fact, he didn't have to do anything, as she was already sleepy, maybe it was the medicine that had put her to sleep. The man squatted on the kitchen floor and placed a funnel into the mouth of an empty *soju* bottle. He poured kerosene from a can. When he had filled one bottle the can was empty. He removed a saucepan from the kerosene stove and unscrewed the cap from the stove's fuel tank. He picked up the stove, tilting it over the funnel. A mix of kerosene and dark red rust poured out. The man watched solemnly as the kerosene filled the remaining bottles. Lastly, he took off his undershirt, tore it into strips, and stuffed the rags into the necks of the bottles.

The man stood the four bottles in a row and brought a cigarette to his lips. He had made a note of the three license plate numbers. The fourth bottle was there in case he needed to create a distraction.

The man lit the cigarette using the welding torch his son had left in the corner of the kitchen. Blue flames danced in waves from the tip. He thought of it as a ceremonial torch in a pre-battle ritual. He dragged slowly on his cigarette. Continuing the ritual, he went inside and put on his old army uniform. It was loose. He pulled the belt tight and tucked the frayed hems of the pants into his socks. He put on his coat, grabbed his backpack, and went back out to the kitchen.

The man crushed the pieces of charcoal into a powder and put it into a metal bowl. He added a few drops of honey, stirred it with his hand, and smeared the mixture onto his face. Looking at himself in the girl's hand mirror, he made sure every inch of his face was blackened. His reflection looked back at him like a warrior from the dark underworld in a Scandinavian folk tale. A warrior who possessed a dark magic that no human weapons could defeat. The man put on a helmet and a face mask too. They were what his son used to wear when he worked with the welding torch. Now he looked less like a warrior from the dark under-world and more like a survivor of a post-apocalyptic battle. The man stuffed the bottles into his backpack and swung it onto his shoulders. It was heavy, as heavy as a flamethrower.

At 3:00 a.m.—the darkest time of night—the man approached the So-and-So Palace apartment complex. He turned off the engine of his scooter. The night was so quiet it felt as if all the stars in the sky had turned off their lights. Standing beside his scooter, he urinated against a wall of the apartment complex—just as he would have done in the jungle. When they were about to go into action, the entire troop would stand in a row facing the direction of the enemy and open their flies, following an order from the staff sergeant. He said they must all empty their bladders unless they wanted to get shot in the head pissing on the battle-field. They agreed that whoever pissed the farthest would march in front. The sergeant's urine went the farthest. Every time.

Pushing his scooter, the man went into the apartment complex. The guard at the security post had dozed off at his desk. The man stopped near one of the apartment buildings and parked his scooter there before retracing his steps. To him, this was not just any building, it was the building where the boy who wanted to be a cosmetic surgeon lived. It was to be the location of his second operation.

The man stopped walking when he got to the building where the other two boys lived—the one who wanted to be a professional gamer and the one who wanted to be a backup dancer. One of his targets was not visible in the parking lot in front of the apartments. It was the target he had been unable to verify the previous evening. There were two possibilities. Either the target vehicle had not returned yet, or it was in the underground garage. The man turned and approached the entrance to the parking garage. Nobody stopped him. It wasn't a matter of luck, or even Providence. It was ninety-nine percent laziness, and one percent total carelessness.

He ran rapidly and nimbly down the ramp into the garage. It seemed to him to be pitch dark, just like in a foxhole. The darkness fueled the dark flames of rage. The man switched on a flashlight. Focusing the beam on a piece of paper he took out of his pocket, he confirmed the location of the security cameras. He turned ninety degrees to his right and took ten swift, purposeful steps forward, pointing the flashlight at each car license plate, one by one. Then he stopped and turned to the right. Now he had his back to a security camera. He turned ninety degrees to his left and walked forward fifteen paces before stopping and turning to the left so that once again his back was to a security camera. The target he had been unable to verify during reconnaissance was nowhere to be seen. The man turned slightly to the left and took nine paces forward, then hid behind a concrete column.

Behind the column, the man took out a lighter and lit the rag in the neck of one bottle. He hurled the bottle at his first target, hitting the windshield. The glass shattered, and flames flared up. There was a sudden, loud honking. It was a car alarm. The man hadn't accounted for this noise so nothing had been marked on the map to suggest it. He couldn't fight an enemy that wasn't on the map. He swung round and retreated swiftly towards the entrance. The bottles in his backpack clinked against one another. He was panting when he reached ground level. Taking off his mask, he caught his breath and moved towards his second target.

When he reached the building where the boy who wanted to be a cosmetic surgeon lived, the man looked around. Nothing was moving other than the breeze. He lit another bottle and threw it at the second target. The bottle exploded and flames burst out in concentric circles. The man looked around and then started to walk towards a car that had a strange sticker on its windshield. The sticker showed an image of a red-faced devil. Its mouth was open wide and it was baring its fangs. Below the picture of the devil there were some words in English — "Be the Reds!"[1] — but the man had no idea what that meant. Although it wasn't his third target, he hurled the third bottle at the car and turned around. Behind him, the alarm was shrieking.

Getting onto his scooter, the man slipped out through the back gate.

1 The slogan of the Korean national soccer team during the 2002 World Cup. (Translators' note)

"Now, Father," he muttered, "I need to get some rest."

The next morning, the first thing the man did when he got out of bed was try to turn on the TV. It didn't work. The electricity had been cut off. He switched on a battery-powered radio and listened solemnly to the morning news. There was no mention of the So-and-So Palace apartments. The man's face crumpled.

Turning off the radio, he made two calls. The first was to the girl's school. He said she had to stay home one more day because she was still sick. He wasn't lying. The girl was burning up with a fever. The electric blanket was cold, so cold it felt like a sheet of chilled metal. The person at the other end of the line said that the girl had to attend school tomorrow no matter what, because it was the last day before winter break. The second call was to his office. The man said he was afraid he couldn't go to work that day because he still wasn't feeling well. That was not a lie. His feet had swollen up and his vision was blurred. He had a fever too. There was no response from the person at the other end of the line.

"Hello?"

"Stay home and rest. Forever."

The line went dead. The man grunted and went into the kitchen. He rinsed some rice and put it into a saucepan. He added enough water to make a thin rice porridge and put the saucepan on the kerosene stove. He lit the burner and turned it up to the highest setting, but the flames flickered. He was low on kerosene. He was low on everything. When the day that even the water was cut off came, they wouldn't be able to manage any more.

The girl was so weak she couldn't even hold her chopsticks. She wouldn't eat any rice porridge, even with dried seaweed sprinkled on top. The man felt her forehead. It was burning hot. Perhaps because his hand was burning hot.

"Have to go to the doctor, no matter what," the man said to no one in particular. There was no response, of course. But he hadn't expected a response.

The man had three doctors' offices in mind that morning, just as he'd had three license plates in mind the previous night. Two of the three targets had been burnt, and two burning hot bodies would go to the three doctors. Lifting the girl and carrying her on his back, the man groped his way down the steep alley. His first stop was a pediatrician's office. Their regular pediatrician was nearby, at the entrance to the local market, but he deliberately went to the clinic in the shopping center attached to the So-and-So Palace apartment complex. As he entered the shopping center, he glanced in the direction of the apartments.

Two women in fur coats were chatting in the waiting room of the pediatrician's office. The man strained to hear what they were talking about. He didn't hear anything that sounded like "fire," but he heard the word "gift" frequently. The girl was given a shot, and there were pills she would need to take. As the nurse handed him the bottle of pills, the man asked if everything was all right; she gave him a perplexed look as if she were wondering whether he was all right. She gave him enough pills for three days and said the doctor's office would be closed until after Christmas. It would be Christmas in two days' time. The man hadn't had a call from his son recently. He couldn't remember exactly where his son was staying; he wasn't sure whether it was Dongtan or Sintanjin, or perhaps Yongin or Uijeongbu. Apparently his son hadn't been drinking lately, because he hadn't called.

The man left the shopping center and stared at the apartment complex for a while, as if to check that it was the same one he had been to during the night. The second clinic they headed for was the one where the doctor had talked about trauma or something. They took a bus and got off thirty minutes later. With the girl on his back the man went down some steps that led to an underground passage. At the bottom step, the man froze. He could see nothing but darkness in front of his eyes. He stood still and waited for the darkness to dissipate. Just as it had done in the past. But even time, which eventually dispels everything, couldn't easily dispel the darkness now. The man's legs shook with fear; fear that he would never again be able to see the light.

When it is time for darkness to descend on a man — a creature that cannot generate its own light — does it ever lift? For the man, who had no inner light of his own, darkness was not something that came and went. It was always with him. Light was what came and went, and came back again. Perhaps this time he would have to wait a long, long time for the light to return. Like a tree, like a solitary tree, carrying on his back the girl who had long ago lost her speech.

A throng of noises burst through the darkness, which now seemed solid as iron: footsteps, a Salvation Army bell, Christmas carols, the clinking of coins, the sound of someone gulping, trying to catch their breath, exhaling a long breath, eyes blinking, heart racing, the menacing roll of dice, time passing by like a crowd bursting out of the subway and bumping into him, and then, from over his shoulder, a weak voice like the voice of an infant.

"Grandpa."

"Yes."

"Are you all right?"

"I'm all right."

"Are you waiting for someone, Grandpa?"

"Yes."

"Who?"

"Someone."

"Are you tired?"

"I'm all right."

"May I sing for you?"

"Go ahead."

"You better watch out, you better not cry, better not pout, I'm telling you why, Santa Claus is coming—to town; He's making a list, and checking it twice, gonna find out who's naughty and nice, Santa Claus is coming—to town."

The Runner

When Eun-jae called, I was jerking off in an attempt to lift my spirits. I was feeling bummed out after getting an email saying I'd been turned down for a job. This was the eleventh time that I'd made it to a final interview and then been rejected. Recently it seemed my resume was being tossed out without even calling me for an interview. It was clear that new college graduates were preferred. I'd begun to notice the change the previous year. Interviewers started asking me what I'd been doing since graduation. They were like shopkeepers checking the expiration dates of new deliveries.

I was frustrated at being interrupted before I came, but I picked up my cell phone.

"Where are you?" I asked.

"At Oksu Station."

"Why so early?"

Eun-jae didn't reply, but asked "What's the matter with your voice?"

"I was working out. On a stationary bike."

"Come on out."

I took a quick shower and pulled on some clothes. Standing in front of a full-length mirror I checked how I looked. I was ready to go. I automatically started to put on dress shoes, but then stopped and took a pair of sneakers from the shoe rack. The Nikes I had bought a couple of days earlier. I'd gotten them for jogging around the neighborhood, but it had been raining on and off ever since, so I hadn't worn them yet, and the tags were still on. "Why does she want to go hiking?" I mumbled abstractedly as I tied the laces. The sound of my own voice startled me. It had been the sound of people mumbling to themselves that had caused me to leave—you might almost say sneak out of—the low-cost rooming house before my lease was up. The disheveled men never looked one another in the eye when they passed in the hallway, and certainly never said hello. In the bleak bathroom, they would mutter as they relieved themselves. And that wasn't it. I often couldn't sleep at night because of the mumbling sounds coming through the thin walls. I was weirded out, afraid that I would become one of them.

Outside, the sun was so bright that I had to squint my eyes. I shaded them with my hand, and looked around. The roof of Oksu Station seemed to be pulling down the hem of the sky. The wide expanse of blue was so cloudless it looked like it had just been swept clean. It was a perfect day for taking pictures. *Oh, I almost forgot!* I dashed back to my room and picked up my camera. It was a Lomo LC-A. I had bought it for myself as a graduation present. I bounced down the rusting stairs, knowing that soon, for the first time in a long while, I'd have some pictures to upload to my blog. I was even whistling a song, almost forgetting that I had been rejected after a final interview for the eleventh time. *To hell with those interviewers! They're too dense to recognize an outstanding candidate. And damn this whistling!*

Eun-jae was standing under the roof of Oksu Station, and she waved when she spotted me. She was wearing a hoodie and a denim mini-skirt with black knee-socks and expensive, imported running shoes. She must have modeled her look on pictures from a Japanese magazine like *Non-no* or *Ryuko Tsushin*. She looked grown-up for her age, perhaps because of her defined facial features, or because of her curvaceous figure.

Eun-jae flashed a smile as I approached. The braces on her teeth gleamed sharply. Embarrassed, she quickly closed her mouth. She was clutching a book to her chest—a biography of Che Guevara. It was unlike her to read about someone like him, and she explained that her favorite band admired him.

After exchanging a few platitudes about the weather, we set out toward the Han River. I asked if her music lesson had ended early, and she began to complain that even though they had the day off for her school's founder's day, she still wasn't allowed to just relax. Eun-jae had been taking viola lessons.

She asked me suddenly where my place was, and on the spur of the moment I pointed to the tall building of studio apartments that had recently been put up among the old buildings on the hill along Dokseodang Road. Eun-jae gave a long look at the handsome building that was like a swan surrounded by ducks. The way she looked at it made me think of a real-estate investor scoping out a property to buy. In fact, Eun-jae already had an apartment in her own name. It was bound to appreciate in value because it was in a complex in Jamsil that had been officially designated a redevelopment site. Eun-jae's family had a few other apartments too.

"What number?" Eun-jae asked with a cheeky smile.

"Forget it."

Eun-jae pouted.

We crossed the road and headed toward the riverbank.

"Let's go rent a bike."

"A bike? In that mini-skirt?"

Eun-jae had already dashed away.

The bike rental shop was run by the town council. A large wanted poster hung on the door of the prefab structure. The wanted man was a suspect in the kidnapping and murder of a series of women who lived in upscale villas and apartment complexes throughout Gangnam. The last victim had been found dead on a mountainside near Paju. The photo on the poster was grainy because it was a screenshot from the security video at an ATM. Besides, the man was wearing a face mask and his cap was pulled down over his forehead.

Eun-jae's face froze when she saw the poster. She said the victim found in Paju had lived in the same apartment building as her.

"They should beat him to death. He's like a rabid dog."

"I heard that dogs that have rabies are afraid of water, so if you get bitten by a mad dog you get hy…."

"Hydrophobia."

Eun-jae blushed when I finished the word for her. Her Korean was halting because she had left for America in third grade and had come back at the beginning of high school. Compared to her peers, she had a fairly weak vocabulary, and she knew hardly any words that came from Chinese. That was why she had been taking Korean lessons from me. I had no idea why she had quit studying in America, which is something everyone desperately wants to do. I once asked her why she had come back to Korea when she'd never be a top student here. This question reduced her to tears, and I was somewhat embarrassed. She had started taking viola lessons right after she came back.

"When I was a kid I was chased by a dog and nearly drowned," said Eun-jae, frowning. "Since then I've been scared of water. I think I might have hydrophobia."

The bike rental shop was quiet. Unsurprisingly, since it was three o'clock on a Wednesday afternoon. Just inside the entrance was a small booth. A middle-aged man was sitting hunched up, dozing in front of a heater. He jumped when Eun-jae tapped on the window. We said we'd like to rent a bike, and he told us to leave our IDs with him and take our pick. He explained that the rent was three thousand won for the first hour plus one thousand for every additional fifteen minutes. We could pay when we returned the bike, he said.

"You have to return the bike before sunset," the man shouted to us as we wheeled the bike out through the gate. "Be careful. The days are getting shorter and it'll get dark before you know it."

I got ready to ride as Eun-jae climbed onto the carrier behind the seat.

Although I'd been living in the neighborhood for almost a year, this was the first time I had taken the path along the bank of the Han River. I didn't even know the name of the bridge that led to Oksu Station. Eun-jae didn't know either. I was surprised that she knew so little about Seoul, given that it was her hometown. My ignorance was excusable, because I had lived here only since starting college. There were too many bridges over the Han River, she explained, and besides, she rarely needed to cross them; that was why she knew so little about them. This was only the third time she had crossed the river since she'd come back from America.

In the open space under the bridge there were various pieces of outdoor exercise equipment, but no one was using them. There wasn't a soul on the bike path that ran alongside the river either. Dragonflies hovered over yellow wildflowers, and waist-high silver grasses waved gently. On the other side of the path the deep blue water ran quietly by. Seen up close, the water looked darker. In contrast, the sky was clearer and brighter than usual. It was like a photo taken with a Lomo LC-A.

The pictures I took with my camera were dark around the edges because of a distortion in the wide-angle lens. It was a kind of tunnel effect. Seen through the deformed frame, the focal object stood out and had a unique quality to it. When she had seen the photos I'd posted on my blog, Eun-jae had said how fabulous my pictures were and nagged me to take one of her. Since she was my most valuable student, I thought it would be worth my while to take a photo of her for free. Her mother had told me that she was going to introduce me to another potential student, the son of a friend of hers.

Eun-jae was already posing in front of the bike. I took my camera out of the case and removed the lens cap. Estimating the distance, I squeezed the shutter.

"Super cute!" said Eun-jae, snatching the camera and looking at it closely.

"It's so cool. I can't believe Russian spies use this type of camera!"

"I have no doubt that a scientist at a KGB research lab invented it, but there's probably no truth to the rumor that Russian spies use it. Think about it. Accuracy is crucial for spies, so why would they be okay with photos that are dark around the edges and where the subject of the photo is distorted? They aren't artists, are they?"

"Wow! You're so smart. Take another shot of me, please."

"I never take pictures of people. But I'll make an exception for you."

"Why don't you take photos of people?"

"I only photograph inanimate objects. When I use this camera I feel like inanimate things have souls. It feels like this camera imbues them with a spirit. Besides, objects are silent and submissive. They don't mutter or nag me to give them a copy of the photo. In the online photography community they call me GPO—the Guy who Plays with Objects."

"A camera that breathes soul into things! You're so unique!"

Right at that moment a roaring sound came up behind us, then flew past with the popcorn beat of uptempo music. It was an old man in cycling gear riding down the riverside path, already receding rapidly into the distance. The insistent beat lingered in my ears until the man and his bike were just a tiny dot. We took off in the opposite direction, following the river upstream.

"Go, *Oppa*!"[2] Eun-jae shouted, grabbing me by the waist.

The sweet scent of Eun-jae made my nostrils tingle. It felt unreal, like I was in a romantic movie, playing a man going out with his girlfriend. At first I couldn't balance the bike with both of us on it, and it kept wobbling, but I sped up gradually.

"Look over there! Those flowers are called cosmos, aren't they? Look at that pampas grass. There's a crane!" I wasn't the slightest bit bored because Eun-jae chirped away, and the view around us was changing all the time. The chilly air on my face was refreshing, and I was eventually able to push the pedals without any trouble.

We had just gone past the pampas grass when a runner came into view. He was running quickly with short strides, his elbows held close to his sides. As we drew closer, I could see him more clearly. Despite reports that frost had set in on the mountains of Gangwon Province, he was wearing a short-sleeved shirt and shorts, and he had even rolled his sleeves up all the way to his shoulders. The number seven was printed on the back of his shirt. A red shirt and white pants: Isn't that the uniform of the Manchester United soccer team? There were some white words sewn above

2 A term of address used by girls and young women to their older brothers or older male friends, increasingly used in a flirtatious manner. (Translators' note)

the number: _____ Morning Soccer Club. The stitching of the first word had come undone, leaving only a few loose threads. The man was wearing a baseball cap and white cotton gloves. He was of medium height and slight build, though his biceps and thighs were disproportionately muscular. Above his black ankle socks, his shins were covered with curly hair. He looked particularly fit, perhaps because he was tanned.

"Whuh, whuh." I could distinctly hear the staccato rhythm of his panting as we came closer. I noticed that the man's running shoes were similar to mine. A tiny logo was printed in the middle of the heel. The words on the logo looked odd, and I stared at it so long that I almost ran into the man. I braked abruptly.

The man was running right along the center line of the bike path. I found it really exasperating, particularly given that there was a pedestrian path right next to the bike path. I could have steered to one side and passed him, but for some reason I didn't feel like doing so. I rang my bell. Ding-ding. The man didn't budge from the center line. Ding-ding, ding-ding. I rang the bell again, frantically. The man didn't so much as swerve, let alone look behind him; he just kept running. Holding back the anger that was boiling up inside me, I steered to his right. I wanted to get a look at the damn fool, but that wasn't easy either, because of the cap and face mask he was wearing. He kept looking straight ahead as he ran, as if he were wearing a neck brace.

I pedaled harder to overtake him, but he wouldn't let me. In fact, he was speeding up too. The harder I pedaled, the faster the man's legs moved. We went along side by side, like an athlete and his coach, both going our fastest. I have no idea how long he and I continued like that. The burning hostility inside me began to surface as he fell behind. Even after I'd outstripped him, I didn't slow down. Rather than feeling relieved, I was left with an uneasiness. I was desperate to turn around and look at him, but I forced myself not to.

"Did you see?" Eun-jae spoke after having been silent throughout the bizarre race. "His tattoo. I thought it was a pile of poo, but when I saw it up close, I realized it was a coiled snake."

I glanced quickly at the handlebar mirror. I could see the man behind us, running steadily in silence. His feet doggedly pounding the yellow line.

We reached a fork where one path led to Eungbong Station and the other to Seoul Forest Park. We decided to go to the park. It would be a better place for taking pictures. The path leading to the park ended at a bridge that was suspended across a stream. The bike path started again on the other side of the bridge. We followed the hairpin bends of the trail until the Han River appeared directly in front of us. The water had risen right up to the bike path, and I felt as if I were riding on the water. Eun-jae's grip tightened.

I stopped and propped up the bike on its kickstand while I took a few pictures. I pointed the camera at Mount Namsan and the Seoul Tower, which were framed by the tall apartment buildings across the river. I wondered how the pictures would turn out. It was a clear day, so the tower would gleam magically in the evening sunlight. I would get more impressive pictures when the sun was lower in the sky. And if a train happened to be passing with its lights on, that would be icing on the cake. I was excited for sunset.

We went under the orange trusses of a bridge supported by giant concrete columns. Eun-jae, showing off her knowledge, said it was the Seongsu Bridge.

"I thought you had no idea of the names of the bridges?"

"I couldn't possibly forget this one. I crossed it just ten minutes before it came crashing down. We were in an ambulance going across the bridge, and my grandma was holding me in her arms. My mom was pregnant and her water had just broken. Grandma was so flustered that she dressed me in a short-sleeved shirt that belonged to Pippi. Pippi was our little dog."

"Wasn't it autumn when the bridge collapsed?"

"What do you mean? Do you think I'm lying?"

"No, I mean . . ."

"My grandma still calls me 'My dear puppy' every time she sees me."

Leaving the Seongsu Bridge behind, we saw another bridge

up ahead. It was an ordinary-looking bridge. Neither of us knew what it was called. The Mapo Bridge, Golden Gate Bridge, Seongsan Bridge, Pont Neuf . . . We joked around, listing off the names of famous bridges. Then there was a roar as a motorcycle came up from behind. It passed us very fast and very close, making our bike wobble. I swerved and just barely managed to stay upright. A dog was panting along behind the motorcycle. It was running frantically, almost being dragged along, by a chain attached to the back of the motorcycle. They were gone in a flash.

"How horrible! Who would even think of doing that to a dog?"

"Did you see? The dog's legs couldn't all touch the ground at the same time."

"Poor dog."

"Didn't you see it? It was really flying along like it had wings."

"I'm scared."

"Of what?"

"It's like 'speak of the devil.' I mentioned my old dog and then a dog appeared. Has that ever happened to you?"

"It's just a coincidence. If you really think you have that sort of psychic power, don't mention that asshole jogger back there. I don't want to come across him again."

"Who? The guy with the snake . . ."

Eun-jae had barely spoken when a figure suddenly appeared on the path. It was the man in the Manchester United uniform, or the something-or-other Morning Soccer Club uniform. It really was a case of "speak of the devil." I felt a shiver down my spine, as if I had been doused with ice-cold water.

The man suddenly pulled in front of us on our right. "Whuh, whuh." The staccato rhythm of his breathing hadn't changed. Neither had the way he held his torso straight and controlled his arm movements. I tried once again to get a look at his face, but because of his cap and face mask only his nose was visible. He went on running in exactly the same way, looking straight ahead. I put more weight on the pedals to stay ahead of him, but it felt like the pedals were pushing back against my feet. In fact, we had come to a slope, smooth but uphill. Damn it! What bad timing! I bit my lip, overwhelmed by a feeling of despair.

In a matter of seconds the man would overtake us. Yet he seemed to be taking care not to race ahead, as if he were a marathon runner watching his pace. He seemed to be pacing himself in order to stay with the bike, which had slowed down. I felt the hair on the back of my neck bristle, and I broke into a cold sweat. I tried to swallow but my throat tightened. I had the sudden urge to stop the bike. But what if the man stopped too? Then I'd have no way out. There are two things you should always avoid: a blind alley, and guys who don't make eye contact. I didn't even want to think about being in a blind alley with a guy who avoided eye contact.

"Whuh, whuh." The sound of his breathing crept up my spine and gave me goosebumps. The path climbed even more steeply. My thighs seemed ready to burst with each push on the pedals, and as the pedal came back up, my calf shook uncontrollably. I gritted my teeth and struggled not to groan like a dying man. At last I could see the top of the hill up ahead. I stood up on the pedals, leaned forward, and pushed with all the strength I could muster. It felt like riding through sand.

The moment the bike crested the rise and set off downhill, it started to gather speed like a cheetah chasing its prey. The pedals turned by themselves. The bastard also started to sprint, as if to catch up with me. "Whuh, whuh, whuh." The sound of his breathing quickened and became irregular, while his torso jolted and he pumped his arms dramatically. Keep up the pace. I guarantee your heart will explode and your muscles will rupture. I felt triumphant. The bastard couldn't keep up. He was bound to get left far behind.

The bike had built up speed, and it careened forwards like an arrow flying through the air. "Woaaaah!" I let out a spontaneous scream. The crisp air was sucked into my lungs. The pedals were spinning crazily, and I instinctively took my feet off of them. The handlebars shook. My surroundings looked distorted and the path seemed to be rising toward me. I was suddenly gripped by fear. I had to fight the urge to squeeze my eyes shut, and I clutched the handlebars even tighter. At least there was no one else on the path. The ground leveled out and the bike continued to barrel along for a while. Wild flowers and bushes whizzed by, along with a bike standing beside the path, a helmet hanging from the handlebars. The old man in cycling gear resting on the grassy bank, a plastic juice box in his hand, a straw sticking out of the box, and the insistent beat of pop music. Everything whirred swiftly past. But that's impossible . . . That old man disappeared in the opposite direction a while ago. I thought I must be hallucinating. I gave my head a brisk shake and pedaled wildly, pushing the bike on and on without pause until I was gasping for breath.

"We're okay now, *Oppa*."

I had almost forgotten that I had Eun-jae behind me. I sat back down on the seat, shuddering as if I'd just had to relieve myself outside in the cold. Without warning, another bridge appeared up ahead. It was old and shabby. It looked like a soldier anxiously awaiting discharge after having endured the worst perils and dangers imaginable. I turned around, but that bastard runner was nowhere to be seen.

Heaving a sigh of relief, I rode slowly under the bridge. To the left, a wide lawn spread out between the bike path and the road. A sign up ahead said "Ttukseom Resort Park." The children's playground in the corner of the lawn was empty except for the wind which was whipping up eddies of dust and kicking around a black plastic bag. Had the river swallowed up all living creatures around there? It was so quiet that I couldn't believe I was in the middle of a city.

Another bridge appeared some distance ahead. It was supported by Y-shaped columns and had a distinctive double truss, so I recognized it as the Cheongdam Bridge, a popular backdrop where people would come at night to take photos. A guy in the online Lomo photography community uploaded photos of this bridge, and nothing else, every day. He called it "A Journal of the Cheongdam Bridge" or something like that. In fact, the street lights along the road leading to the bridge were far more remarkable than the bridge itself. The narrow overpass supported on slender pillars curved elegantly toward the bridge, like an art installment. Just past the bridge, I stopped the bike and took some pictures of the surrounding cityscape.

Eun-jae said she was getting hungry and pulled me toward a nearby snack bar. I followed her more than willingly, since all I had eaten so far that day was some instant curry and rice. I bought a cup of noodle soup, a can of beer, and some sausages. The man at the bar put a kettle of water onto a portable gas burner. His bald head was shiny. He wore thick glasses that made it difficult to tell what he was looking at, but I had the sneaking suspicion that he was ogling Eun-jae.

"Look!" I shouted brusquely, "the water's boiling." I felt the man glaring at me as he poured the hot water into the cups of noodles. His thick lenses made his eyes bulge out from his face and did nothing to hide his glare of outright hostility.

Eun-jae and I sat at the bottom of some steps that led down to the riverbank. While we waited for our instant noodles to be ready, I stood up and went back up the steps to fetch my bike, which I had left beside the path. When she saw me carrying the bike on my shoulders, Eun-jae jeered at me and said that I was showing off and wasting my energy since there was no one around. I said nothing.

Eun-jae took a lunchbox and a thermos out of her backpack. She opened the lunch box—a pink Hello Kitty one—and said "Surprise!" Inside the lunchbox were *gimbap*, pieces of dark seaweed wrapped around a filling of white rice and vegetables. They had some seeds sprinkled on top, and they looked good.

Eun-jae, her eyes sparkling, watched me as I took a piece and tasted it. It was nowhere near as good as it looked. The rice was too sticky, and the other ingredients were bland and unsalted. What was worse, Eun-jae seemed to have used perilla seeds instead of sesame seeds. It tasted weird. It looked like *gimbap* but didn't taste at all like it.

"I made it myself. Do you like it?" asked Eun-jae, eagerly awaiting my reaction.

"It's delicious. When did you learn to make food like this? This is the best food I have ever eaten." I gave a thumbs-up, and Eun-jae's face brightened.

"It's just a recipe I found online. I'm so relieved you like it."

"Why don't you eat some?"

"I'm all right with coffee."

"Did you make the coffee too?"

"No. I bought it at Starbucks. Do you really mean it that this is the best *gimbap* you've ever had?"

"You know I never tell a lie. It's so good that I can't help thinking that maybe you bought it at *Gimbap* Paradise."

"Gimbap Paradise? I've never heard of it."

"I'm going to eat my noodles too, so have some *gimbap* yourself."

"I'm really all right."

"It's a shame to have them all to myself . . ."

"Let's go in one of those boats later, shall we?"

Eun-jae pointed at some paddle boats that were bobbing in groups around a floating restaurant.

"That's just for rednecks."

"But it could be fun . . ."

I deliberately said nothing, and Eun-jae didn't say anything more about it.

A group of middle-aged men were fishing from the riverbank; some of them were drowsing and others sipping *soju*, their fishing rods dangling over the water. They all looked similarly scruffy. A few of them looked at us. I loathed the fishy smell of their glances and pretended not to notice them.

Across the river stood a series of identical apartment blocks that looked as if they had been made in a mold. They were like the walls of an impenetrable fortress, with the river as a moat. On the other side of the deep, wide moat and beyond the tall, strong wall stood Eun-jae's apartment. Inside the fortress were the school Eun-jae attended, the private tutoring centers she went to, and the department stores and restaurants she frequented. Twice a week I crossed the moat to go to Eun-jae's apartment and teach her Korean. On my first visit, the security guard had looked me up and down before asking me a series of questions: Which apartment are you visiting? What is the purpose of your visit? What is the name of your student? It was only after he had talked with Eun-jae's family over the intercom that he stopped treating me with suspicion. And he automatically asked me for the license plate number of my car. He explained that every visitor who parked there had to check in with the security office, even if they were only staying for an hour. When I told him I didn't have a car, he gave a weird grin, lifting one corner of his mouth. It was the kind of grin that made me suddenly wonder if I had a stinking sore on my face, oozing and putrid. Subsequently, I was delighted whenever I saw the "On Patrol" sign in the window of the security office.

"By the way, the man who was following us . . ."

"What about that jerk?"

"He kept looking at my thighs. I thought I was going to go crazy trying to pull down the hem of my skirt all the time."

"It's your own fault," I blurted out. "Who would think of riding a bike in a miniskirt?"

Eun-jae's eyes widened and she stopped sipping her coffee. Her lips quivered and she looked as if she was about to cry. I spoke more gently, putting my hand on her shoulder.

"I wish you had said something. You should have told me at the time."

"And if I'd told you, then what?" she asked, looking me straight in the eye.

"That crazy bastard! I'm gonna smash his skull in. How dare he . . ."

"Seriously?"

"Of course. Trust me, I will. Hey, you little rats! What the hell are you doing?"

Three little boys, of roughly elementary-school age, stopped throwing stones at the paddle boats and turned to look at us. One of them gave me the finger with a defiant look.

"You little punks! How dare you?"

I roared and stood up. The kids immediately fled towards the park, shrieking like monkeys.

"Calm down, *Oppa*," said Eun-jae, pulling at my pant leg to stop me, though she sounded amused.

I ripped the tab off a can of beer and drank to quench my thirst.

"You know, I think the woman who was kidnapped from the parking garage of my apartment building lived very near us. I saw her in the elevator. I was on my way to my music lesson and I was waiting for the elevator. When it stopped she walked out. It seemed like she thought it was the ground floor. You know our apartment is on the second floor, right? And you know what she muttered when she got back in the elevator? 'Kids these days have it so easy.' I still can't believe she said that! It's not my fault that my family happens to live on the second floor, is it? You don't know what it's like going down the stairs carrying a viola case. I was already sick of hearing my mom nagging me about it, after I told her I wanted to quit viola lessons. Mom said I was mollycoddled and spoiled, and she wouldn't even drive me to my lessons, so I had to take a taxi by myself. When I got out of the elevator I muttered, 'I wish ogres were real, so that she'd get gobbled up.' I was shocked next day when I heard that she'd been kidnapped. Mom told me not to talk to anybody about her."

"Why?"

"She said our apartment would lose value because of it." Eun-jae snatched the beer can from my hand and took several gulps in rapid succession. "Do you think the woman could have heard what I said?"

I didn't know how to respond.

Eun-jae drained the can of beer. I peeled back the plastic packaging and handed her a sausage. She took a bite and frowned.

"What kind of sausage is this? It tastes funny."

Then she said we should be getting ready to go back, but I didn't hear her because the white rapids under a bridge in the distance had caught my attention. It was the weir at the Jamsil Bridge, which I had only ever seen in photos. I thought it would be a shame not to see it, now that I was so close. Besides, I hadn't finished my roll of film yet and I wasn't sure when I'd get out here again now that the weather was getting cold. I figured that I could get over there, take a few pictures, and still get back to the Cheongdam Bridge in time to capture it in the glow of the setting sun. I managed to talk Eun-jae into going along with my plan by promising to buy her a nice dinner. We got onto the bike. I kept glancing in the mirror. There was nothing behind us but the deserted path.

Just after we left Ttukseom Resort Park we stopped because Eun-jae suddenly needed to go to the bathroom. She didn't usually drink beer, and it seemed to go right through her. I looked around, but I couldn't see a restroom.

"If it's so urgent why don't you go behind that clump of pampas grass?"

"Are you crazy? I'm a respectable girl. I'm not gonna pull down my panties in such a bewildered place!"

"I think you mean 'wild place.'"

"Whatever!"

Eun-jae got off the bike and started to walk back the way we had come.

"Where are you going?"

"I remember seeing a restroom next to the snack bar."

"Let me give you a ride."

"Never mind. It's just around the corner. I'll wait for you there. Hurry up and come back quickly when you've taken your photos. You'll get there and back quicker without me. And the sun's already sinking."

"Are you sure you're all right by yourself?"

Eun-jae waved without turning back to see me. Apparently, besides needing to go to the bathroom, she was also getting bored with the picnic. Eun-jae was impulsive, and she rarely finished what she had started. She changed private tutors as often as she changed her accessories. I was her fifth Korean language tutor. But at least I was the only one she had stuck with for more than three months.

The sun really had sunk quite a bit, as Eun-jae had said. It was down to the level of the bridge and the light had grown weak and pale. I climbed onto the bike and hurried off. With each push on the pedal the bike rolled smoothly forward. If I hadn't had Eun-jae behind me before I wouldn't have had to sweat blood to get ahead of that asshole runner. As the bike raced along at top speed I felt I didn't have a worry in the world.

Dusk was falling when I reached the Jamsil Bridge. I left the bike beside the road and hurriedly took pictures of the bridge and the surrounding scenery. Only two of the five sluice gates at the northern end of the bridge were open. The stream gushed into the still water below. The two bodies of water didn't exactly combine but rather shattered into one another, forming whirlpools and turning the river into foam. The roar of the rapids was extremely loud, perhaps because the rain we'd had on and off over the last few days had raised the water level.

Below the bike lane there was a gravel beach that spread out in a fan shape, curving along the riverbank. I walked down onto the pebbles to take a closer shot of the weir. Three little kids were skipping stones. They were the same boys who had been throwing rocks at the paddle boats. The stones were sinking close to a man in a black jacket who was standing waist-deep in the water, a fishing rod in his hands. The stones—which seemed to be stepping across the water on the rings that they formed—flew closer and closer to the man, inch by inch. Every time a stone fell near the man, the boys giggled.

"Hey, you brats!" I yelled.

The kids turned around and started throwing stones at me. I dodged instinctively.

"What the hell!"

A deafening shout came from behind me. A group of men, their silhouettes sharply defined, sat around a large iron pot near one of the columns of the bridge. A fire was licking the bottom of the pot and seemed about to devour it whole. Empty *soju* bottles were scattered around. The men stared at me, their eyes glistening with hostility. One of them rose to his feet, rubbing his back lazily.

"It wasn't me . . ."

When I turned around, the kids had already disappeared without a trace.

"You fucking asshole!" the man snarled. "You wanna die, don't you?" He looked as if he was about to charge. The men were all glowering in the same menacing way, it seemed to me, perhaps because I could hear the sparks spitting from the flames. I staggered backwards. Tripping over a stone, I fell flat on my back. The men's laughter reverberated in the clear air like the screech of metal on metal. The man who had been rubbing his back waddled forward, his eyes glaring, but then fell, knocking over a motorcycle that was standing nearby. There was another burst of screeching, metallic laughter. A motorcycle with a metal chain! It was the one that had been dragging the dog behind it. The dog was nowhere to be seen. The man picked himself up slowly, as if he had to push aside the curtain of dusk before he could stand. I bolted toward the bike path, kicking up gravel with every step I took. Jumping onto the bike, I pedaled as hard as I could, but it slumped and lurched. I strained myself to no avail, then stopped and examined the bike. The rear tire valve had been opened and the cap was missing.

"Fuck!"

I started to run, dragging the bike along beside me. The pedals, turning by themselves, kept hitting my shin, but I was so focused on dashing ahead that I didn't feel any pain. I ran like this for quite a while until I was soaked in sweat from head to toe. My shin was throbbing and aching.

Night fell abruptly. The street lamps all came on simultaneously, as if they were frightened by the sudden darkness. At least there was no sign of the motorcycle following me.

Without knowing why, I looked over my shoulder, and almost froze on the spot. The same asshole was running towards me in the middle of the path, through the crisscrossed shadows of bare branches. His face was still hidden behind the baseball cap and face mask. His posture hadn't changed: he was still holding his torso straight and his arms close to his sides. His eyes, though they were in shadow, glared and almost seemed to smolder. He was bearing down on me rapidly.

Hurling the bike aside, I ran for my life. "Whuh, whuh." His panting was so close I thought it would grab me by the back of my neck. I raced, my heart almost exploding. My mouth fell open, and my face twitched. The bastard didn't seem the slightest bit tired. It was as if he had just started out, and yet he had been running all that time and was now only thirty feet behind me. He seemed intent on chasing me into the fires of hell.

The bright lights of the Cheongdam Bridge suddenly came into view just ahead. The light of the setting sun lingered, making the bases of the columns glow. Dark except for its neon sign, the floating restaurant sunk into the dusk. The fishermen had left the riverbank. The snack bar was closed, yet the door of the restroom was wide open.

Where had Eun-jae gone? What was wrong with that asshole runner? Who the hell was he, anyway? A flood of questions throbbed in my temples. There was no one around to help me, and if something should happen to me there was not a single eyewitness—in the middle of this vast city—to testify that some crazy asshole who I didn't even know had assaulted me for no reason. I felt like I was being hunted down by that jerk. I was desperate but I didn't know what to do, I was unable to move.

Just then the paddle boats caught my eye. I scurried down the steps to the river and dashed toward the dock. Grabbing randomly at the ropes that were tied to the handrail, I fumbled in my haste to untie them, then flung myself into a boat. I pedaled the boat away from the dock as fast as I could. It was a good thing I had been working out on a stationary bike, doing more than six miles a day without a break. I was lousy at running, but I sure could pedal. The paddle boat slid forward rapidly. The rest of the boats drifted away, rocking on the agitated water. The bastard wasn't at the dock or on the riverbank. No doubt he was hiding somewhere in the looming darkness, glaring at me.

Wondering where Eun-jae had gone, I fumbled in my pocket for my cell phone, but it wasn't there. I must have left it at home.

My camera had disappeared too. When and where had I dropped it? I scanned the path that I had run along so frantically. There was nothing there but the gathering darkness, silent, as if nothing had happened.

A train rattled past on the bridge. It was packed with people on their way home from work. The windows, glowing with a yellowish light, were misted up from the warm breath of the commuters, some sighing with contentment at the end of the day, others tired but indifferent. The train, sliding uphill at the end of the bridge, seemed about to take off into the sky, the way Galaxy Express 999 did in the anime cartoon I used to watch on TV as a child. It really did look like that, like it was heading for a distant planet in that galaxy where it's said people can buy immortal life, if only they have enough money to pay for it. But scarcely had the stream of yellow light slipped across the bridge when it disappeared behind the impenetrable wall on the other side of the river. The gigantic structure that spanned the river looked forlorn as the train left it behind, like a deserted space-train station on an abandoned planet. I kept pedaling away in silence. The other side of the river was still very far away.

Ninety-Nine Percent

I sometimes get a craving for something sweet. It happens when I've lain awake all night and still haven't come up with a single workable idea, or when I've presented my concepts for an ad campaign and I'm waiting to hear the result, or simply when something makes me anxious. Then my sweet tooth kicks in and torments me. Chocolate works best. As it melts in my mouth, the sweet chocolate boosts my heart rate and sends blood pumping to every region of my brain, taking the edge off that nagging need for something sweet. What works best of all is chocolate with almonds. Apart from the pleasant crunchiness of the nuts, there's the fact that almonds are good brain food.

The first time I met the guy, I felt my craving switch on and start bugging me. I had never experienced this before: having a craving for chocolate when I was introduced to someone. It was bizarre, and I was puzzled.

Even the way the guy first showed up was out of the ordinary. It was a Monday morning in early spring of last year, we were having the worst dust storms on record. The boss himself walked around the office to personally introduce the guy to everyone. All I was thinking at the time was "Here we go, just as expected," because a rumor had been going round that the agency was going to recruit this guy. We'd won far fewer new contracts than expected during the first half of the fiscal year, so everyone was speculating that there would be a shake-up of the organization, or that the agency would be taken in a completely new direction.

In fact this wasn't the first time the company had struggled. The advertising industry had become very polarized. A handful of giant companies with significant resources had snapped up most of the major contracts. At the same time, boutique agencies were targeting niche markets, where they could make the most of their unique creative approach. It was medium-sized businesses like ours that were having the greatest difficulty. There had been some rumors around the office that our company might merge with another agency of similar size, but most of us were expecting a round of heavy layoffs to be announced at any moment.

None of us dared to be away from our desk even for a few minutes; we were all painfully aware that unemployment had worsened and even if you had an outstanding resume you weren't going to be able to find another job easily. Even the creative director, who always used to go to the sauna on his lunch hour, began to show up in the cafeteria every day. I was watching my back too and I tried to avoid using the online messenger to chat with Miseon. She worked in accounting. We had been dating ever since we met at a company cycling event, but we'd been keeping our relationship under wraps.

A wunderkind of the advertising industry who had the Midas touch; a genuine global expert with hands-on experience working in America, the hub of capitalism ... I couldn't believe my ears—I was embarrassed for him—when I heard the company president praising the guy, especially given that the boss was never one to compliment his employees. Nevertheless, standing there beside the president, the guy looked self-assured and composed. His chiseled features gave him an aristocratic air. The president was ecstatic. He was like a school principal introducing a new student he had been scouting and had finally persuaded to transfer from a big-city school. I was suddenly reminded of the principal of G_____ School—the principal who had personally led me into a classroom and introduced me to the class.

Before transferring to G_____ School, I'd been at a high school in the city of B_____. It was shortly after my father had had an accident and had had to quit his job as a cab driver. G_____ School offered me a scholarship that covered all my tuition, board, and other expenses. Otherwise I would have had to quit school. It was a private school located in the city of G_____, on a nearby island. The school had plenty of money, and they were eager to scout gifted students from other high schools in the vicinity. What was really amazing was that they were offering full four-year college tuition to any of their students who got into Seoul National University.

The principal had great hopes for me because I had been a top-ranked student at my previous high school, which was one of the most prestigious schools in B_____. When he introduced me to the other kids, he made his expectations clear. Not only was it rare for a school principal to introduce a new student in person, but what he said about me was very flattering, so I was too embarrassed to hold my head up in front of the class. "Well now, I'm very pleased to introduce an outstanding student, a future star of our school. Now, Choi, who stands in front of you today, was a first-rate student at the highly reputed B_____ high school . . ."

"My name is Steve Kim. Nice to meet you." The guy greeted everyone individually, reaching out to shake hands. He offered his hand to me too, saying the same thing. The instant I shook hands with him I was struck by a strong sensation of déjà vu.

"Have we met before?" I asked.

He blinked rapidly.

"Well, I couldn't say, but a lot of people ask me that," he answered, smiling, "because I guess I have a rather generic look." He had straight, white teeth.

Mi-seon started an online chat.

"You sucked up to him pretty fast. I didn't know you were that kind of person."

"What are you talking about?"

"I heard that you suggested to Steve Kim that you'd met him before."

"Who said that?"

"Everyone's talking about it."

"That's ridiculous."

"Didn't you ask him if you'd met before?"

"How does that amount to sucking up?"

"That's what it sounds like. Had you two really met before, by the way?"

"No."

"You didn't know him but you asked that question anyway? That sounds to me like sucking up. It's impressive that he's already a vice-president at his age. Wait a second . . . you're the same age!"

"I'm busy."

"Do you want to get spaghetti for lunch today?"

I closed the live chat window. Taking a chocolate bar out of my desk drawer, I stuffed the whole thing into my mouth at once. Apparently the guy was already a topic of conversation around the office. The nonsense about me sucking up to him was clearly because they were all so interested in him, not in me.

Whether they were eating in the cafeteria or drinking coffee around the vending machine, all they talked about was the new guy. Whenever he put in an appearance, they all started gossiping about him the second he walked away. The women mainly rattled on about his clean-cut looks and elegant manners.

"He's so handsome!"

"He has such nice manners!"

"He's the perfect American gentleman."

The men revealed, one by one, what they thought about his job title.

"Has there ever been a new hire who's been named vice-president right off the bat? Even if he is very capable?"

"I heard they created the position so they could persuade him to sign."

"It's like a rookie being put in as relief pitcher."

"It's got to be a bit of a blow to Sauna Park, since he's got ten years' seniority on the new guy."

Everyone fell silent when Sauna Park, our creative director, appeared.

"Anyone got a cigarette?" he asked, trying to sound nonchalant.

Nobody answered.

"Oh dear! No smokers here. Ha-ha!" Then he turned to me and said, "Mr. Choi, I know you smoke."

"I quit a few months ago."

"You're so damn strong-willed! You know fathers don't let their daughters marry a quitter, right? Ha-ha! Oh, all right then. I hope you guys all live a long and healthy life. Ha-ha!" Forcing a laugh, Sauna Park turned and walked away.

"It's enough to make anyone nervous," someone mumbled. "Even a person who's as self-possessed as a Buddha," and everyone looked at me.

Sauna Park and I came from the same town. He was one of the first people to be hired at the agency, and he was a close friend of the boss. Away from the office they were on first-name terms. Furthermore, Sauna Park made no secret of the fact that he liked me and looked back with pleasure on my early days with the agency, when he was my boss. The fact that I'd been promoted to assistant manager before anyone else who'd joined the company at the same time was not due to any favoritism on Sauna Park's part. But my co-workers thought differently. Their true opinions would come out when they'd had a few drinks.

"Your friend Sauna Park always has your back." I found this annoying.

"You all know that Sauna Park doesn't play favorites and he's always fair. He doesn't get into arguments, even when he should. If he gets steamed he just heads off to the steam bath. That's how he got his nickname, right?"

As he retreated toward the end of the bleak hallway, Sauna Park's back looked like a crumpled cigarette packet.

That afternoon, the new guy showed up at a meeting of the creative department. Everyone was clearly surprised. A vice-president sitting in on the meeting? And on his first day at the agency?

"I want to get familiar with what's happening in the agency as quickly as possible. That's why I'm here. Please don't let my presence inhibit you. Just go ahead as usual," he said with his trademark sly smile, his glance sweeping around the table.

The purpose of the meeting was to brainstorm concepts for a cup ramen commercial. We'd had the advertising contract for this brand of cup ramen for the past two seasons, but sales had fallen off recently. There were rumors that the client was going to put the contract out to bid, and everyone at our agency was worried. The economy was at a standstill, so new contracts were few and far between, and the last thing the company wanted was to lose an existing client. The atmosphere in the meeting couldn't have been tenser.

A variety of ideas came up: that we should go with animation to target the primary market segment, or that we should use an emerging pop singer as our new spokesperson. I put forward an idea too.

"An ad for cup ramen needs to differentiate it from regular ramen products. What's the chief benefit of cup ramen? That it's very easy to enjoy, anytime, anywhere. Picture this: a group of climbers is scaling a perilous-looking snow-capped mountain. A blizzard leaves them stranded in their tent with the summit, their destination, right ahead. They're all shivering with cold. Their teeth are clattering. All they have to eat is canned food, which has all frozen. Then a Sherpa melts some snow and boils water. He takes a cup ramen out of his backpack, pours hot water into the cup and starts eating it. Once the storm is over, the Sherpa leads the group up the mountain and reaches the summit first."

The meeting fell silent for a moment. This usually meant one of two things: either the concept someone had suggested was ridiculous, or quite the opposite. If it was ridiculous, people didn't avoid making eye contact with the person who proposed it. They would give the person a sympathetic glance which was often a thinly disguised look of scorn. If the opposite was the case, and the concept was a good one, they tried to look away so as not to reveal the envy burning inside them. A couple of people nodded. Even the office manager, who was notoriously scathing and outspoken, didn't dismiss the idea.

"A group of climbers with cup ramen . . . Maybe going the humorous route will work," said Sauna Park, approvingly.

I was beginning to think I'd struck gold when the new guy started to speak.

"As you all know, the Jungfrau is one of the most challenging peaks in the Alps and is often called 'the rooftop of Europe.'

It rises 13,635 feet above sea level, and is capped with snow year round. As the peak's name, which means 'virgin,' suggests, few people have managed to conquer it."

Everyone looked puzzled. "Didn't he say he was here to familiarize himself with our work?" my colleagues seemed to be saying to themselves. "So why all this stuff about Jungfrau?" "He's supposed to be the wunderkind of the industry, but he doesn't have a clue about what we've been working on." Unfazed by the perplexed looks, the guy went on.

"At 11,332 feet above sea level there's an observation platform with a view of the summit. Cup ramen is the top-selling item in the cafeteria there. As you may already be aware, they started selling cup ramen there because Korean tourists kept asking for it, and then it became popular among Western people who weren't very used to spicy food at that time. As this example shows, there's a good chance that there are still some new market segments we can explore. Besides, showing that cup ramen has become popular overseas will help promote it in domestic markets as well. Come to think of it, let's go with the slogan 'The spicy Korean flavor enjoyed around the world,' and feature it in a series of commercials. Eskimos serve their most highly valued dish when their friends come to visit. How about this? An Eskimo has a Korean friend over and serves him cup ramen. They sit side by side enjoying cup ramen in an igloo. Then we show people all over the world eating cup ramen: at Niagara Falls, at Machu Picchu, at the Great Wall of China, at the Eiffel Tower and so on. 'Anytime, anywhere, taste the spicy Korean flavor enjoyed around the world!'" The guy ended his lengthy speech with the slogan he had made up on the spur of the moment.

"Bravo!" someone shouted. A few people even applauded.

"Your strategy is to capitalize on how Koreans go crazy for anything that's popular overseas, right?"

"This feels like the beginning of a new era in cup ramen advertising."

"What we have here is the strategic exploitation of consumer psychology."

"I'd like to be part of your team when you shoot footage overseas."

"Machu Picchu! Cool!"

One by one they all gushed over the new guy's proposal. His face settled into a smug smile.

"Do you know how much the world's most expensive wooden chopsticks cost?" the guy went on, apparently emboldened by the positive response to his idea. "At first the staff at the cafeteria gave Korean tourists hot water for free whenever they asked for it. But then they noticed that the Koreans were using the hot water to eat something. The Swiss are very business savvy. They saw their opportunity and began selling cup ramen. But then they realized they needed to sell hot water as well, because the Koreans weren't buying cup ramen. They were just asking for hot water. The cafeteria sold hot water for three euros. And then a pair of chopsticks for one euro. People often forgot to bring chopsticks for their cup ramen. Then the Korean tourists stopped bringing their own cup ramen with them."

Everyone burst out laughing.

"But the Jungfrau is actually 13,641 feet above sea level, isn't it?" I blurted out the question.

Everyone immediately stopped laughing, as if in response to a prearranged signal. They just studied the guy's face. He and I stared fiercely at one another. His white-hot gaze stirred up something that had been buried deep in my memory. I remembered seeing a gaze like this once before.

When the principal introduced me to my new classmates, I noticed a look of envy and caution in their eyes. There was one particularly unforgettable glare that had struck me at the time. It was from a kid who was seated at the very end of a row, next to the window. He looked at me the way a boxer glares at his opponent before the start of a fight, when the referee is reminding them of the rules. The cold gaze of his narrow eyes gleamed with the enmity of a beast whose territory has been invaded, with jealousy toward someone praised in a way that he had never been. This was the gaze of my classmate Tae-man, who, until I came along, had always been the top-ranked student in the school. Kim Tae-man was his name.

"You have a very good memory, Mr. Choi," the guy said with a smile. "The Jungfrau was 13,641 feet high, as you say. But I'm sorry to say that the glacier on the summit has melted and so the mountain has lost about six feet. Because of global warming, you know." His smile lifted one corner of his mouth slightly, giving him that sly look.

"I'm honored to work with you, sir," someone proclaimed. Someone else suddenly stood up and applauded like an ancient Roman welcoming a general back from a victorious campaign. The corner of the guy's mouth, which had been raised in a sneer, now relaxed, and he looked like the picture of congeniality. I felt a sudden craving for something sweet.

The client was overjoyed with the new guy's advertising concept. In fact, the new vice president put together the presentation and pitched it himself. The client accepted it without blinking. Rumor had it that just the slogan, "The spicy Korean flavor enjoyed around the world," had been enough to captivate the client. Although some of our staff had concerns about the cost of shooting footage overseas, the guy won approval for his entire proposal, including the series of TV commercials. There would be as many as five or six ads based on the global landmarks theme. For our agency, this was like winning the lottery.

There were no more complaints about recruiting the guy. Instead, everyone was talking about how young he was and saying that it showed how dynamic our company was. The mystery surrounding how the firm had set about recruiting him sparked the employees' imaginations and had them concocting a series of dramatic stories about the guy: that the boss had promised to hand over the business to the new guy; that the boss had gone to see the guy as many as seven times before he finally succeeded in hiring him; that the boss and the new guy met for the first time when they both got lost hiking on Mount Jiri; and so forth. There was even a rumor that the boss had hired the guy with the intention of getting him to marry his daughter. The swirl of unconfirmed rumors added to the hype around his unconventional start with the company.

He came to every single meeting. People were puzzled by this at first, but they soon got used to it. He would listen to everyone else and then trot out his own idea. The concept he presented always ended up being chosen and put into production. Every decision that was made, from creating the storyboard for a commercial to selecting a model, came from one of his suggestions. He had rapidly occupied the agency like a military commander invading a less developed country.

One evening we all got together to celebrate our success in getting a contract renewed, but the festive atmosphere changed, and everyone started brown-nosing Steve Kim, falling over one another to flatter him. Even the people who had been fuming about how crazy it had been to hire the guy were now praising his keen intelligence and his skillful way with words. These were the same people who, until just a short time prior, had been flattering me and saying that I was the genius of the agency and an endless source of ideas. As for the women, they were all trying to catch his eye. Miseon was no exception. She even stood next to him and drained the glass of beer that the guy had filled for her. Then she handed the glass back to him. I couldn't believe this was the same Miseon who usually sat with a beer in front of her but didn't touch it, as she said that just a few sips would go right to her head.

The conversation drifted to the guy's distinguished career and his Ivy League degree and his MBA. He told us that after working briefly for a consulting company in America, he had taken his career in a new direction and gone into the advertising industry. He explained that he had wanted to do something creative even if it wasn't as well paid. Then someone asked him why he had decided to return to Korea.

"I stopped in my tracks one day when I saw a billboard in Times Square in New York," he explained. "It was an ad for a Korean company. Right there and then I realized that if my work was going to help sell anything, I wanted it to be products from my native land."

People nodded and some even applauded.

"My cousin goes to the same college you went to," said Ms. Jeong, a copywriter who had joined the company earlier in the year. "I heard that there's some really bizarre hazing that goes on there. Was that the case when you were there?"

The guy drank deeply as if to quench his thirst and then began to speak.

"I was a very shy kid, and when I went to college I was still suffering from social anxiety. It was so serious that I used to spend all my time holed up in my dorm room. I skipped a lot of classes. The other students gave me the nickname 'Ghost,' which goes to show what I was like back then. One day I went to one of my core classes for the first time in a long while. Before taking attendance, the professor turned to me and asked me to let Steve Kim know that if he skipped one more lecture he was going to flunk him. I laughed sheepishly, thinking it was a joke. But, you know what, no one tried to tell the professor that I was the person in question. When I looked around, I was the only one who was laughing. It came as a real shock to me. I wondered if I'd really turned into a ghost, and I became really worried. The very next day I went to a clinic and made an appointment with a therapist."

The festive atmosphere around the table had suddenly turned somber.

"I'm sorry. That was a stupid question," said Ms. Jeong, her voice trembling slightly.

"That's all right. It's ancient history now. You guys, don't be loners. It's not cool."

Everyone relaxed again.

"I heard you went to America when you were still in elementary school," said Ms. Kang, a designer. "But you speak Korean very well. In my case, I had a really hard time getting used to speaking Korean again, and I didn't go to America until after I graduated from high school."

Ms. Kang, who drove a Mini Cooper and wore nothing but

Louis Vuitton, was proud of having graduated from an American university. Mi-seon's face darkened. She often got angry, saying that Ms. Kang treated her like she was an ignorant country girl. And the other young women were no different. They all had well-to-do parents, they didn't even need to work. They weren't trying to make a living. They were just working for the extra spending money for clothes and makeup. They might consider getting married, but only if they happened to meet a wealthy man. Otherwise, these were the sort of women who were contemptuous of conventional marriage. Their careers allowed them to make an easy life for themselves. That was all. Doesn't it sound glamorous? The concepts behind most commercials in the 1990s, which targeted young career women, weren't workable any more, because what they used to dream about had now become reality. Women no longer just fantasized about that kind of life. "They're different from us," said Sauna Park one day. "They're blue-bloods. They even smell different, don't they?"

The employees who had joined the company after it became successful were indeed distinct. They'd been to elite schools, and their families were filthy rich. They all drove expensive imported cars before they'd even gotten their first job. They each had a good command of a foreign language, besides English. Mi-seon, who had graduated from a little-known college, stuck out among her co-workers. When she was hired, various rumors went around: that she knew the right people; that her father owned a local construction company; that her father was a big shot in the world of payday loans; that she was a close relative of the boss. These rumors all turned out to be false. Mi-seon's father worked at a local government office. Once they found out the facts about Mi-seon's background, people started to make fun of our boss and his odd way of interviewing people. The boss—who I'd heard had been the caretaker of a mountain cabin on Mount Jiri before he started the agency—would ask job applicants the date and time of their birth and read their palms. Rumor had it that when he interviewed Mi-seon he nodded approvingly and said that her birth date was a good omen for any company where she happened to work. Whether or not it proves his point, it was true that Mi-seon had as many as five bank accounts and they all had plenty of money in them.

"My mother made me speak Korean at home," said the guy, with a wistful look. Everyone nodded.

There had been a gigantic shipyard on the island I had moved to for my studies, and people had arrived in large numbers when it was built. Then money came flooding in. Blue-eyed foreigners became a common sight. Nine times out of ten they were ship-builders. Most of these engineers came from places like Britain, Greece and Sweden, where the shipbuilding industry had flour-ished. The mother of my rival student Tae-man ran a bar where foreign engineers were regular customers. She would often speak in a mix of English and Korean. When she asked what someone's father did for a living, she would say, "What is your father's *ji-geop*?" and inquiring about a person's ambitions, she would ask "What's your future *ggum* job?" She was known across the island for her beauty. Her skin was fair and smooth, and she had big, sparkling eyes. What's more, she was friendly and likeable and she could persuade even the British engineers — the most reticent men in the world — to open both their hearts and their wallets. Tae-man, however, was nothing like his mother; so much so that the townspeople used to gossip about his birth. He didn't have a father. No one believed him when he said his father was a crew-man of a deep-sea tuna fishing vessel.

"What elementary school did you go to?" I asked Steve Kim.

Blinking rapidly, he replied. "I don't remember, because our family emigrated right after I started elementary school. When we arrived in America, it was as if my memory had been wiped clean." He shrugged. "I'm pretty sure of one thing, though, that I didn't go to the same elementary school as Mr. Choi."

My co-workers burst out laughing. While they all bustled about ordering another round of drinks, I snuck out, taking Mi-seon with me. We went to a bar that we often liked to go to. I was thirsty, and I gulped down a bottle of Budweiser.

"You know his idea for the cup ramen commercial?" I said.

"Strictly speaking, that was my idea, and he stole it from me. I was the first person to come up with the idea of eating cup ramen in an unexpected place."

"Did we slip away just so you could talk about this?" Mi-seon said, in a sarcastic tone of voice.

"Maybe you don't understand, because you weren't there when it happened."

"I know what happened. I heard all about it," said Mi-seon. "But you don't really think a snow-capped mountain is the same as the North Pole, do you? Besides, the point of the vice-president's concept is to show people from different countries eating cup ramen together, isn't it?"

"It makes no difference whether it's a snow-capped mountain or the North Pole," I replied. "The idea of a unique location is what's distinctive about the concept. I mean the idea of suggesting that even people in distant lands enjoy cup ramen. Besides, a Sherpa and an Eskimo are pretty much the same to Koreans, since they're both strange and foreign. So basically Steve Kim copied my idea."

"You still don't understand the main point of the vice-president's concept, do you?" said Mi-seon, speaking so earnestly it was as if she were defending her own work. "The idea is to show the Eskimo tradition of serving what they value most to their guests. And the implication is that Eskimos value cup ramen highly."

"Even if I concede he didn't actually copy my idea, at the very least he still exploited my idea to come up with his Eskimo version."

"You haven't mentioned this to anybody, have you?" Mi-seon asked, sounding like she thought I was pathetic.

"You think I'm being ridiculous?"

"I don't see a problem, even if the vice-president was inspired by your idea. That's the kind of thing that always happens in brainstorming meetings, isn't it?" Mi-seon was unusually insistent.

"The problem is how arrogant he is when he discusses those ideas, as if he were the one who thought them all up."

"So this is all about you being unhappy because you aren't appreciated for what you contribute, is that it?"

I took off my jacket.

"It's not a question of how unhappy I am. I just want to tell you the truth. The reason I'm telling you this is not to try to get you to say how good my work is, but just to open your eyes to the truth. When you're wounded by a lie, revealing the truth is the only cure."

We were beginning to attract attention. Apparently I was talking loudly.

"All right," said Mi-seon, suddenly becoming amenable. She liked it when I was argumentative, and, sure enough, respect showed in her eyes when she looked at me. It was the kind of look that made me feel important, the look of envy and esteem that always used to follow me in the city of G____.

"Don't you think Steve Kim is odd?" I asked abruptly, as if the notion had just come into my head.

"In what way?"

"He seems reluctant to talk about his life in America, doesn't he? Especially his student days."

"That's because he's modest. Otherwise he'd be bragging about it nonstop. You know how everyone in the office always shows off about studying abroad? Honestly, the vice-president is so different, telling embarrassing stories about himself so frankly. Successful people like him wouldn't normally reveal themselves that way. I thought at first he was one of those ruthlessly ambitious types, but I realized he's not and he's actually full of heart. He became a marvel of the advertising industry after overcoming social anxiety! He's pretty impressive!"

I was beginning to regret having opened up to Mi-seon about Steve Kim. But now that I'd started, I went on.

"It makes no sense that he couldn't remember the name of his elementary school just because his family emigrated right after he enrolled."

"Oh, that can happen. I sometimes have trouble remembering my own cell phone number or my address. Jet lag really could have made his mind go blank, who knows?"

"Jet lag? Oh, please! Do you seriously think it was because of jet lag?"

"I didn't mean it seriously. Anyway, why do you get so upset every time the vice-president is mentioned? I guess you would be jealous, wouldn't you?" Mi-seon looked at me with a cheerful smile.

"Jealous? Don't be silly! I don't even know the meaning of the word! And how come you treat him with so much deference when he's just joined the company? You drank every drop that he poured for you, and you haven't even touched the drink I bought you. You'd think he gave you honey and I'm giving you poison."

"Oh, so it's true! You are jealous of him!" She smiled as if she was enjoying seeing me betray my emotions. I was fed up with the mystery of Steve Kim, and with our pointless conversation.

Steve Kim continued to excel, making my suspicions about him seem more and more foolish. He rose to dizzying heights that my skeptical mind could never have imagined, and there he shone brilliantly.

"Apparently Steve Kim has won every contract he's bid for."

"That's seven in a row, isn't it?"

"They say Steve Kim caused total panic when he left his former company. The owner himself tried to talk him out of it and promised him everything he could think of, a bonus or stocks. But Steve Kim didn't bite. He left. That's when he joined our company. There might be some truth to the rumor that the boss promised to make him his successor."

"It's just a matter of time till we see the youngest president ever in this industry."

Steve Kim was becoming a legend.

The more dazzling his achievements became, the more my suspicions grew. I found it particularly hard to believe that he had quit a world-famous consulting firm out of sheer patriotism, and had left behind all he had achieved to come back to Korea. Everyone in this country is desperate to fly across the Pacific to America, to the extent that they'll give up a decent job because they say that they want to advance their career or that they're willing to take a gamble on anything in the New World. Why would he do the opposite? Just because he wanted to help sell products from his home country? What crap! And what about his mysterious past? It was strange that my co-workers didn't notice any of the inconsistencies about Steve Kim that were so obvious to me. What was especially ridiculous was how they portrayed his return as being like the Jews' return to Israel. The uncertainties surrounding his past just fed their imaginations and gave rise to a series of myths about him.

I had to admit, however, that he was extraordinarily gifted. His skills particularly came into play when we found ourselves in a quandary. There was one time, for instance, when we were previewing footage for a new milk commercial. It went like this: it's dawn, and the city is silent; a young woman in workout clothes is jogging briskly along the streets; a little while later, she sees a newspaper and a bottle of milk on her doorstep; wiping perspiration from her forehead, she opens the bottle and drinks the milk with obvious enjoyment. Then came the voice-over, which I had written: "A glass of milk in the morning satisfies you all day!" When we looked at the client's face, we could tell he wasn't happy.

"It's a milk commercial," said the client grumpily. "Why are the actress's boobs so pathetic?" And he got up and left, his marketing team following him.

"The actress's breasts aren't that bad," said Sauna Park. "That old man has a thing for huge boobs."

Everyone tittered.

"Are you seriously laughing when the client has just said no?" said Steve Kim sharply. "What kind of professionals are you? Do you have no pride in your work?"

Sauna Park's face reddened as if he had just come out of the steam room. I had to look away.

"The actress's figure has nothing to do with their sales figures," I muttered.

"Mr. Choi!" said Steve Kim, raising his voice. "We're not selling milk, we're selling a milk commercial!"

"Do something about the actress's breasts. Then we'll meet again."

"Well, sir. Umm . . ." said Jang in a barely audible voice. "The actress is away in Australia on a shoot."

This was a snag that no one had anticipated.

"Don't you know everything is supposed to be on standby until the client signs off on it? What's the problem with you? Are we a junior high advertising club?"

This was the first time we'd seen Steve Kim get angry. It was excruciating. There was a heavy silence in the room. After a few minutes Steve Kim continued.

"Let's use CGI to fix it. Tell the production team to get to work on it. Let's make the breasts look as full as possible and get them to bounce dramatically when the actress is jogging."

"But, that's . . ." Jang looked baffled.

"What's wrong?" Steve Kim asked.

"Well you see, this actress is trying to shed the pin-up girl image . . ." Mr. Jang's voice trailed off as he waited to see how Steve Kim would react.

Kim began to speak slowly and clearly, as if he were giving instructions to a child.

"Call the actress's manager and tell him the client is asking for a different actress. She wants to change her image? That's something only an A-list actress can afford to do!"

As he was leaving the room he turned around, as if he'd just remembered something.

"Mr. Choi, rewrite the copy, please. Now that we're going with a different actress. The wording we have now is boring. You'll have it ready by tomorrow morning, right? And the rest of you, let's go out for a drink after work."

"Are you buying?" someone asked facetiously.

"Of course!" he answered, sounding upbeat.

I worked late that evening, alone, sipping a glass of milk and struggling to write new copy.

"Milk?" Miss Kim, an assistant who took care of miscellaneous things around the office, dropped a black plastic bag down on my desk. It was full of cartons of milk. They were our client's products. When I asked her what they were for, she said that the vice president had sent them with the message that the milk would help me come up with some fabulous slogans.

"Do you need anything else?" Miss Kim asked, with a cheeky grin.

"Some Lacteeze," I said, forcing myself to smile.

My mind began to wander. I stared at the computer screen and kept clicking the mouse. Every now and then I would snap out of it and find myself snooping around the website of the school they said Steve Kim had graduated from. I even googled the words "social anxiety," "ghost," and "Steve Kim." Then, as I stared numbly at the words "Steve Kim" on the screen, a thought struck me. Steve Kim can't be his real name, because he wasn't born in America. He must have a Korean name. I felt stupid for not having thought of it until now.

The following day I invited Mi-seon to lunch in an Italian restaurant. She dreamed of seeing Venice, and she was crazy about everything Italian. Coincidentally, the name of the restaurant was Venezia. She smiled broadly as she read the menu. The food was more expensive than I had expected. Mi-seon ordered seafood lasagna and spaghetti alle vongole for herself and me.

"What's the matter? You've been so careful not to draw attention to us in the office, and now you invite me out for lunch," said Mi-seon sarcastically.

I got straight to the point.

"Do you by any chance know Steve Kim's real name?"

"The vice president's real name? How could I possibly know it?"

I was disappointed, but I wasn't ready to give up.

"Aren't you curious?"

"What? About the vice president's real name?" Mi-seon was on the defensive. "I don't understand. Who cares about his real name?"

"You're afraid your fantasy about him will be shattered, aren't you?" I tried to provoke her a little.

"Fantasy? Nonsense! I'm not a teenager!" She snapped. My attempt to provoke her had worked. I saw it as a good sign and decided to go on prodding her.

"He submitted his banking information for his pay, didn't he?

You could easily find out his real name if you took a look, right?" The idea had struck me early that morning while I was jotting down some slogans on a piece of paper. Thank God for the accounting system! I was so pleased with the idea I almost let out a shout of triumph.

"What's going on? What in the world are you trying to find out?" Mi-seon asked, narrowing her eyes.

"I'm just curious." My excuse sounded weak even to my ears. Fortunately, our food arrived right at that moment.

"Sir! Mr. Kim!" Mi-seon cried out, rising to her feet abruptly.

Steve Kim stopped on his way out of the restaurant and turned towards us. He was about to leave because there were no tables available. Mi-seon asked if it was just him, and he nodded. Without attempting to disguise her pleasure, she invited him to join us.

"I'm not interrupting you?" he asked politely.

"Not a bit." Only then did she ask what I thought about it. "It's all right with you, isn't it?"

I just barely stopped myself from saying Speak of the devil! and motioned him to join us.

"Please take a seat, sir."

"Have you ever been to Venice, sir?" Mi-seon asked, pulling her chair closer to the table.

"Venice?" He repeated.

"I mean Venezia."

"Oh, Venezia! The city the Italians built on the sea so that they could get away easily if Attila the Hun invaded. You know who Attila the Hun was? An Eastern emperor, the most feared enemy of the Eastern and Western Roman Empires."

"Wow! So you've been to Venice. I really want to go and see it before it sinks."

"Don't worry," he said, laughing. "The city is a UNESCO world heritage site, so it won't be allowed to disappear. Actually, I heard that UNESCO is planning a vast project to prevent the ground from subsiding. They're going to build a seawall to hold back the tides. It will cost an unimaginable sum, which is why they raised the fee for using public toilets. Do you know how much it is? It's one euro! It's a kind of environmental fee. The city makes money from selling water and charges for flushing the toilets. It's literally 'a city of water.'"

Mi-seon's jaw dropped in awe at Steve Kim's eloquence and vast knowledge.

"Why don't you order?" I interrupted.

"Mi-seon, you'll find that garlic bread is best dipped in olive oil and balsamic vinegar. Could you bring me a pizza margherita and gnocchi? And some six-year-old balsamic vinegar too, please," he said to the waitress, without looking at the menu.

"Sorry, but we only have three-year-old balsamic vinegar," said the waitress apologetically.

"That'll be better than nothing," he said. "A six-year-old vinegar would have been perfect, though," he added, with a hint of dissatisfaction.

I dipped my garlic bread in spaghetti sauce and ate it unconcernedly.

"Sir," I asked as we were having coffee after the meal, "what do you think of the new copy for the commercials?"

"What copy?" he asked, sounding puzzled.

"The copy for the milk commercial," I said, my voice sounding brusque in spite of myself.

"For the milk commercial? You rewrote the copy? Why? It was fine the way it was."

"Are you certain you don't remember telling me to rewrite it by this morning? I spent all night at the office working on it." I didn't go as far as to mention the milk cartons.

"Did I? Thank you for trying, then. I'll check it out when I get back to the office. Mi-seon," he said, avoiding my gaze, "coffee is best enjoyed while it's still hot. Finish it before it cools down. Colombian coffee is the finest, by the way." I felt a flare-up of anger in my chest.

Kim left, saying he had somewhere to go, and Mi-seon and I walked back toward the office.

"It's strange," I murmured.

"What is?"

"A person who lived in America for many years would say

'Venice,' not 'Venezia,' wouldn't you think?"

"That's right. Because Venice is English for Venezia." This time, Mi-seon agreed with me.

"You think so?" I said, glad that she agreed.

"So what?" Mi-seon asked, looking puzzled that I was pleased.

"When you asked if he'd been to Venice he hesitated. But he understood right away when you called it 'Venezia.' You remember that?"

"So?" Mi-seon asked, glaring at me.

I hesitated. Then she lit into me.

"What the hell are you thinking? It's totally ridiculous! Are you trying to suggest that Mr. Kim padded his resume? That it's fraudulent? Do you think the agency is that stupid?"

"People lie about their education to get university jobs, you know."

Mi-seon let out a sigh and said nothing more.

When we got into the elevator—there was no one in it but the two of us—I said quietly to Mi-seon, "Don't forget what I asked you."

She didn't answer, but she cast a reproachful glance at me.

The following afternoon, Mi-seon started an online chat.

"What's cooking?"

It was our secret code for starting a conversation, to make sure that there was no one around to see our messages.

"No food for three days."

That was code for "All clear."

"The gentleman's real name is . . ."

Gentleman? What crap!

"Get on with it, will you?"

"Kim Hyeon-bin."

I was disappointed because I had expected it to sound lower-class. I assumed he had even changed his Korean name.

"That sounds so slick!"

"It sounds like the name of the hero in a romance novel. I like it much better than 'Steve Kim.'"

"A romance novel? Don't be ridiculous!"

"You know, nine times out of ten, when the heroine finally meets her Mr. Right, he has a name just like that. Oh, Hyeon-bin!"

"Oh, please! Quit writing a screenplay. Wait a second!"

"What? Do you want me to change my hero's name?"

Just then, in the darkroom of my memory, a picture of a summer day in my freshman year of high school began to take shape. Although it was summer break, all the students had come in that day for extra classes. Our math teacher, who was in charge, stopped by our classroom while we were studying.

"Which of you is Kim Hyeon-bin?" he asked, holding a pink envelope in his hand. None of us responded. Naturally, since there was no one by that name in our class.

"Maybe I have the wrong classroom. That's odd. It's supposed to be this room."

"It's for me." A gruff voice came from the back of the classroom. It was Tae-man. He stumbled towards the door.

"Why didn't you come and take it right away? Let me see, you're Kim Tae-man, aren't you?" the math teacher asked, pushing his glasses firmly into place.

"That letter is for me, really."

Tae-man confessed to the math teacher that when he wrote to his pen pal he used the name Kim Hyeon-bin. Even so, he wasn't allowed so much as to touch the letter, but was ordered to clean all the restrooms in the school by himself for seven days. Subsequently, every time the math teacher saw Tae-man he would make fun of him and say "Hyeon-bin, are you still writing to your pen pal? Don't let Tae-man be Delay-man! Make sure you write back to her promptly."

Could Tae-man really be Steve Kim? I shook my head vigorously to dismiss the thought. After work I went straight home and looked through my high school yearbook. I couldn't find Tae-man anywhere. I lit a cigarette, which was something I hadn't done for a long time, and tried to think back to my school days. Once I had enrolled in G_____ School, Tae-man was no longer able to maintain his position at the top of the class. The teachers would post the class rankings at the main entrance of the school building. My name was always at the top of the list, except for just one occasion. Tae-man and I never spoke to each other. He was quiet—almost invisible—in class, but rumor had it that he knew how to have fun outside school. Whenever I passed by his desk, during recess or at lunch break, he would be giggling behind a comic book.

I didn't make friends in the new school because I spent all my time studying. Frankly, I saw my years on that obscure island as just a brief period that had to be endured before I could set foot in the real world. It was windy on the island and I often felt lonesome like a single piece of clothing fluttering on a washing line. To escape the loneliness, I immersed myself more and more in my textbooks, studying late into the night. Quite a few of the high school kids were anxious to get into prestigious universities, but they were way behind the students in my old school. It was a piece of cake for me to take the title of top student in my year and to hold onto it, even though in my last school I had barely managed to make it into the top five. Once I'd overtaken him, Tae-man wasn't able to narrow the gap, let alone catch up with me. His grades were getting worse and worse. Considering what a good student he had been, his deteriorating grades were a mark of extreme failure. When he suddenly left the island toward the end of my second year, he still hadn't been able to get his grades back up.

At that time, Tae-man often used to brag that a British shipbuilding engineer—who he said had fallen for his mother—was going to take them to live in Britain with him. Everyone, however, was curious about the real reason Tae-man and his mother had left the island without any explanation. There were various rumors: they had to beat a hasty retreat because his mother's affair with a married man had become public; they were forced to flee because his father, from whom they had been hiding, had tracked them down. Since Tae-man had voluntarily dropped out of school, some people really believed that he and his mother had left for Britain.

I eventually found Tae-man's picture in one of my old photo

albums. It was a group picture of my freshman class on a picnic. Tae-man was at one end of the back row, just like in the classroom. Narrow eyes, snub nose, square chin, and darkish, acne-covered skin. He stood with his arms crossed, looking standoffish, as if he felt he didn't belong there.

I studied Steve Kim's face during our next meeting. Large, well-defined eyes, a sharp, straight nose, elegantly curved chin, smooth, spotless skin — he exuded pure elegance, as if he had just walked out of a fashion magazine. He had such a composed and self-assured air that anyone who looked at him would think he had never in his life experienced failure. In every respect he was the total opposite of Tae-man, as if he had been created to compensate for everything Tae-man lacked. I couldn't find a single thing that Tae-man and Steve Kim had in common.

"Do I have something on my face, Mr. Choi?" Steve Kim asked, putting his hand up to his cheek.

"No, no. I was just thinking how clean and clear your skin is." I mumbled, scratching my head.

"Mr. Choi, you haven't been overdoing it lately, have you?" asked Steve Kim. "Your face looks rough. Have you thought about visiting a skin clinic?"

"What? I'm not a woman."

Every woman in the room looked at me sternly.

"Men get skin care too, these days. Inner beauty? That's just some pretty nonsense beauty pageant contestants used to like to spout. Inner, outer, we need to be beautiful, inside and out. Besides, as ad men, our job is to project attractive images, isn't it? Keep in mind that a sloppy appearance can suggest negligence on your part."

The next day, while I was surfing the internet, I came across the website of a beauty clinic. They offered not only skin care but also cosmetic surgery. I read through the FAQs and found out that men quite often go in for cosmetic surgery. I texted Mi-seon and asked her if dermabrasion was really worthwhile, but she just scoffed and told me to get real. I thought of texting her back and saying it was unfair of her to say that it was cool for Steve Kim to get cosmetic work but that I was crazy to ask about it. I didn't text her back, though. I took a chocolate bar out of my desk drawer and bit off a chunk.

Steve Kim continued to do an excellent job. Thanks to his extraordinary skills, we got the opportunity to compete for a contract with a car manufacturer. This could be our big break. The office was complete pandemonium; just bidding for a contract like this was far from easy. If we could clinch the deal, it would be a golden opportunity for our agency to advance to the next level.

The product being advertised was a new model of crossover SUV that looked on the outside like a sedan. The market for conventional SUVs had been saturated. If we were going to hold the attention of the existing market and simultaneously target a new market, we needed to create a commercial that highlighted both the characteristic sporty qualities of an SUV and also the upscale image of a sedan. Sportiness and elegance. Our commercial would need to combine these conflicting features into a single concept.

It was such a big project that the agency set up a special team to work on it. Steve Kim was put in charge. There was nothing unusual about putting together a special team when something came up that needed an exceptional degree of commitment. But it was unusual for someone at such a high level in the agency to be appointed as a team leader. As a matter of fact, there was some griping about the arrangement, mostly from senior people.

"Steve Kim is competent. I don't deny it. But the agency has ground rules for organizing projects."

"A vice president taking charge of a team? What are we here for then? Does this mean we should be preparing our letters of resignation?"

"I don't understand why Steve Kim still needs to attend every meeting. It was fair enough in the beginning, because he needed to know what's been going on. But why does he still need to be here?"

"Do you think he's watching us with an eye to laying some of us off? I heard a rumor that there's going to be a big shake-up in the organization, and I'm beginning to think there's some truth to it."

"I heard that Steve Kim's specialty is restructuring organizations."

"Restructuring?"

"That means cutting any non-essential positions."

"So the boss has brought him in to do the dirty work?"

"Steve Kim hasn't formed any kind of network here yet. So we don't have any relationships to rely on, right?"

"That's right. Apparently he said he didn't even remember the name of the elementary school he went to."

"So he was basically saying 'Keep your distance,' huh? If he was trying to create a smokescreen by responding evasively like that, then he's a lot more cunning than we thought."

"Young people are so calculating these days," one of the senior people said, and they all turned to look at me.

"I just wondered what elementary school he went to. That's all. He looked familiar, so I asked." I threw up my hands in protest.

"Why are you so defensive?"

Some of them were clearly disappointed to learn that I had no connection with the guy, and others pretended not to care. They all studied Sauna Park's face to see how he reacted, but he said nothing.

Steve Kim invited the special project team to lunch. We gathered at a nearby Japanese restaurant in a room carpeted with tatami mats. He reminded us how significant the current project was and told us we would all need to buckle down. He poured a cup of sake for each of us as a gesture of encouragement. After eating and drinking together, we were leaving the room when I noticed a pair of brown Ferragamo dress shoes sitting beside the door. Inside the right shoe there was a thick pad. The shoes belonged to Steve Kim. He kept a shoe horn in his pocket and used it only for his left shoe. I almost let out a shout; I knew someone else whose feet were different sizes. It was Kim Tae-man. He was the only person in our whole class who wore Nikes. How could I forget his feet? He had such expensive shoes, and he treated them so carelessly, crushing down the back of one shoe. His left foot was bigger than his right, just like Steve Kim's. And then I realized that Kim was left-handed, like Tae-man. I suddenly felt sweaty and nauseous, my heart pounding.

Struck by this series of coincidences, I felt like I was possessed. I felt that I was on the cusp of the final revelation, as yet unknown, about Steve Kim's true identity. I couldn't focus on my work. The harder I tried to dismiss the mystery from my mind, the more stubbornly it stuck, like a piece of gum on the sole of a shoe.

It was near the end of summer vacation during my second year of high school that Tae-man talked to me for the first time. I was on my way home to see my family and I was standing on the deck of a ferry. Tae-man recognized me and said hello. In our second year we had been assigned to different classrooms, so we had little interaction. If we happened to meet in the hallway, we pretended not to know each other. But on this occasion, Tae-man turned toward me as if we were old friends. A girl was standing beside him. She had big, sparkling eyes. She said she had moved from Seoul the previous year, following her father, and had started at a nearby girls' school.

I said, "Nice to meet you," awkwardly, blurting it out before I had finished bowing to her.

"You're the brilliant guy that the school recruited to send to Seoul National University, aren't you? I'm honored to meet you. Let's be friends." Looking straight into my eyes, she extended her hand.

As the ferry was approaching the port of B_____ the girl told me she and Tae-man were going to see a movie and suggested I should join them. I hesitated, but then Tae-man backed her up, saying it would be more fun if I went along. Every time the girl caught my eye she smiled. I felt as if something I had deliberately buried deep inside me was erupting. I don't remember the name of the movie we saw. Sitting next to me in the theater, the girl smelled of a pleasant perfume I had never smelled before. Tae-man had his arm around her shoulders all the way through the movie. His fingers played with her hair. When we left the movie theater, we made our way to the beach to hang out.

At the beach Tae-man and the girl changed into their swim suits. I lay under an umbrella and watched them playing in the water. The sand glittered like tiny gems in the sunlight, and I felt the lid I'd been keeping on my emotions ever since puberty begin to loosen. My eyelids felt heavy from the sunlight and the sea. A gleaming white yacht was receding toward the distant horizon, and it seemed unreal, like a boat in a dream.

"That's a nice yacht," said Tae-man flopping down next to me. Looking longingly at the boat, he talked on and on about a movie he had seen. It was about jealousy, revenge, murder, and the grim fate of the young protagonist who, being from a disadvantaged background, didn't have a chance to put his talents to use. He was, however, exceptionally gifted, and was tempted to try to change his fate, but, Tae-man recounted in a gloomy voice, his abilities failed him when his luck ran out. He said he would never forget the last scene. Moments before the protagonist was to see the fulfillment of his dreams, the body of his friend floated up to the surface of the water. It had been held down by an anchor, but now the truth was revealed. Tae-man said he had actually shed tears at the sight of the body surfacing. Tae-man's description formed images before my eyes as vivid as the clouds floating across the sky above the blue sea. I actually felt as if I had seen the movie. We watched the gleaming white yacht disappear into the haze that hovered above the horizon. Tae-man said that before setting sail you should always weigh anchor and make sure there's nothing to hold you back. He went on to say that there was a tribe of indigenous people who believed that they could free themselves from whatever they feared by getting a tattoo of what scared them. His words were puzzling, and in the back of my mind I felt uneasy. Many years later I saw the film Tae-man had described. He was wrong. The body hadn't been trapped by an anchor; it was caught in the boat's propeller.

Every day was hectic as we worked frantically on the proposal for the car commercial. We had endless meetings and worked through the night. My suspicions about the guy's background—which I had somehow managed to suppress for a while—surfaced again whenever I saw him. And once aroused, my doubts prompted me to nose around for more inconsistencies, like an animal waking from hibernation and searching hungrily for food. *Aren't you curious to know what he's hiding behind that suave mask?* whispered a voice in my mind. *What's behind that bright smile? Don't you really want to know?* Fed by silence, these suspicions, which I had to keep to myself, grew bigger and bigger and took root deeper and deeper inside me. It would be better for my career and my life if Steve Kim were not the same person as Tae-man. Things would have been easier for me if all my doubts were groundless. As more evidence confirming my suspicions surfaced, I hoped more fervently that the guy was not the person I had known. It felt like I was caught in a trap. A trap that was all the more treacherous because I had set it myself.

It was so bad that one day, when I was staring at my computer screen, someone asked me, "Why are you clenching your teeth so hard? Are you in pain?" In the afternoons I would grow numb as if I had plunged myself repeatedly into hot and cold water. I felt heavy all over as if an anchor were tied to my ankle. When Miseon chatted to me online I didn't respond. One moment I would feel all alone and slip into depression, and the next moment I would fly into a rage, feeling that the whole world was an enemy I had to destroy. I would often find myself in a daze watching the dawn break after spending an entire night sitting on the couch, or I would drift off to sleep behind my desk at the office. Every time I nodded off I had the same nightmare: an anchor was being pulled out of the water, a swollen body dangled from it. The face of the corpse was Steve Kim's. But when the blue, rotting skin was peeled back, it revealed Tae-man's smiling face. Or sometimes my face.

"What do you think of 'Transformer' as a concept for the car commercial?" I said during a brainstorming meeting, looking straight into Steve Kim's eyes. "By presenting the image of a transformer, we can highlight the fusion of a sedan's elegance with the power of an SUV. As you all know, a movie about a car that transforms into a robot was a big hit recently, particularly among men in their thirties and forties."

I stressed the word "transformer," but he didn't seem at all ruffled. He looked as confident and poised as ever.

"What? Are you talking about a car that's a transformer? A sedan transforming into an SUV?" said one of my colleagues with a laugh. I felt dejected.

"I saw the movie because my son nagged me to go to it," said someone else. "It was dumb. I mean, a robot turning into a car and then into a plane? There's even a risk we'd be seen as misleading consumers."

"I enjoyed it. It brought back all my childhood memories of the transformers I used to play with."

"The CGI was cool. But the plot was weak."

"That's because it's based on a comic book."

"I didn't know it wasn't an original story. The little kids in the front rows were talking the whole time. It was really annoying. Little brats!"

They argued back and forth about the movie, and my proposal was forgotten. Then Steve Kim, who had said nothing up till then, started to speak.

"I can see you're all pretty excited about transformers. But I'm sorry. That's not what we're creating a commercial for. Otherwise, I'm sure we could beat our competitors hands down."

Everyone laughed.

"Let's imagine we're in a medieval city. It could be Rothenburg in Germany or Orvieto in Italy. We're looking at a Gothic cathedral in the middle of the city. A wedding is going on. Hey, Mr. Choi! Get away from the altar. It's not your wedding!"

Everyone giggled.

"The bride and groom are a blond couple. After the ceremony the newlyweds, dressed in medieval costumes, walk outside. A new SUV is waiting. It's decorated with colorful balloons and ribbons and there are empty soda cans hanging from the rear bumper. A strip of red carpet leads to the vehicle, and knights on horseback are lined up along each side holding flags and forming a guard of honor. The newlyweds get into the vehicle and a driver in a coachman's uniform drives them away. The husband and wife share a kiss in the back seat. Then they quickly take off their medieval clothes, revealing equestrian outfits underneath. As the vehicle picks up speed the medieval city recedes rapidly into the distance. And then comes the tagline: 'The choice of the chosen few. In the country or the city, the choice of Korea's top one percent!'"

There was silence, followed by applause.

"You never disappoint us, sir. It's a shoo-in."

Everyone congratulated him. The concept that I had prepared for the car commercial was now destined to be thrown away without ever seeing the light of day. So, dear reader, let me take the opportunity to present it here, at least: an SUV is driving rapidly up a mountain; it's splattered with mud. The driver, who has been enjoying the scenery, looks at his watch with a worried expression. The vehicle goes at top speed over the mountain and across a river. With just one hand on the wheel, the driver blows up balloons and drinks from a can. The vehicle—now decorated with balloons and empty cans—pulls up in front of a cathedral. A newlywed couple gets in, and the car drives smoothly away. And then comes the message: "When you want the best and more for every situation."

Thank you, but please hold your forced applause. What I need is not a cheap expression of sympathy but the courage to face the truth. Don't worry. No matter how messed up my mind has been these days, I still have enough sense left not to say out loud to my colleagues, "That guy took my idea again and reshaped it. Damn it, it's just because we've all been kicking around ideas about transformation."

"It's a rather elitist advertising strategy," I said. "I think there's some risk of a backlash. There are some people who are prejudiced toward the rich."

I wondered whether I would feel this way if I were standing on the Jungfrau. A gust of chilly air whirled round me, as I sensed everyone in the room was listening to me.

"You make a good point." His voice was completely calm. "We're tapping into people's contradictory feelings about the message behind the concept. By focusing on the one percent, we're targeting the other ninety-nine percent. The ninety-nine percent who despise the one percent but at the same time want to belong to it. We're going to light the fuse of this complicated envy of the one percent. And then . . ." He paused. "Boom!" he said, stretching his arms out wide.

For the first time in a long while, Mi-seon and I went out for dinner. We went to a restaurant beside the Han River. Now that the concept for the car commercial had been decided we had a little while to relax. The ad would be made soon, and as everyone had predicted, it would be just the way Steve Kim had proposed. Shooting it would be easy, based on the storyboard he had created. The wording was ready too. He was such a genius it was certain that ours would be the winning bid. Mainly because he knew exactly what the client wanted, if not what the consumer wanted. Another glorious victory was going to be added to his stellar resume.

"Why are you so downcast?" Mi-seon asked, pausing as she cut up her salmon.

"Am I?" I said, glumly. Dusk, like dark syrup, was settling densely over the water.

"Is something the matter?"

"What? I don't think so . . ." I hesitated. Should I tell Mi-seon about my suspicions regarding the guy? She might take me seriously.

"You're hiding something from me, aren't you?" Mi-seon could easily read my mind. "Tell me what it is. Right now. You'll only make it worse if you keep it to yourself."

I gazed quietly into her eyes as she prodded me to confide in her.

"Before I tell you, there's something you have to promise me."

"What is it?"

We demand promises from people not because we don't trust them but because of fear within ourselves.

"No matter what I tell you, don't laugh at me."

Mi-seon nodded briskly. I revealed all my suspicions about Steve Kim, every lingering doubt that had been weighing on my mind. I also told her that every detail proved he was the same person that I had known in the past.

Mi-seon sat in silence for a long time after I finished talking. I had expected to feel some relief once I had gotten it all off my chest, but I didn't. Instead, I felt as if I had just been made to swallow something sour.

"So," Mi-seon said finally, "you're saying that the vice president, I mean Steve Kim, is like the Count of Monte Cristo, covering up his past and becoming a totally different person. How do you explain the fact that his face looks so different?"

She stared at me, looking interested.

"Plastic surgery," I answered unhesitatingly.

"That's possible. After all, there was all that uproar recently about the actor who showed up with a totally new face. He was completely unrecognizable." Mi-seon frowned as she spoke.

The water had now blended completely into the darkness. Something was flowing, but it wasn't clear whether it was the river or the night. Lights came on one by one across the bridge. They looked like the lights fishermen used to lure fish, and below them ran the darkness, moving silently into the unknown. I felt all the blackness of the universe closing in on my mind.

"But there's one thing I'm still not clear about. This was a long time ago and you and the other person weren't close friends, so how can you be so sure your memory is reliable?"

This suggestion of the unreliability of memory struck me as surprising. Would she believe me if I said that back then every day was the same, and so that day stood out in my memory? At that time, I was completely focused on winning a scholarship, and that period of my life was abysmally monotonous. In a period of such profound boredom there's always a moment when something gleams out of the darkness. Gazing at the inky black water, I continued hesitantly.

"You don't have to believe me, but I'm certain my memory is reliable."

"I didn't mean I don't believe you." Mi-seon blushed defensively. "What I'm saying is you need something concrete that would corroborate your memories."

Instantly the image of an anchor came into my mind.

"An anchor." I said involuntarily.

"An anchor?" Mi-seon's eyes opened wide.

"Yes, an anchor." It has to be tattooed somewhere on his body. That summer night, the three of us were drinking on the beach. It was the first time I'd ever had a drink, and I passed out. When I woke up I found myself lying in a seedy motel room. I had a pounding headache. The girl from Seoul was sleeping next to me. She was naked. Tae-man was nowhere to be seen. It felt unreal, but I didn't need to pinch myself to see if I was dreaming, because the smell of mold was tingling in my nostrils. I couldn't help looking at the girl, though I was petrified with embarrassment. And my eyes lit upon an anchor. An anchor tattooed on the girl's body, below her belly button, close to her pubic hair. It looked as if it had been dropped there deliberately to catch in the black seaweed and anchor her navel.

The image of that anchor stuck in my mind for a long time, resurfacing whenever I came across Tae-man at school. I was certain the same anchor must have been tattooed on his body.

When we took our first test after summer vacation, I was ranked second. I saw the words "Kim Tae-man" above my name. It was the one and only time that I lost the title of number-one student in the school.

When I said that the guy's naked body would explain everything, Mi-seon's face froze as if she'd bitten on some grit.

"I would sell my soul to see him naked and I . . ." I mumbled, looking imploringly into Mi-seon's eyes.

"Are you out of your mind? Is that really what you want in order to satisfy yourself? That's totally insane. I don't even recognize you these days. What's come over you?" Mi-seon's voice trembled.

"If my memory is correct and I've made the right deductions, he's got to have a tattoo." My voice trembled too. I regretted having unburdened myself to Mi-seon. I bit my lip, realizing it was too late.

"Your memory? My ass! Do you even remember what day it is today? Have you any idea how stone cold you've become when we run into each other at the office? You won't even hold hands with me anywhere near the office, for fear that someone will spot us together. Are you that afraid that they'll find out about our relationship? Are you ashamed of me? Because I'm not an Ivy-League graduate like them, or because my parents aren't stinking rich? Why me? Why did you even start seeing me?"

She burst into tears. Only when I was left there watching her dash out of the restaurant did I remember that it was her birthday. And I realized one more thing: Mi-seon looked like the girl from Seoul who I'd hung out with at the beach that summer.

Things were rough after that. Mi-seon ignored me at the office, and she didn't respond when I tried to start a conversation online. Sauna Park applied for early retirement. We were all surprised by his sudden announcement, and he explained he had been mulling it over for a long time. He said he didn't want to live alone anymore and was going to join his family in America. But people didn't believe him, and they whispered that he'd decided to take matters into his own hands before he got laid off.

We all got together for his retirement party. When he left to go to the restroom everyone changed the subject and began speculating about who the company would recruit to replace Sauna Park. I couldn't bear it.

"Guys!" I shouted. "Honestly! Have you forgotten that we're here to bid him farewell?" They all turned to look at me. It was as if they were looking at an alien creature.

We moved on to another place and drank all night. By the early hours of the morning, as we left a karaoke bar, there were only five of us left, including Steve Kim. Sauna Park looked at his watch and suggested we should go for a sauna. He said it would be fun for all of us to go together for the last time before he quit, especially since we'd stayed up all night and it was just a few hours before we'd have to go to work. He said he had to get to the U.S. consulate first thing in the morning. One guy tried hard to bow out, but Sauna Park wouldn't let him. Just then an idea struck me and left me stone-cold sober. This was certainly an unexpected opportunity. My heart pounded and my palms began to sweat. I fumbled in my pocket for a chocolate bar.

"Are you hungry, Mr. Choi?" Steve Kim asked.

"This man is a fiend for chocolate," Sauna Park said in a booming voice.

"Chocolate with almonds in it? You're so behind the times! Try this. The cacao content is what determines the quality of chocolate. British aristocrats used to enjoy chocolate that's ninety-nine percent cacao."

He rummaged in his pocket, took out a bar of chocolate, and handed it to me. The cacao content was printed in large, gold type on the package: 99%. I tore it open and bit off a piece.

"How do you like the taste of Great Britain?" asked Sauna Park.

As it melted on my tongue, the chocolate released a bitter taste that grew terribly strong. It felt like I was eating pencil lead or had taken a gulp of brandy. I frowned and they all giggled.

"There's supposed to be a slight lingering sweetness, though," Steve Kim said, tilting his head curiously to one side.

In the steam room, I kept sneaking a glance at the towel that covered the lower part of Steve Kim's body. It was wrapped around him and firmly tied above his belly button. I left the steam room and went to take a dip in the hot and cold tubs. I cooled down in the cold water and then settled myself into the hot tub. I sat facing directly toward the door, waiting for Steve Kim to open it and walk in. I waited and waited, but he didn't appear. My eyes felt heavy, just as they had under the dazzling sun at the beach that time long ago. I rubbed them to keep from falling asleep.

Eventually the door swung open and Steve Kim walked in. Without a towel. My vision was blurred by either the steam or my sweat. I blinked rapidly. I could see a little more clearly now. Beyond rising clouds of steam I could see the dark hair of his pubes. I swallowed anxiously. I suddenly felt the bitter taste of the ninety-nine percent cacao chocolate spreading through my mouth. I searched every corner with my tongue, trying to find a trace of the lingering sweetness that Steve Kim had mentioned.

The Ups and Downs of Hurricane Joe

When Hurricane Joe called me I was inhaling ice cream, devouring it straight out of the carton. I was waiting for a text from a woman I had met on a blind date the previous week. I had free tickets to a movie and I was going to ask her out but it had taken me three days to finally send her a text. The reason I'd procrastinated was that I was afraid of being rejected by a woman yet again. Once I summoned up the courage to text her, however, I wasn't afraid any more. By the time I was scraping the bottom of the ice cream carton, I was afraid she would say yes. Frankly, I was afraid of getting any response at all. Luckily, or unluckily, my cell phone rang, showing an unknown number.

"Hello."

"Is this The Ups and Downs?"

It was a booming voice. I flinched as if I had just switched on a radio with the volume turned all the way up. Catching my breath, I said "Yes." I had a habit of speaking quietly, and teachers often used to have to call my name twice when they checked attendance. I cringed when I was around people who spoke clearly and distinctly.

"Is it true you ghostwrite autobiographies for people?"

Despite his strong voice, he sounded cautious. Which indicated the odds were good he would wind up being my client. I set down the ice cream carton and grasped my cell phone firmly.

Histories are written by victors, memoirs by losers, and autobiographies by aspiring authors. In other words, would-be authors ghostwrite autobiographies for other people. The person who got me started in the ghostwriting business was another aspiring author. He had graduated from the same college as me and tried for years to launch his career as a writer. We were in the same year of the creative writing program. At first I was baffled as to how to address him, because, although we were in the same class, he was a good ten years older than me. I talked to him about my dilemma and he told me to call him *seonbae*[3], since, as he pointed out, he had started his career in the real world before I had. Later I learned he'd had an unusual education. He was a physics dropout but had a BA in philosophy, and even students who were older than me also addressed him as *seonbae*.

The *seonbae's* personality was as unconventional as his background. He always wore a suit, with the result that the security guard at the main gate of the college took him for a professor and would bow to him. When I asked him why he insisted on wearing a suit, he answered with characteristic erudition by launching into a speech about the origin of the suit and its political and aesthetic significance. His encyclopedic knowledge was particularly noticeable during our creative writing workshops. Prefacing his remarks with his usual opening statement—"I have some small knowledge of this topic"—he would home in on every error in other students' writings. For example, if someone had a scene where a pop singer and his fan were in a love-hate relationship, he would say, "Let me help you with this, because I have a friend who is the road manager of a singer, and he gave me all the lowdown on this pop star and his fan club."

It was the *seonbae* who advised me to change the name of my business to The Ups and Downs.

I'd originally called it The Mirror and the Lamp, a title I borrowed from a book I read in college.

The Mirror and the Lamp.
No matter who you are, your life is worth recording.
We admire the lives of ordinary people, and
we chronicle your life on your behalf.

I rode the subway and put advertising stickers on the priority seating for the elderly, and on benches in Tapgol Park, where retirees would often gather, but the response was disappointing. I got just a few calls and they were to ask if I did interior design.

---

3 Honorific used to address a fellow student in a higher year or a colleague with more seniority than the speaker. (Translators' note)

When I had new stickers printed up with the new business name, I got far more inquiries. It was thanks to those calls—many of which turned out not to be serious inquiries—that I had developed a gut feeling about people who called. I was able to pick up on who was serious and who was not, just from their first few words.

I was certain the elderly man was a genuine client. He sounded inquisitive and cautious, and he was guarded about telling me any details of his life. He was the kind of man who yearned for an autobiography but had no ability to write it on his own. A man who firmly believed that his life was special enough to merit an autobiography. A rare and precious client!

"Yes. I ghostwrite autobiographies, but only for ordinary people."

I emphasized "ordinary people."

Three days later I met the elderly man at a coffee shop in Insadong. Although he had wanted to come to my office, I insisted on meeting at the coffee shop. I didn't have an office as such, and I knew the coffee shop would be perfectly okay for recording an interview, because it was quiet on weekdays.

I walked into the coffee shop and looked around for an elderly man wearing sunglasses, which was how he said I'd recognize him. He was sitting in the farthest corner wearing aviator sunglasses that hid half his face. Seeing me headed straight towards him, he stood up. He was of medium height and had a stocky physique. His sturdy, muscular torso was clearly perceptible under his tight t-shirt. I could scarcely believe it was the body of someone who would turn seventy in just three years.

He sat down again and took off his sunglasses. There were deep wrinkles at the corners of his narrow eyes and he had a long scar just above his left eyebrow. His nose was crooked as if it had been broken and not subsequently straightened. Dotted here and there with liver spots, his face was much more distinctive without the sunglasses. Perhaps because his robust body seemed to belie his age, his face, in contrast, looked old and gaunt, hinting at a harsh life. The weird contrast between his strong body and his wrinkled, shrunken face reminded me of a centaur.

After we had introduced ourselves, the old man handed me his business card. Jo Min-gu. Director, Seongdong Branch of the Nation of Justice Campaign; Member, Crime Prevention Volunteers of Seongdong District; Adviser to the National Council of Sports for All; Advisory Committee for the Center for Missing Children; Member, Lions Club International.

I gave him my business card. Taking his reading glasses from the inside pocket of his suit jacket, he perched them on his nose. He looked intently at my business card, and asked me how many autobiographies I had ghostwritten so far. The question took me by surprise. Nine times out of ten, the first question was how much I charge. Potential clients would often sit quietly, looking nervous as they waited for me to ask them questions, and feeling doubtful about whether their lives were really worth recording. This time, however, I was the one being questioned. I took two books out of my bag. They were the two autobiographies I had ghostwritten, one for an old woman who had supported all four of her children by selling *gimbap* until they graduated from college, the other for a man who had worked for thirty years as a railroad stationmaster and retired when his station was closed down.

The elderly man leafed through the pages inattentively, then looked carefully at the author's profile inside the back cover. He scanned both books without saying a word, good or bad. There was something about his silence that would have made anyone feel tense. The look on his face—his eyebrows drawn into a frown and his lips pursed—gave the impression that he was struggling to control a mounting anger inside and was looking for a chance to vent it. I swallowed anxiously as I waited for him to say something. After a few minutes, he finally spoke.

"Is this all?"

I took a thick book out of my bag. It was the autobiography of the CEO of a well-known company. I had ghostwritten for him too. It was my trump card, which I was reluctant to produce, but his excessively cautious attitude hurt my pride and made me determined not to give up. On the other hand, I was becoming very curious about him. I could feel my curiosity bubbling inside me.

"Did you really ghostwrite for this man too?"

"Look inside the back cover."

On the last page was the signature of the entrepreneur—who had started his business from nothing and grown it to a Fortune 500 company—and above it was my name with the words "All my thanks to."

"Didn't you say you only work with ordinary people, sir?"

He sounded more good-natured, and even addressed me as "sir," which implied that I had passed his test. I was relieved, but I was uncomfortable with his show of respect. It felt like I was deceiving him.

"I used to ghostwrite for celebrities. It was before I started The Ups and Downs."

"That must have been a good business. Why did you quit?"

It wasn't the first time I had been asked this question.

It was Christmas Eve two years previously. The *seonbae* and I were drinking silently in the corner of our favorite bar, trying not to make eye contact. Neither of us had received the call we had been hoping for. We had both entered an annual writing contest for the tenth time, and yet again we had both failed to win. Every year, when we got the bad news, we would go out drinking, lamenting over "our doomed masterpieces." We would drink and dwell over our misfortunes until we finally passed out, like a cicada that suddenly stops chirping at the end of summer, but this time things ended differently. The *seonbae* muttered gloomily that he would never enter the contest again. Since he had repeatedly failed to win, I was puzzled by how badly he was taking it this time and how depressed he was.

"The stories I've written so far are all phony. They're just a sham. I'm doomed and I can't write my authentic story."

"Your authentic story?"

"I mean my own unique story. That no one can imitate, even if they've had the same experience. A story that tells the truth, not just a catalog of events. A story that amounts to far more than just a series of facts."

"Why can't you write what you want?"

"It's been stolen from me."

"Stolen? Your authentic story?"

"That bastard Park Jin-seok won the contest with my story. I told it to him when we were out one night drinking together. So now I can't write my true story anymore."

Park Jin-seok, one of our classmates, had won the Spring Writing Contest when he was still in college and had already published two collections of short stories. It had been eight years since Park Jin-seok had won the contest, so it seemed odd for the *seonbae* to bring this up only now. Although his grievance appeared to come out of the blue, the words "authentic story" stuck in my head until late that night.

When the *seonbae* called me the following day, he sounded completely sober, as if he had already shaken off all the despair and anguish from the previous night at the bar. He said he'd been approached to ghostwrite the autobiography of a politically influential figure, and he suggested that I should take on the job since he had already committed to a similar contract.

"I don't want to do this work any more," I said.

"Why not? It makes good money, you know."

"I want to write an authentic story of my own."

"An authentic story?"

He didn't remember what he had told me the previous night. An authentic story. Now that I'd uttered the words myself, it felt as if they had always been dear to me. Although I didn't know exactly what they meant, I was certain they signified something more than the overblown success story of a famous person. It was right at that moment that the idea of ghostwriting for ordinary people came to me. Besides, it seemed like it could be a smart business move. Ghostwriting for celebrities had grown increasingly competitive, with more and more writers getting into the profession every year.

I needed to get some experience before launching my new business. My father was thrilled when I suggested ghostwriting his autobiography. Ever since he'd retired from teaching, he'd been spending his days drinking. After I interviewed him, he would call me early in the morning to tell me something he had forgotten to say. I couldn't believe he was the same man who used to be a hopeless recluse. But when I finally completed the manuscript, he didn't want to get it published. He said he would rather keep it to himself. I should have realized it at the time. When the majority of their days are behind them, what people really want is not a wonderful autobiography but someone who will listen to their life story.

Since then, I had ghostwritten and published only two memoirs. I'd had a few other contracts, but those clients had changed their minds and cancelled. One client even demanded his down payment back because he said he didn't like the manuscript and the project had fizzled out. I'd lost the confidence I'd had when I started the business. I was seriously thinking I might have to start ghostwriting for celebrities again.

"I wanted to do something meaningful."

The old man nodded but said nothing.

The discussion about terms then followed smoothly. We agreed that he would pay half the fee up front and the other half after I had completed his memoir and published it. He was more concerned about the date of publication than the fee.

"Do you have any particular reason for being in a hurry?"

"I don't have much time."

He sounded very solemn. It was the solemnity you might see in a man who has focused on a single goal all his life and has borne every hardship with patience.

He took a newspaper clipping from inside his coat and put it down on the table. It was a report saying that a former world boxing champion was fighting Parkinson's disease. As his nickname, Iron Fist, suggested, the boxer had knocked out almost all of his opponents. He was especially known for roaring the words "A KO is the only way to win!" right after knocking out a powerful, long-time champion in the final round.

I asked the old man what connection the bedridden boxing legend had to his autobiography.

"He lived my life on my behalf."

I instinctively took my tape recorder out of my bag, eagerly anticipating that I might be on the trail of an authentic story. I pressed record right away, and without a moment's hesitation the old man started to recount one story after another. He spoke for four hours, and this is what he told me:

In his younger years, he had been a boxer known as Hurricane Joe. Spurred on by having won a boxing contest in the army—the commander of his battalion, who was crazy about boxing, had offered a three day and four night leave of absence to the winner—he'd gone into the world of boxing when he was discharged. Systematic training brought out his latent talent immediately. He quickly distinguished himself through his innate power and endurance. It took only six bouts for him to earn the nickname Hurricane Joe. He had beaten all of his opponents by KO. (Without missing a beat, he listed off the opponents' names.) By then, people were starting to talk about him, saying that he was certain to be a future world champion. When he sent his tenth opponent packing, it seemed that no one in Korea or anywhere in Asia was a match for him. At that time, the world champion in his weight class was a Mexican in his mid-thirties. The tide favored the challenger, who was on a roll, rather than the Mexican champion who had been resting on his laurels. (This was the old man's way of saying that it was just a matter of time before he clinched the World Boxing Champion title.)

Then an unexpected obstacle arose. A promising boxer from the next highest weight class dropped down to his class. In the world of professional boxing, losing as little as a kilogram means enduring grueling workouts, so getting down to a lower weight class amounts to putting one's life on the line. This foolhardy boxer was none other than the Iron Fist. The reason he changed weight class was that there were too many tough competitors in his former class. (At this point the old man's voice began to get louder.) What's more, the world champion in that class had a record of all wins and no defeats and he had knocked out all of his five challengers.

The Iron Fist lost weight through murderous workouts, and his blows were still as murderous as before. (The old man used the word "murderous" a lot, and his voice shook slightly when he described what the Iron Fist's punches were like.) The Iron Fist's two back-to-back wins by knockout—right after changing weight class—shattered all the negative talk that had been going around. Some people had criticized him for running away to avoid fighting tough opponents, and others had worried that his iron fists would have turned to jelly in the weight loss. After these decisive victories, he had to take a long break because no one wanted to take him on. There were only two boxers in the world who were considered a match for him. One was the reigning world champion and the other was Hurricane Joe. After many twists and turns, a match was finally arranged to decide which boxer—Hurricane Joe or the Iron Fist—would challenge the world champion. The two sluggers—neither of whom the World Boxing Champion wanted to take on—were finally going to meet in the ring.

"I have a meeting to go to. Let's call it a day," the old man said, glancing at his watch.

He hurried out of the coffee shop without pausing to schedule our next meeting. He was as quick on his feet as the lightweight boxer he had once been. I sat back, stunned, perhaps because the story had been interrupted at its climax or perhaps because of the way the old man had vanished so swiftly.

My eyes fell on the newspaper clipping he had left on the table. As I read it again carefully I noticed a place where it had been corrected in red, something I hadn't seen the first time. Where the article mentioned the former champion's boxing record it read that his record was thirty-two fights: thirty wins and two losses. A correction in red ink said it was thirty-one fights: twenty-nine wins and two losses. Apparently Hurricane Joe didn't acknowledge one of the Iron Fist's recorded wins.

Even the *seonbae*, who was very well informed, said he had never heard of a former boxer named Hurricane Joe, although he knew a Japanese comic book about boxing titled "The Challenger Hurricane." And he offered to help me out, explaining that one of his friends worked for the Korean Boxing Association. Although I was just a ghostwriter, I felt I had to check out the old man's story. There was a serious risk of defaming the legendary boxer who was battling illness.

I played back the recording over and over while I waited to hear from the *seonbae*. The old man's story was very specific and detailed. It didn't seem like he had made it up. To my mind, his sturdy physique and swift movements were solid evidence that he had in fact been a boxer. I felt a strong urge to call the old man and hear more about his life, but I decided to wait until the *seonbae* called me back, just in case the old man's story turned out to be a lie and I had to void the contract.

It was not the *seonbae*, but the old man who called me first. He suggested we should meet the following day. Once again, he was insistent that he wanted to come to my office. I had to work hard to talk him out of it, saying that the interview would probably take a long time, so it would be best for us to have dinner and talk at our leisure.

The old man ordered a chicken salad, nothing else. He even asked for it without dressing. I asked him if a salad was really all he wanted. He said he sometimes ate a simple chicken salad three times a day. I ordered steak for myself. Out of the blue, the old man asked me how much I weighed.

"Eighty-nine kilos."

I actually weighed ninety-one.

"In that case, you're a heavyweight."

"Oh. I see."

The word "heavyweight" stuck in my craw. It seemed to indicate a class of people who have lost some degree of dignity.

"Gaining weight is not a sin, but being too lazy to do anything about it is. If you're a heavyweight, the implication is that you're someone like Muhammad Ali or George Foreman."

Doing something about it. It was my mind rather than my body that felt weighed down when I thought about my flabby gut. I didn't even want to imagine being punched by Muhammad Ali or George Foreman.

"How much do you weigh?"

"Today I weigh sixty-one point two."

"Do you check your weight every day?"

"The first thing I do when I wake up in the morning is stand on the scale, and it's the last thing I do at night too."

"Is there any particular reason for that?"

"Because I have to regulate my food and exercise according to my weight."

The old man didn't touch the chicken on his plate and just picked at the vegetables.

"Is the chicken not good?"

"It's fine, I'm sure. It's just that my weight is in jeopardy today."

"In jeopardy?"

"The lightweight class limit is sixty-one point two three."

"Does it matter that much?"

The old man put down his fork and stared at me. He looked as if he was barely able to contain his fury.

"Of course it does. Once you set foot in a boxing ring you can't stop. Everywhere you go there's always a ring. People say the world is a boxing ring. It's easy enough to say that. But if it's true, shouldn't we always be prepared to fight? It's not just a meaningless metaphor. There's truth behind it. Do you know why the ring is a square? It's because nine times out of ten, the places you go in life are square. Bedrooms, classrooms, offices, elevators, buses, and so on and so on. From the cradle to the grave, we can't get away from squares. A man's destiny is a square."

I thought there was some sense in what the old man said, but I still couldn't understand why he was so obsessed with his weight, not the way a normal person would be, out of concern for their health. It reminded me of the way a professional boxer would monitor his weight closely before a fight.

The question became clear, however, after we finished eating and resumed the interview. The answer lay in a match between Hurricane Joe and the Iron Fist. When the old man finally started to speak about the controversial match, all I could do was sit quietly and take it all in like a tape recorder.

The old man's phrase, "a man's destiny is a square" inspired me. It would be dramatic to start his memoir with a scene where the two powerful boxers, both contenders for the world championship, were set to square off. As I listened to the old man telling his story, I was already starting to sketch out his memoir in my head:

"A man's destiny is a square. It really is for a boxer, at least. A boxer's destiny is determined inside the boxing ring. Outside the ring they just have a tedious fight with themselves to get in shape. But no matter how tedious the fight, it is what eventually determines the winner. A man who can't win the fight with himself outside of the ring brings nothing but defeat into the ring.

"Before he steps into the square ring, a boxer has another square to step onto: a scale. Whatever heaven is like, there's certainly no such thing as a scale there. Because the scale is an instrument of Satan.

"My opponent was a light welterweight. He had such a powerful punch that people called him the Iron Fist. He'd just moved down from a heavier class, so his blows were going to be a whole lot more powerful than anything I'd experienced before. I'd find out from my head, my chin and my abdomen if he was worthy of his nickname. To prepare myself to fight an opponent who had come down a weight class, I had to adopt a new approach. An eye for an eye, I thought, and I made up my mind to gain as much weight as I could without exceeding the upper limit of my weight class, and then to use that weight to deliver some powerful blows.

"There are two ways to gain weight. One is to eat more and the other is to exercise less. I couldn't cut back on my exercise. A cannibal eats the flesh of a man because he wants to gain that man's energy for himself. I would kill and eat things I was fearful of so that I could overcome my fear. I killed and ate nothing but fighting cocks. Their flesh was tough and chewy. After eating an entire fighting cock, my jaws hurt, as if I'd taken a full-body-weight uppercut.

"Finally the moment of truth arrived. The weigh-in was the day before the match. They flipped a coin to decide who was to stand on the scale first. It was the Iron Fist. Since dropping a weight class, he had often had to dehydrate himself to make his weight, but he weighed in successfully that day. He even stood there on the scale and ate an apple, just to demonstrate how confident he was. The apple looked unusually red and appetizing, my trainer had been holding it in his hand, but the Iron Fist snatched it from him. I would normally eat a red apple after a weigh-in. It was a kind of ritual — the sort of thing a warrior would do to ward off bad luck. My mouth filled with saliva as I watched the Iron Fist relishing my apple. I swallowed and stepped onto the cold, square scale. My weight had been 61.19 kilograms when I checked it one last time in the boxing studio. Everything was going pretty well but I couldn't help feeling some tension. That was how I always felt when I was about to step onto the scale. I was as anxious as if I were standing before my Maker on Judgment Day.

"As I said before, a man's destiny is a square. I met my doom on that small, cold square. The needle pointed to 61.32 kilograms. I couldn't believe my eyes. At the second weigh-in two hours later it was no different. I protested and said that the scale must be faulty, but it was no use. What was the matter? Only Satan, the master of the scale, knows.

"After that day, the Iron Fist had a series of victories. But I never again won a single fight. What the Iron Fist ate on the scale that day was not just an apple but the strength that I, Hurricane Joe, had built up."

I was wondering how much of the old man's story to believe when, as if he could read my mind, he told me the exact date of the weigh-in. I felt sorry for the young boxer who had experienced this sudden downfall. I tried — perhaps because I felt so strongly for him — to find something inconsistent in the old man's story. If I could somehow establish that Hurricane Joe was a fictional character, or — if he was a real person — that he had been beaten in the ring rather than disqualified, I wouldn't have to sympathize with him.

"Maybe there was something wrong with the scale?"

"No, it was definitely correct. I always tested the scale personally before weighing in. I brought the dumbbells that I used to train with every day and put them on the scale. The reading was the same as on the scale at the studio."

The old man's face grew dark as if he were thinking back to that day.

"Did you know that the human body becomes heavier when there's a full moon?" he asked.

"No, I didn't."

"One theory says that when the lunar gravity increases, the blood circulates faster and that makes the human body heavier. The moon was full that day."

"But even if we accept that theory, it doesn't explain why you'd get a different reading on a different scale, does it?"

"You're right. The extra 130 grams is more than the full moon would account for."

The old man fell into deep thought, as if he were struggling to solve a difficult problem. After a long silence, he mumbled gloomily.

"I shouldn't have swallowed when my mouth watered. I should have spat."

I was walking into the National Library when my cell phone rang. It was the *seonbae*. I was going to do some research to corroborate what the old man had told me. Since the two boxers were potential challengers for the world championship, the fight would have been reported in various newspapers. Besides, it was rare for a boxer to be eliminated for failing to make weight. The *seonbae* said he had asked around but hadn't found anyone who knew of a boxer named Hurricane Joe. He hadn't found any record of a boxer by that name either, because it was such a long time ago.

When we finished talking I headed to the microfilm room. I looked through all the newspapers dated around the time the old man had specified, but I found nothing. In fact, I didn't come across a single article about boxing. I felt like I had been duped, but I couldn't bring myself to just get up and leave. I couldn't figure out why I felt so disappointed and dejected, given that I had hoped the old man's story would turn out to be a fabrication.

I tried to call the old man to make sure I had the right date, but he didn't answer. As I was leaving the library, a large calendar hanging on a wall of the lobby stopped me in my tracks. It was a traditional calendar that showed both the lunar and solar dates. I immediately remembered that the old man had mentioned the full moon. I searched the Internet on my phone and found out where the date he had mentioned fell on the solar calendar, and hurried back to the microfilm room.

The old man's story was true. I was relieved. Under the headline "Much Ado About Nothing," a news story—dated the day that the weigh-in occurred—recounted how the big match had been called off after Hurricane Joe was disqualified at the weigh-in. It said the situation was so unusual that even the people involved were dumbfounded. It quoted someone close to the situation who described the incident as unfortunate and put it down to Hurricane Joe's obsession with maximizing his weight because he was so conscious of the fact that his opponent had dropped down a class. The newspaper story was very brief, given how much anticipation the match had generated. Other news reports that I looked through were no different. I found just one short feature about the Mexican champion whom the Iron Fist was challenging, but nothing about Hurricane Joe.

I went on scanning newspapers that had come out after the weigh-in. There still wasn't anything about Hurricane Joe, but I did come across a report four months later saying that the Iron Fist had defeated the world champion. It seemed that Hurricane Joe—who, spurred on by his own burning ambition and the public attention, had trained so doggedly—had slid into a dramatic decline after being disqualified from the fight, and had eventually sunk into oblivion.

My cell phone rang as I was leaving the library. It was the old man.

"Did you call me?"

"Yes. I had a question for you, but it's okay now."

"Let's meet up."

"You mean right now?"

"Time is running out, isn't it?"

He must have meant the Iron Fist's time. His illness must have worsened by now. Nonetheless, I couldn't understand why the old man was in such a rush. I set off to meet with him, wondering why he needed his memoir to be published while the Iron Fist was still alive.

He wanted to meet at a boxing studio in Majang-dong. The sign reading "Champion Fitness Boxing Club" stood on the top of a five-story building at the entrance to an outdoor marketplace. The stairs inside the old building were steep, and by the time I got to the third floor, my forehead was beaded with sweat and my knees were starting to ache.

Despite the shabby exterior, the boxing studio was clean and spacious inside. The even planks of the hardwood floor had been polished until the grain shone. Treadmills and other exercise machines stood in orderly rows and a mirror covered one entire wall. The studio looked just like a fitness club, except for the ring in the center.

The old man was wearing shorts and was hitting a speed bag. His sharp, swift arm movements were impressive, and his abs were even more striking. He had a tanned, firm six-pack. After a while he stopped the quivering bag by grasping it with both hands, and he turned toward me.

"You're amazing."

"Do you mind waiting another half hour?"

"Not at all. Don't worry about me. Where's everyone else, by the way?"

"The place is closed on the first and third Mondays of the month. The owner is my *hubae*[4], and lets me come in whenever I want."

"Oh, I see."

"If you get bored, go ahead and do some jump rope work."

I hadn't touched a jump rope since elementary school. I was already overweight back then, and I used to pray for rain when we had PE class. I hated jump rope most of all. I loathed the feeling of getting my ankles caught in the rope. I was often seized by

---

4 Honorific used to address a fellow student in a lower year or a colleague with less seniority than the speaker. (Translators' note)

a delusional fear that if I got tangled I would never return to my normal self. The more frightened I was, the worse I jumped.

The old man read something in my rigid expression. Although I tried hard to refuse, he forced me to take a jump rope. I felt like I was caught in a trap. Closing my eyes tight, I started to jump rope, but I couldn't manage more than ten jumps. I tried again, but it was no better. Every time the rope wrapped around my ankles I felt my heart sink. I became breathless, and sweat started to soak my armpits. Worst of all, the pain in my knees was so sharp it was like being stabbed. Panting heavily, I massaged my knees.

"It's your knees, not your fists, that help you throw a punch," the old man said, winding a bandage around his hand. "Similarly, your knees rather than your feet help you jump rope. We humans walk upright, so our knees are the source of all our strength. If your knees are damaged you lose everything. If you want to win, you have to start by taking care of your knees. Try safflower seeds. They'll make your bones incredibly strong."

He wrapped his other hand, stepped onto the platform and walked toward the center. He stood silently with his eyes closed for a minute and then started to move slowly. Lifting his right heel, he flexed his right knee repeatedly, and then, holding up his arms, he twisted his upper body from side to side. He stared straight ahead—as if he were facing his opponent—and then threw a left jab and a right straight, one after another.

The old man moved his body faster and faster. Sidestepping carefully, he shot a series of punches. Every movement of his body seemed triggered by desperation, as if he were on the edge of a precipice fighting the world's most terrifying enemy. Every time he threw a punch I flinched.

Maybe because I could see his shadow on the mat, I felt like I was watching a ferocious slugfest. Whenever the old man threw a punch, his shadow threw one too; every time he dropped his head his shadow dropped its head down too. The old man hurled his fists, but they just cut through the air around his shadow. Striking at something that could not be struck, he grew exhausted. His arms hung limp and his feet moved sluggishly. His sweat-covered face became increasingly contorted. The eyes that had been glaring menacingly now wavered in fear, the fear of a boxer who has just realized that no matter how hard he strikes, his opponent is invincible. His shadow, feeding on the evening sunlight that streamed through the window, grew bigger and bigger.

We left the studio and ate dinner together at a nearby restaurant. He ordered a plate of raw ground beef. As soon as his food arrived, he wolfed it down as if he was being pursued. Remembering how anxious he had been about gaining just a few extra grams, I was puzzled.

I don't like raw meat, so I cooked mine on the grill set into the table. When the old man had finished what was on his own plate, he started to pick at the pieces of cooked meat, and it was all gone in a flash.

"Do you want me to order more?" I asked.

"What?" His eyes looked blank, as if he were in another world.

"Would you like some more meat?"

"I'm all right."

Looking at the empty grill, his blood-smeared plate, and the chopsticks in his hand, the old man frowned. He put down his chopsticks.

We moved on to a coffee shop, and I was about to start interviewing him when the old man's cell phone rang. He listened silently, a dark look on his face. He hung up and for some minutes he sat there, stunned. At first he looked baffled and troubled, but then he began to mumble the same word over and over again like a terrified child. I couldn't make out the word at first, but the third time he said it I heard it distinctly. *Daijoubu.*

A few minutes later the old man sprang to his feet and, saying he would call me later, he bolted out of the coffee shop.

I haven't heard a word from the old man since that day. When I tried calling him, all I got was a dial tone followed by a recorded message saying that the number was out of service. I was perplexed. I didn't know what to make of a situation where a client who had already paid a deposit disappeared without a word. He was the one who had fallen out of touch, so I was not responsible for the unfinished job. Still, I asked around and tried my best to find out the old man's whereabouts.

I was deeply curious about the untold portion of the old man's life story, and I couldn't get him out of my mind. I felt I had to see him one last time. I tried calling all the numbers on his business card, but to no avail. Some of the organizations said they had never heard of him, and others said they were also wondering what was going on, because they too had suddenly lost touch with him.

I went back to the Champion Fitness Boxing Club. Unlike the first time I'd visited, it was crowded, and almost all the machines were in use. I spoke to a man who was hitting a punching bag. I told him I was looking for the owner, and he pointed towards a young woman who was exercising, or dancing, to upbeat music in front of the huge mirror, all the while throwing punches. A woman, and what's more a young woman—this was not at all what I had expected. A group of people in orderly rows imitated her movements.

When I asked about the old man, the owner shook her head and said she didn't know anyone by that name. She didn't recognize the name Hurricane Joe either. When I described him she said it could be the man who used to clean the studio. She said that the cleaning company had started sending a different person the month before. I didn't mention anything more about the old man—that he had once been a famous boxer and that he used to work out in the studio on the days it was closed. As I made my way out of the studio, my eyes were drawn again and again to the boxing ring. The square platform, the ring where destinies were played out, was empty.

Naturally, I wasn't able to finish ghostwriting the old man's autobiography. How could I? I only knew about the few years he had lived as Hurricane Joe. I had no idea what his life was like before he earned that nickname or after he and his name were both forgotten. I could have speculated. But there was one thing that

I couldn't even guess at: the mystery of the extra 130 grams at the .weigh-in.

I wanted to lose some weight, so I started going to a boxing studio near my apartment. Whenever I did jump-rope training, I remembered the old man's advice. Focusing on my knees rather than my ankles, I found that my fear diminished and I could do more jumps. The better I got at jumping rope the less I thought about the old man.

It was on Christmas Eve that I happened to mention the old man again. As usual at that time of year, I was drinking with my *seonbae* in the corner of our favorite bar, anxiously waiting to hear who had won the literary award. The *seonbae* said I seemed to have lost weight, and I told him I had been working out at a boxing studio. Then, explaining why I'd joined the studio, I mentioned the old man. I went on to recount the mysterious story the old man had told me — how his weight had suddenly increased right before his match with the Iron Fist, and the way the Iron Fist had apparently devoured Hurricane Joe's strength along with an apple during the weigh-in.

"Your story is similar to one I heard from a *hubae* of mine. A friend of his had won a literary contest. And later, when my *hubae* read his friend's award-winning story, he realized it was a story he had told him when they were out one night drinking together. He hasn't been able to finish a single story since then."

He had told me the same story on Christmas Eve two years earlier. But on that occasion he had told the story about himself. One version or the other had to be a lie. Or maybe they were both lies. I was beginning to think that all the stories he had told me up to then were untrue.

"Do you believe the story?"

"You mean my *hubae*'s story?"

"I mean Hurricane Joe's."

"The story about his sudden weight gain?"

"Yes."

"He must have eaten something."

"That's impossible. A boxer would have to be crazy to eat right before his weigh-in, wouldn't he? Particularly when he'd been training so hard for a crucial fight."

I was surprised to find that I was raising my voice. The *seonbae* stared at me as if he was puzzled by my reaction. Slowly, almost imperceptibly, I put a tempting piece of pork tempura back down on my plate.

A few days later an item in the news caught my attention and I found myself thinking about the old man once again. I had eaten chicken salad for dinner and was about to mix some safflower seeds with honey for dessert. The report said that a cremation urn containing the ashes of a former world champion boxer had gone missing from a cemetery in Gyeonggi Province. It was the Iron Fist's urn. They had no idea who had stolen it or why. I was stunned because I didn't even know that the Iron Fist had died.

As soon as the news report ended I started an internet search. I entered "Iron Fist" and a series of articles came up. Most of them were about the stolen urn, so I had to scroll down, skipping about ten stories, before getting to the reports about his death.

He had died on a Monday three months previously. I checked and it was the same day I had seen the old man for the last time. The image of his face when he answered the phone came back to me. And the mysterious word he'd mumbled as if he were trying to banish a nightmare by intoning a magic spell. I searched the internet for the word. *Daijoubu.* It was Japanese and it meant "It's all right."

All kinds of thoughts suddenly cascaded into my mind. Many things were becoming clear, but just as many were becoming obscure. And in the middle of it all there was the mystery of the sudden weight gain of 130 grams. I felt that I was close to solving the mystery which had derailed the career of Hurricane Joe, when suddenly I was surprised to find myself shoveling safflower seeds into my mouth. I had no idea how much I had already eaten. I felt a sudden chill run down my spine. The truth had been right there all along, like a murderous opponent. Covering my mouth with my hand, I dashed to the bathroom.

Heinrich's Heart

Dawn was breaking in the eastern sky as Kang Min-sik (male, age fifty-four) made his way to the scene of an accident. He kept rubbing his knees. The younger detective, who was driving, glanced at him, and then, when their eyes met, immediately looked away as if he had seen something he shouldn't have. The pain was coming more frequently, and in both knees.

Kang had had a check-up the previous month, and the doctor's report was tucked into the inside pocket of his frayed jacket. He kept rereading the part where it said he had developed arthritis and should have another medical exam. He read it again and again, both in the early hours of the morning when he couldn't get to sleep because of the piercing pain, and during the stake-outs when he drank endless cups of coffee to fight off sleepiness. He read it like a love letter full of private memories. He had, however, never received or written a love letter. He had never even received an ordinary personal letter, let alone an intimate one. But there had been just one occasion when he had written a personal letter.

Most of the writing Kang had done consisted of police reports, where cause and effect were always clear. That world—where a man set fire to his girlfriend's house because she had dumped him, or a teenager stole money from a gas station for a night out—was contemptible, but straightforward. Even so, he was finding it harder and harder to draw up a police report. It seemed like the world of cause and effect was coming undone and a different world—one that needed a totally new system—was taking its place.

The previous year Kang Min-sik had arrested a boy who had beaten his father to death with a dumbbell. The boy was in high school. His academic record wasn't bad, and he had gotten along well with his peers. In short, he was just an ordinary young man. His father was a pastor and his mother was a professor. Kang Min-sik saw no trace of either anger or regret on the boy's face, and he couldn't believe anyone could kill their father for no reason and not show a shred of remorse. But the boy—sitting impassively in front of Kang—was clear evidence to the contrary. The boy's eyes seemed to be asking what the matter was. When Kang looked into those eyes he saw the depths of hell.

The boy's attorney requested a psychiatric evaluation, but the boy refused it. He knew what he had done. However, the questioning about his motive for the murder went on and on for hours, because the boy wouldn't say a thing. When he eventually spoke, his voice was frail.

"I want to eat a *Cheonha Jangsa*."

Kang didn't know what the boy was talking about until the rookie officer whispered to him that it was a type of snack food. The rookie fetched a package from a nearby convenience store and gave it to the boy, but the teenaged murderer just stared at it. The boy's eyes flickered with anxiety and agitation. He even began to sweat.

"May I eat this?" the boy asked, in the same frail voice. It sounded like he was both begging for permission and also anxious not to make any missteps.

Scarcely had Kang said, "Go ahead, kid," when the boy scarfed down the whole packet of fifteen fish-flavored snacks in one go. Apparently they stuck in his throat, because he asked for milk. He specified strawberry-flavored milk. His voice was still barely audible. The young detective went out again to get the boy a carton of strawberry milk.

The fish snacks and strawberry milk seemed to break down the boy's resistance, and he began to speak. He had had no intention of killing his father. He had just wanted to beat his puppy to death, because it kept annoying him. But he found himself killing his father as well without knowing why. The boy added that there were lots of things he had never eaten because his mother wouldn't let him have anything but organic foods. He looked depressed when he said he'd never even eaten noodles in black bean sauce. His mother was a professor of nutrition.

"What do noodles in black bean sauce taste like?"

"Why did you kill your father?"

"He had bad breath."

The first private letter Kang Min-sik ever wrote, which was also his last, was to his nine-year-old daughter. It had already been more than twenty years since then. He had taken his daughter to a Chinese restaurant. He ordered sweet-and-sour pork and noodles in black bean sauce. He also asked for a bottle of Chinese *kaoliang* liquor. His daughter didn't eat anything but just watched him cautiously. As he poured the liquor into his glass, Kang said to her, "Go ahead, kid." He looked closely at his daughter's face, which he had rarely done before. He had tried to avoid looking at her face so that he wouldn't be overwhelmed by regret, wishing that he had never gotten drunk, that the one-night stand on his first furlough had never happened, and that the woman had never come to see him in the barracks, with a newborn baby.

His daughter took a bite out of a slice of pickled daikon and put it back down on the plate. The way her mother used to do. Lying atop the pile of untouched daikon, the slice showed the marks of her teeth.

"You shouldn't put food back down on the plate once you've touched it with your mouth."

His daughter's face brightened in spite of his rebuke.

At the end of his last meal with his daughter, Kang pressed a letter into her hand. And he didn't forget to say, "Read it when you get home. Be sure and read it once you get home."

"Will I turn into a pillar of salt if I read it on my way, Father?" she asked, with a twinkle in her eyes.

"Yes, you might. Why don't you call me Dad, like other kids?"

His daughter blushed and just smiled wanly.

The rookie shook Kang by the shoulder, rousing him. They could see a vehicle at the accident site a little way ahead. It was a white

Hyundai Elantra. It looked to be in good condition, although it was an old model. Kang noted the license plate. It ended in an even number. Which meant the car had gone through the toll gate the previous day since only vehicles with odd-numbered license plates were allowed on the roads today.

A traffic patrol officer was directing traffic around the accident. When the rookie held out his ID the officer saluted. He said the crime scene investigation team would be arriving in ten minutes or so.

Putting on white cotton gloves, Kang opened the car door and looked inside. A young man and woman sat in the front seats. They both had slim faces, thick eyebrows and thin lips. The man was wearing a white dress shirt under a black suit, and the woman had on a black dress. It looked like they were taking a little nap after having been to a funeral.

It was at his ex-wife's funeral that Kang saw his daughter again for the first time since they had parted outside the Chinese restaurant. She was heavily pregnant, but she didn't have a man with her. Kang was drunk and yelled that she was having a bastard child as a way of paying him back. They were at a Chinese restaurant again, and though she ate two servings of noodles in black bean sauce, she didn't touch the pickled daikon. She took a drink of water and said, "There isn't a woman in the world who would have a baby out of revenge, Father." Then she held out a dog-eared piece of paper. He recognized his own handwriting.

"Could this have been a suicide pact?" the rookie asked.

"Then why were they wearing seat belts?" Kang responded.

There were no visible wounds on either the man or the woman.

"They were poisoned, maybe?"

"There's going to have to be an autopsy."

"If it's a case of poisoning, then it must have been a love affair, right? Or money, perhaps. What relationship do you think they had? They can't have been husband and wife anyway, because if they were, they wouldn't have driven out here to end it all. They'd have stayed home to finish themselves off."

The young detective was always garrulous when dispatched to the scene of a crime or an accident. Kang searched the man's pockets and found his wallet and cell phone. The wallet contained the man's national ID card, his driver's license, three credit cards, 43,000 won, and five business cards. His name was Choi Yeong-jun, thirty-seven years old. The change-of-address box on the back of his ID card showed that he had lived in Bangwha-dong until recently. All the business cards had his name on them, but each one showed the name of a different publishing company.

In the woman's shoulder bag Kang discovered a wallet, a passport, a couple of cosmetic items, a cell phone, a children's book, and three pills: vitamins. He opened the passport. Her name was Jin Yeong-ju, thirty-five years old. She'd lived in Bongcheon-dong. It had been issued five years prior, and didn't show any evidence that she had traveled outside the country. Kang found other items in the wallet: nine coupons of various kinds, 58,000 won, and calling cards for eight realtors. The rookie found another fourteen cards in a small pocket of the shoulder bag, all from different realtors. According to her ID, the woman had never moved. One thing at least was clear: the couple was not married.

The rookie's cell phone rang. It was the chief inspector.

"Got to go back to the precinct, sir. Been reassigned to the missing child unit, effective immediately."

"But we can't leave until the crime scene investigation team gets here."

"Umm . . . He only mentioned me . . ." The rookie scratched his head, his voice trailing off.

"Off you go then. One person is enough here. Looks like a case of love or money, as you said. No doubt about it. We'll check their phone records and talk to people who knew them. Then everything will become clear. It'd be a waste to have two detectives on a case like this, wouldn't it?"

If the rookie hadn't been so hesitant Kang wouldn't have attempted an explanation. He winced in spite of himself as a shooting pain ran through his knees. With knees this stiff he couldn't even chase a dying dog. I can't stand your mother any longer. So from now on don't try to find me. I'll still pay your school fees, so focus on studying. Kang didn't know why the words he had written in the letter came back to him just then. He bit his lip. I can't stand your mother any longer. So from now on don't try to find me. The logic of what he had written was absurd. That's what he found intolerable.

Chae Mi-jeong (female, age twenty-nine) almost dropped her coffee cup when she heard that the police had called the office. She blushed when her office manager—who had delivered the news—teased her, a grin on his face, and said she must have something on her conscience.

"Oh, let me get a look at you. You're hiding something, aren't you?" he said, even more playfully.

"Is it really so much fun to tease me?"

Scowling slightly, Chae Mi-jeong looked askance at the manager. It was a look that her fiancé—whom she had been dating for six years—would make fun of, saying that it made her look old.

"You look so cute when you make that face," the manager said, still grinning. Chae's ears turned red.

The manager said the police had called to ask for help with an investigation. He handed Chae a sheet of paper with the names and cell phone numbers of two customers, and asked her to check their call histories. The customers were a man and a woman. Their names were similar to one another, but the numbers were completely different.

"Why do they want it?" Chae asked.

"They wouldn't be cops if they explained why. You have the phone and fax numbers for the police there on that sheet of paper. Give it your best shot."

The manager winked at her and left. A strong scent of lavender lingered after him. It was a cologne that Chae had given him. He kept it in his desk drawer. He would put it on when he got to the office, and then spray odor neutralizer on himself before he left in the evenings. His wife was pregnant with their second child.

"Something wrong?" the manager asked her later that day through the online messenger they used to chat. "You look worried."

"Nothing's wrong." Chae replied, but she was lying. A number of things had happened to her that day. All of them were depressing.

When she had arrived at the office and opened her email account, she had found a threatening message. It read: "Repent. I know you're in an improper relationship. If you want peace of mind, deposit ten million won in the bank account shown below. You have one week." The email address was unfamiliar. She stared at the screen until her eyes grew sore. She had no idea how long she had stared at it before she finally reassured herself that the email was just a prank or it had been sent to her by mistake.

Chae entered the woman's phone number into the search window of the call log. The results showed that the woman was a new customer. She had switched mobile service providers a month ago, but had kept her old number. In the past month she had made thirty-eight calls, and received twenty-nine. Chae noticed that many of the outgoing numbers included the Gangwon Province area code. There were fourteen of these calls and they were all to the same number. The woman had called the number every other day. She hadn't called any other numbers more than three times, and none of her calls matched the man's number. Chae then checked the log of the woman's text messages. She had sent thirteen text messages and received seventeen. No numbers came up more than three times, and the man's number didn't appear. Chae made a few clicks of the mouse and the printer began to spew out documents.

Chae thought hard about whether she ought to talk to her boss about the threatening email. She was afraid she would look ridiculous if she brought it up, but decided she had no choice. Yet she was hesitant. She wondered what her relationship with her boss really amounted to. Then she realized that what was upsetting her was really this: the uncertainty surrounding their relationship. What was certain was that she could do nothing to put her failing relationship with her fiancé back on track, and that she had been feeling chest pains that were sometimes so severe she couldn't even breathe. That made one uncertain matter and two certainties. None of them were going to be easy to deal with.

It wasn't until she got a call from her fiancé that Chae realized the suspicious email was just the start of her problems. He said he was leaving for Prague. His voice sounded flat and detached when he explained he had made up his mind to go, and that he thought he could get by for about a year. The previous night, after they'd been talking on the phone for a long time, Chae had yelled at him and told him he needed to make a choice: either marry her or break up with her. After a certain point in their relationship they had started arguing regularly and especially when they talked on the phone. They talked on the phone almost every day, which meant they argued almost every day. They argued casually, as if it were part of their routine. Recognizing the problem, they avoided talking on the phone on days when they'd seen one another. But yesterday they'd met in person and talked on the phone. Chae trembled when she came to the conclusion that, by announcing that he was leaving for Prague, her fiancé meant he wanted to break up with her. He'd said so much over the phone.

Prague, my ass! It's just like a poet to be evasive like that! What a freaking loser! Chae could barely stop herself from swearing aloud. She coughed uncontrollably. It was a violent and prolonged coughing fit. Chae had trouble breathing and felt her chest tighten. The doctor she had seen said it was caused by postnasal drip. That literally meant that mucus was flowing backwards into her throat. He added that if it worsened it would probably develop into a sinus infection.

"But you don't have any money, do you?"

Chae wished she had held her tongue. The situation couldn't get much worse. She felt as if she was suffocating. When she had urged her fiancé to decide on one thing or the other, all she'd really wanted from him was just a few heartwarming words. Like "Cheer up" or "Hang in there"—not to mention "I love you." Was it really because it was so hard for him to utter those words that he had finally decided to fly to Prague, even though he was penniless? Dumbass! He couldn't write a poem that didn't include the word "love," but he couldn't bring himself to say the word aloud.

Chae suddenly recalled the lines that she had read somewhere in her fiancé's first collection of poems, which had come out seven years after he first began calling himself a poet. Which love would you choose: the love that starts for one reason and ends for ninety-nine reasons, or the love that starts for ninety-nine reasons and ends for one reason?

When that first book was published, the writer and his friends invited Chae out for drinks to celebrate. An old friend of his—a woman—asked Chae what she thought of those lines of poetry. The woman stared icily at Chae.

"Ninety-nine reasons are too few to fall in love, and one reason is one too many to bring love to an end," Chae answered.

The woman whistled and handed Chae a bomb shot of liquor and beer. Although she knew that a single glass of beer was enough to cause the blood to run to her head and make her short of breath, Chae knocked back the drink. At that moment, she would have drunk anything this friend of her fiancé's offered her, even if it meant risking her life. Perhaps this was her real problem: that she had nothing special to risk her life for.

While Chae kept drinking and putting her life on the line, her fiancé and one of his friends were arguing and betting one another the cost of the fried chicken and beer.

"Andong is bigger than Seoul? Nonsense!"

"Yes, it is."

"No. It can't be."

"You always contradict everything I say!"

"Well, well, you're the VIP today, so let me drink to whatever you say."

"Drink to whatever I say just because I say it? No way! Because Andong is bigger than Seoul."

"All right, let's just say it is."

"No. You should just admit that it is, because it is."

"You're going to regret this."

"See? You obviously think I'm wrong."

"Let's stop. Your girlfriend is here."

"Fuck off! She's not my girlfriend, she's my fiancée!"

Their drinking and arguing continued into the early hours of the morning, and it was Chae who'd had to pay for all the drinks and broken beer glasses: 400,000 won.

Out in the street, the two men who had been fighting and hurling glasses at one another were now squatting down next to a utility pole, one of them repeating "I'm sorry" and the other "Congratulations." They hugged, and they even kissed one another on the cheek.

"You'd best go on home. Those guys won't budge from there until they sober up," said the woman. Then she pressed something into Chae's hand, saying, with a shrug, that she had swiped it from their table in the bar. It was the button used to call the server. "You've never stolen anything, have you? At first it's not easy. But once you get started there's nothing to it."

On her way home in a taxi, Chae pressed the button over and over again. She got no response. She wished she had answered her fiancé's friend differently and said that one reason is too many to start to love someone, and ninety-nine reasons are too few to stop loving them. Chae now had too many reasons to stop loving her fiancé: his first publication of poems after a seven-year delay, the way the woman had whistled in response to what she'd said, the bomb shots, Seoul, Andong, the two men calling her "girlfriend" or "fiancé," the broken beer glasses, the utility pole, the two men squatting down beside it, the stolen call button, the goddamn fact that nothing and nobody responded no matter how hard she pushed it, and Prague.

Picking the police request back up, Chae entered the man's cell phone number. Six outgoing calls and seven incoming. That was his call log for the last six months. Not six days but six months. And four of the seven incoming calls were automated marketing calls. Not one of the outgoing or incoming numbers matched the woman's number. Chae typed the man's number into the search field and she set the search to the maximum time period, which was six months. She got the same result. There were no text messages. Not a single one.

Chae gazed abstractedly at the screen, and, without realizing it, spoke the man's name under her breath. It sounded like the name of a forgotten and forsaken place. Then she suddenly started coughing. She felt her chest tighten and she couldn't breathe. She wanted to cough up so much more than just air. When the coughing subsided, she pressed a key on her cell phone. It was the shortcut key for her fiancé's number. Listening to it ring she still didn't know what she was going to say.

Kwak Woo-cheol (male, age forty-eight) was checking out share prices when a detective came to see him. A rumor had hit the Asian stock markets that the US Federal Reserve was about to raise its interest rate. The Nikkei and the Hang Seng Index both plummeted. The KOSPI index also plunged below its previous record low of 1300. The fact was that the big foreign investors had already sold their shares.

Kwak was looking for the right moment to sell his stocks. The price was certainly going to be weakening for the time being. He might have to sell out before it was too late, and start to buy gold or euros. He'd probably be better off waiting for a sharp rally, even if it meant risking a big loss. But then he suddenly remembered a photo taken the year the Olympics were held in Beijing. It was a photo of a swarm of frogs that had carpeted a road right before an earthquake in Szechuan Province. The frogs had clearly sensed the imminent disaster and were escaping from it. And all of a sudden Kwak wondered where the frogs could have been heading.

The detective held out his ID and took it back again so quickly that Kwak didn't manage to get even a brief look at it.

I seem to remember that in Hollywood movies detectives work in pairs. Why don't you have your partner with you? Normally in a situation like this, Kwak would have cracked a joke by asking that kind of question, but today he wasn't at all in the mood for it. The price of every stock he owned was going down. Kwak asked the detective what his visit was about, and the detective replied by asking if he could sit down. He sank into a sofa. He looked as if he was taking a break rather than pursuing an investigation.

"Ms. Jo!" Kwak called, drawing out the vowel sound.

A plump woman walked in.

"Two coffees," said Kwak.

"Could I have a glass of cold water instead of coffee?" the detective asked.

Kwak made an eye contact with the plump woman and nodded.

"Coffee keeps me awake at night," he mumbled, rubbing his knees.

The detective took his time drinking the water, and he said it tasted good. When Kwak offered him more, he declined. Taking a business card from his jacket pocket, the detective put it down on the table. He pushed it toward Kwak, who leaned forward and looked at the card without touching it.

"You know him, don't you?"

"He was an employee here."

"He worked as a senior editor, didn't he?"

"Yes. And he was the only employee I had. He quit last year. I treated him like a brother but . . . Young people these days, they don't know how to behave. Besides, they're impulsive. I had such a hard time finding someone to replace him."

"He's dead."

"Oh!"

When the detective told him the details, Kwak realized that the death he had happened to hear about on the news was someone he had known, and his former editor, no less. Kwak was totally shocked. The former editor was the last person he expected to see in the news reports. He tried to remember what the man looked like, but he couldn't picture him clearly.

Kwak remembered many things about his former employee: he had never left the office early or taken a day off during the two years he worked there; he always brought lunch and ate it alone; he liked hot tea, even in summer; he used to wear headphones while he worked; he never talked unless someone spoke to him; he didn't like karaoke; he looked gloomy most of the time, but often laughed. However, Kwak couldn't remember what he looked like.

"What was he like?" the detective asked, studying Kwak's face.

"What do you mean?"

"I mean his financial situation, his relationships with women, that kind of thing."

"He was sensible with money, and he kept mostly to himself."

"Did he have a girlfriend?"

"No. I asked him once what he did during the weekend. He just smiled."

"Are you sure about that?"

"About what?"

"That he wasn't dating anyone."

"I'm one hundred percent certain."

The detective closed his eyes for a moment and opened them again. He was clearly disappointed. He asked for another glass of water, took some pills out of his pocket and swallowed them with a mouthful of water.

"Did the forecast say it would rain today?" the detective asked, after drinking the rest of the water.

"Sorry, but I have no idea. I stopped watching the weather forecast a long time ago."

"I understand."

The detective fumbled in his pocket and took something out. It was a citizenship card. He asked Kwak if he recognized the person in the photo. Kwak looked closely at it and suddenly remembered what his former editor looked like. The woman in the photo and the editor looked alike, he thought. Still, the woman wasn't anyone he knew. Kwak shook his head. The detective lapsed into silence. A heavy silence filled the air until the detective spoke again.

"What kind of books do you usually publish?"

"Children's books."

"What kind of children's books?"

"Fairy stories and folktales."

"I see."

Another heavy silence descended on them.

"Do people still give a baby a gold ring on its first birthday?" the detective asked.

"Sorry?"

"I mean, when they have a party for a baby's first birthday."

"What's that got to do with your case?"

"Never mind. It was just something that came into my head."

"I'm sorry, but it's been a long time since I was invited to a baby's first birthday party."

"That's all right. Forget it."

"Ms. Jo!" Kwak called out. But the detective stood up with a dismissive gesture. He winced as he got up. Kwak also rose, half sitting, half standing. Only then did he realize he had felt uneasy throughout his conversation with the detective. He couldn't figure out what was making him uncomfortable, but he was certain he'd had a similar feeling when he'd seen the photo of the swarm of frogs.

"He was a model employee."

The detective said nothing in response. Kwak guessed he was brooding on things like a baby's first birthday party or a gold ring.

"Why did he quit?"

"He said he wanted to go back to school."

"What was he studying?"

"I don't know the details."

"That's odd. He started working for a different publisher."

"Really?"

"You didn't know that? I'm sorry."

Kwak didn't understand why the detective was sorry. Was it because his former employee took a job with a different publisher, or because Kwak had had no inkling of it until now, or because the detective had let it slip by accident? The detective held out his hand, thanking Kwak for his time. His palm was damp with sweat. As soon as the detective left, Kwak rushed to the bathroom to wash his hands. He made sure to use soap.

Back at his desk, Kwak opened his investment website and

bought eighty shares of S_____ Pharmaceuticals. The owner of the massage parlor on Yeoui Island that Kwak frequented had whispered to him that the company was close to developing a new vaccine against the mutated bird flu virus. A crisis for everyone is an opportunity for someone.

Kwak dialed an international number. He would often feel better when he heard his daughter's voice. She was at a school in New Jersey, in the third grade. When they talked on the phone, they spoke English. Kwak was always pleased when he found that his daughter had learned a new English word.

"Did you have fun today?"

"Yes, Daddy."

"What did you do after school?"

"I went to a friend's birthday party."

"Was your friend Korean?"

"No. She's American."

"Is she black or white?"

"She's white. Her name is Judy. Her hair is red, and she has lots of freckles on her face."

"What's father doing?"

"You're talking to me, aren't you?"

"I mean Judy's father."

"Dunno. Do you want to talk to Mom?"

"No. That's all right. You remember what I always tell you, don't you?"

"Yes."

"Well, let me test you then."

"All right, Daddy."

"What should you do if a stranger starts a conversation with you?"

"I should yell."

"What should you do if anyone touches you?"

"I should run straight to Mom and tell her."

"You're such a smart girl."

"When will you come see us, Daddy?"

"As soon as possible."

"I miss you so much, Daddy."

"I miss you too."

Putting down the receiver, Kwak leaned back in his chair and closed his eyes. He suddenly heard rain. The raindrops hitting the road sounded like a swarm of frogs croaking. Like a swarm of frogs racing towards a dead end.

For a long time, Byeon Yeong-ae (female, age forty-seven) had been in the habit of judging a man by his shoes and a woman by her purse. The man was wearing running shoes, which she thought was unusual for someone his age. The white shoes were new and had thick soles but there was no visible logo. His clothes were shabby. His appearance suggested he hadn't been around women for a long time. He didn't seem to be looking for an apartment. Byeon watched him out of the corner of her eyes, but she didn't stop what she was doing—sitting on a couch and singing a hymn.

> Are we weak and heavy laden, cumbered with a load of cares?
> Precious Savior, still our refuge, take it to the Lord in prayer!
> Do thy friends despise, forsake thee? Take it to the Lord in prayer!
> In His arms He'll take and shield thee, thou wilt find a solace there.

The man stood quietly until the hymn was over, his eyes fixed on the neighborhood land registration map on the wall, as if he didn't know where else to look. Only when she had said a closing prayer and ended her small worship service, did Byeon acknowledge the man's presence. She apologized for making him wait, and he said he was sorry for interrupting.

Byeon saw helplessness in the man's face. She gradually began to picture an alleyway full of twists and turns behind his eyes. The alley was dark and quiet. The fate of a wanderer in that soundless, shadowy lane: a lonely and doleful life. Byeon tried to imagine what the man's life was like. He would have to trudge along that gloomy, silent alleyway wearing the running shoes he had just bought. No one could tell how many pairs of shoes he would wear out before he reached the end of his journey.

Because her work involved meeting new people every day,

Byeon had gotten in the habit of accurately picturing people's lives just by observing their appearance. When she asked a client a question, it was because she wanted to see if what she had imagined about them was correct. Sometimes she was wrong, but she often guessed correctly. She was sure she would soon master the art of knowing everything about a person at first glance.

When Byeon asked how she could help the man, he said he was a detective. The three women who had been worshipping with Byeon stood up from the sofa, stealing a glance at him as they rose to their feet.

"We'll wait for you at the restaurant. No hurry," one of the women said to Byeon.

"Go ahead and order. I'll be right there." Byeon said loudly as the women left.

"I won't take up much of your time," said the detective.

Byeon didn't even ask him to sit down. He took an identity card out of an inside pocket of his jacket and asked her if she recognized the face in the photo. It was a young woman.

"She was here a month ago."

"You have a good memory."

"I rarely forget a person's face, even if I only saw them once."

"Was she alone?"

Byeon remembered the woman clearly. She had been alone, and she had carried a Michael Kors purse. If Byeon had to choose one of two empty seats — either beside a woman with a Michael Kors purse or a woman with a Louis Vuitton one — she wouldn't hesitate to choose the former. Because a woman with a Michael Kors purse would never talk unless you spoke to her first. Besides, a Michael Kors type wasn't the type to brag. Byeon loathed show-offs, because they wouldn't let her get a word in. The woman in the photo had confirmed Byeon's theory about the two types of women.

Although it was an outdated style, the woman's purse looked brand new. It must have meant a lot to her. The woman's clothes were plain, unlike her bag. She was wearing flat shoes, which had gone out of style.

She must have splurged on the purse as a big treat for herself.

The odds are high that she's not married, because she isn't here with a man. She's a working woman. That's clear from her appearance. But it doesn't look like she takes the purse with her to work. Her job must involve a lot of standing, because she wears flats even though she's not tall.

Byeon made wild assumptions about the woman and she wanted to find out whether or not they were correct. She asked the woman where she lived, and she said she lived in Bongcheon-dong. When Byeon went on to ask her what neighborhood of Bongcheon-dong and what type of home she lived in, she snickered, saying she had an apartment in a multi-family unit. When asked if she was married, she snickered again, mumbling "Not yet."

Oh, this is fun! So far so good. Byeon got excited and asked more questions one after another. Not serious ones, but just the kind of casual questions that anyone would ask a stranger sitting next to them, and yet a certain curiosity lay behind them.

Byeon didn't see the woman as a potential customer. Still, having taken up so much time with her questions, she couldn't pretend she had an urgent appointment and ask the woman to leave. Instead, she offered her a cup of coffee. She figured the coffee would be worthwhile if it saved her the thankless task of traipsing around showing the woman a host of apartments she wouldn't want. The woman said she'd prefer tea. Byeon brought her hot water and a teabag from a package she had bought in the duty-free shop in Heathrow Airport. The woman seemed to enjoy every sip of the steaming hot drink. She drank three cups of tea while Byeon had just one cup of coffee.

The woman laughed a lot. She laughed when she was asked an awkward question and when their conversation stopped abruptly. There was an air of aloofness and loneliness about her laughter. Like the smell of wet earth after rain. She constantly snickered, as if doing so was what made life bearable for her. When Byeon asked if it was part of her nature to laugh so much, the woman abruptly stopped smiling and asked, "Did I laugh?" Her unsmiling face was cold and resolute.

Byeon asked if the woman was by any chance a school teacher. She replied without smiling that she was, sort of. She said nothing more. Byeon didn't ask any more questions either, guessing that the woman would just smile and say nothing regardless. They sat in silence for a moment. The dark eyes of the woman—who was lost in thought—were quiet, quieter than silence. The woman asked Byeon if she looked like a school teacher. This was the third question the woman had asked. The first question was insignificant, and Byeon couldn't remember what the second was. As a matter of fact, she was not used to being asked questions. Byeon didn't answer. Instead she tried following the woman's example. She smiled. She was aware that this was the first time she had smiled at her, but she didn't know it would be the last.

The woman was looking for a two-story house with an attic room. She insisted that it had to have an attic room. Byeon asked her why she was so anxious to have an attic when she didn't have children who might enjoy it. The woman said nothing and just smiled, as she had before.

As they visited prospective homes, Byeon asked questions and the woman answered. It was as if Byeon were the house-hunter, and the woman was the realtor. At one of the houses, the woman stayed in the attic room for a long time, as if just that room rather than the whole house was what mattered to her. She looked around carefully, with a wistful expression, more like she were giving her old room one last look before leaving it forever. She briefly glanced at the rest of the rooms. She liked the home, but only because of the attic room. She didn't ask the price right away, though. It was only after they had left that she suddenly asked about the price, as though she had almost forgotten to inquire. When she heard the price she reacted neither positively nor negatively, as if she were completely indifferent. Perhaps what she really wanted to know was what it would cost for her to rent the attic room. Byeon headed back to her office, skipping the last two houses she had planned to show the woman.

"Did she mention who she was going to move in with?"

"No, she didn't."

"Did you notice anything unusual about her?"

"Hmm, not really."

The lines in the detective's forehead deepened.

Byeon was going to tell him that the woman had been obsessed with having an attic room, but she decided not to. She had a lot on her mind. She had arranged to go and see a psychic at Donam-dong after eating lunch with the other church members. When someone was considering buying some land, this psychic could pinpoint the best land to buy. Besides the matter of the land purchase, Byeon had plenty of other things to ask the psychic. Why her husband was going on so many business trips these days, and what major her son, who was a senior in high school, should choose at university, and why he too, like his father, was so careful to avoid her. There was nothing she wanted to ask about her own life. The person she was least curious about was herself. It wasn't that she already knew everything about herself, but rather that she didn't know anything at all about herself.

"What is this all about, anyway?"

"Nothing special. Are the offices of Prosperity Real Estate and Luxury Realty nearby?"

The first one was a block away, and the second was in the commercial part of a nearby apartment complex. Byeon gave him directions to both.

A cell phone rang. You're born—to be loved; you're born—to be loved, went the ringtone. It was Byeon's.

"I'll be right there. Would you order for me? Yes, the usual. Steak. Medium-well. All right."

The detective took a notebook out of his pocket and leafed through it. He found the name Byeon Yeong-ae and crossed it out.

A helicopter flew overhead, and the windows shook. The dogs barked frantically, and the cats yowled loudly. Animals that had been abandoned were highly sensitive to the smallest sound or slightest movement. Kim Gyeong-hwan (male, age forty-one) had had a summer job at the Children's Grand Park when he was a college student. His main duty was to take care of the animals in the park, but when the park got very crowded, he was asked to watch the kids who had lost their parents.

The lost children reacted in many different ways. Some cried uncontrollably and others sat still and remained calm. Most of the kids ended up finding their parents the same day, but some did not. Abandoned children knew that they had been abandoned. Abandoned kids neither cried nor stayed calm. They would crouch down in the corner of the waiting area, biting their lips. Their eyes brimmed with tears as though they were about to start crying, but they never cried. They seemed to be afraid that they'd be kicked out if they did. If you listened closely you could hear a sound—shush, shush—escaping from their bodies. It's the sound you hear when a man's soul shrinks. People say that a man loses twenty-one grams with his last breath. From the moment a child is abandoned, its soul starts to shrivel, little by little, until that last twenty-one grams escapes. In short, a child starts to die from the moment it is left behind by its parents. Children's Day was when they had the greatest number of lost kids who never found their parents.

The helicopter had been flying overhead all day, spraying disinfectant. The public health authorities were placed on alert, because of a mutated bird flu virus that was reported to be highly contagious to humans. The only emergency measure they took was to bury live chickens and ducks that were thought to be infected. The World Health Organization also issued a public warning that the mutated virus could spread to four-legged animals, which meant the barrier between species was meaningless. The number of abandoned dogs and cats increased drastically.

As the noise of the helicopter died away the animals became quiet. Kim Gyeong-hwan continued to do what he had been doing—examining newly arrived animals. An animal control agent had brought in three Persian cats that morning. He said they had belonged to a young man who had died. They were found and reported by the owner of the building where the young man had been renting an apartment. The owner lived in the same building. The agent didn't know how the young man had died. It must have happened suddenly. Otherwise he would have asked someone to take care of his cats.

All three cats were in good condition. Their fur was long and shiny. Two of them were white, and the third was white and black. They all had green eyes, but up close, there seemed to be a blue tinge to them. Kim wondered what kind of person the cats' owner had been. Dog lovers were usually people who liked touching and being touched, while cat lovers were not. Dog owners would usually ask him first how much the dog's treatment would cost, while cat owners would ask how long it would take their cat to recover. Dog owners would tell Kim what their dogs were like, and cats would let him know what their owners were like. The owner of the Persian cats had probably been someone who would wait quietly, no matter how anxious he was to know something, until the other person explained it to him. As quietly as a ghost.

Kim placed the cats on a scale, one at a time. This was always the first thing he did with newly arrived animals. The city council paid the shelter a subsidy according to the weight of the animals. The three cats weighed exactly the same: three point eight kilos. It had to be a coincidence. Still, it struck Kim as very unusual. The cats were all male, none of them neutered. They must have weighed a little more before their owner had died. At least twenty-one grams more, perhaps.

Kim passed a microchip scanner over the cats. It showed nothing for any of them. Under the new animal law, every owner had to have their pet implanted with a chip that recorded the animal's breed, medical history, and the owner's name and address. Anyone who didn't comply faced a fine of up to one million won. It was supposed to reduce the number of abandoned pets. A human conscience implanted into the body of an animal. Some animal rights groups came out in strong opposition to the law. Other groups warned that the measure would lead to human microchip-implantation—even quoting the Book of Revelation.

Kim forced each cat's mouth open and checked the teeth. They were around six years old, give or take a year. The cats were docile, like innocent children totally unaware that their parents had left them behind. Kim liked these cats, particularly because they were not microchipped. The day would probably come when humans would be branded on their foreheads and wrists like animals, as the prophet said—when all humans would have to be microchipped. When that happened, would humans stop abandoning one another? It was anyone's guess. The prophet also said that, when that day came, anyone who wanted to know the human population would have to count animals. As a vet, Kim interpreted the phrase as saying that the barriers between species would break down. A virus that was deadly to animals would attack humans. No one would be immune. Maybe the Creator made the virus on the seventh day. As a kind of insurance.

Kim was supposed to enter the three cats into his record book, take photographs of them, upload the photos to his animal hospital website, wait for ten days, and then, unless someone had showed up to adopt them, put them to sleep. This was what he usually did, following the regulations, but he thought of another plan for these cats.

There were ten animals that had not found a home in the time allowed: six dogs, three cats, and one lizard. Kim was starting to prepare a muscle relaxant to euthanize them, when the man who sold dogs arrived. He stopped by Kim's animal hospital once a month, but this time he was two weeks early. It was his busiest time of year. He chose seven animals this time, including four that Kim was going to put down, saving Kim a lot of work. The man weighed the animals he had picked and paid Kim five thousand won per kilo. He seemed interested in the lizard, so Kim gave it to him for free.

Kim injected a muscle relaxant into the remaining animals: two dogs and three cats. The animals died within a minute. There was neither resistance nor struggle. Kim wrote in his log: "Euthanized six dogs, three cats, and one lizard." He could claim twenty thousand won for each animal. His seven-year-old son did not know that his father's job included injecting abandoned animals with a chemical to put them to sleep. His son didn't know the source of the smoke that escaped under cover of darkness from the chimney of the animal hospital or that some dogs were "dispatched" without smoke. All Kim's son knew was that his father worked at an animal hospital.

Kim had been meticulous about what he let his son know about his job. That's why Kim was going to give the three Persian cats to the boy. He injected the cats with an anesthetic. Each of them was wearing a collar with a silver tag. Each tag was inscribed with a name of a philosopher. Plato, Spinoza, and Nietzsche. The one with the black markings was Nietzsche. Kim knew just one thing about the three philosophers: they were never married.

The three cats went limp as the drug took effect. Once they were completely unconscious, Kim would castrate them so that they would make a suitable gift for his son. The boy's birthday—that is, the day Kim had adopted him—was two days away.

It was the first sunny Sunday in a long while. Yi Hye-ryeon (female, age thirty-two) was busy preparing the elderly residents for their visitors. She was so busy bathing and dressing the old people that she couldn't even take a moment to catch her breath. The last thing she did was check their nails. If they were neat and clean the residents were ready to meet the world outside—the world that they'd forgotten or that had forgotten them.

Yi didn't see one of the residents, Jin, anywhere. She went up onto the roof. She found the old man crouching down in a space between two water tanks—it was the same spot she had found him in several times before, always hunkered down in the same way. Jin had arranged some sheets of plywood across the tops of the water tanks. He called this "the attic room." The moment he spotted Yi, he stood up unhesitatingly, like a little boy who had been found in a game of hide-and-seek.

"You want to look clean and nice for your daughter, don't you?" Yi asked loudly, holding Jin's arm.

Jin's youngest daughter visited him every Sunday, like clockwork. Of all the visitors, she arrived earliest and left latest. Every time she visited she read fairy tales to her father. She once said her job was reading to children. No matter what kind of story she read to him—sad, cheerful, or downright comic—Jin would smile in a simple-minded way. Just once or twice a serious look passed fleetingly across his face, as if an old memory that he had long forgotten had come back to him. A look that suggested he was hearing names from a world that had perished long ago. Although it was Jin's son who had put him into the nursing home, the young man had never visited his father. Neither had Jin's other daughters.

Yi undressed the old man, revealing his thin, shriveled body. He sat down on a plastic bath stool and leaned forward, his back towards her. His arms, dangling from his hunched shoulders, were as thin as twigs. The slightest tug could pull them from their sockets. His protruding ribs seemed about to pierce through his sides. Yi started to rub the old man's body all over, every crevice of it, with her soapy hand. Holding a shower head in her other hand she sprayed water over him. Reaching unsuspectingly into the old man's groin, she was startled and pulled her hand back. His penis had grown stiff. This had never happened before.

The new director had restricted visits to Sundays. It was the first thing he had done when he was transferred to this nursing home. Then he had changed a lot of other things. Almost everything, in fact. Everything but the residents themselves. He immediately changed anything that was unsightly in his eyes. He even fired a senior nurse who had been there for six years, just because he said she laughed while he had been giving her instructions. No one knew why she laughed, because he didn't ask and she didn't offer an explanation. After that, no one laughed in front of the new director.

From a very early age, Yi had always laughed readily. The slightest thing would set her off. This tendency had been more of a help than a hindrance to her. For her coworkers and the elderly residents her childlike smile was what they liked most about her. But this was no longer the case. Every time the new director appeared, Yi and the people around her all grew tense—on her part it was because she was struggling not to laugh, while the others were afraid that she would laugh nonetheless.

Yi's parents had run a public bathhouse, and they often had her sit in the cashier's booth. The Plexiglass window of the booth had been covered in colored cellophane so no one could see into the booth or out of it. All sorts of things were handed back and forth across the desk through the small opening: bills and coins, bath towels, disposable razors, shampoo, soap, a sense of curiosity. A feeling of shame, too, at times.

One day, when she was a teenager and was sitting in the booth, Yi handed a towel, a razor and shampoo to her art teacher, whom she idolized. She recognized his voice and the silver ring with his initials engraved in it. There was another thing that led her to believe it was her art teacher: a pair of brown dress shoes with pointed toes. Yi blushed with embarrassment, as if her teacher had recognized who was in the booth. From the moment the shoes disappeared up the stairs until they appeared again, she didn't laugh once. This rarely happened to her. Meanwhile, in her imagination, she was picturing her teacher's naked body. Doing so somehow alleviated her embarrassment but then she realized what she was doing and felt ashamed again. After that, whenever Yi had to be certain not to laugh in front of someone, she would picture them without their clothes on. No one could or should laugh in front of a naked person. No matter what that person's body looks like.

Cars were starting to arrive, one after another, bringing the visitors. Many of the cars were imported models, because the residents were from the wealthiest district of Seoul. The original plan had been to build the nursing home in that part of the city, but the project had to be relocated to the Gangwon Province because the residents' association in the wealthy neighborhood had filed a civil complaint, saying that building the facility there would decrease the value of their apartments.

The parking lot was downhill from the nursing home. To reach the building, people had to walk up 108 steps. Did this mean that every visitor, knowing the significance of the number in Buddhism, would release all their worries and anxieties as they walked up? There were actually ninety nine steps, but people referred to the stairway as the 108 steps.

The nursing home was surrounded by picturesque mountains and valleys. The trees were in full leaf. Most of the family members who came to visit were dressed in brightly colored outdoor clothing. To them, the nursing home was probably a kind of ticket office to a scenic park. Contrary to expectation, the number of visitors had increased when visiting was restricted to Sundays.

Yi couldn't see Jin's youngest daughter anywhere. She had borrowed a children's book from her last Sunday. It was about the friendship between a spider and a pig. When the family members had finished their sightseeing and began to crowd into the building, Jin's daughter still hadn't shown up. Jin was sitting vacantly at a window that overlooked the parking lot. It was where they would sit when his daughter read to him.

Visiting hours were almost over when the director appeared unexpectedly. He was wearing a track suit and had apparently just come back from a hike in the mountains nearby. He walked around among the tables shaking hands with the family visitors. Park, one of the residents who was known for his pranks, went up behind the director and pulled down the man's pants. It happened in a flash. The old man must have pulled hard—the director's boxers came down along with his trousers. The director hurriedly hitched up his underwear. This all happened in the blink of an eye. Everyone stared at him, their mouths agape. The pattern printed on his boxers was of the Kiri card from a deck of Japanese Hanafuda playing cards. Throughout the room, people began to laugh.

In a matter of seconds the dining room was in uproar. Residents started reaching for the person in front of them and pulling down pants or lifting skirts. The shrieking and laughter became contagious. One moment they were screaming and the next they were laughing, or what started as a laugh became a scream. To stifle her own laughter, Yi tried to picture the director's naked body. She didn't need to imagine his buttocks, however. She had just spotted a large birthmark on his right cheek. And the laughter she had struggled to suppress spurted out. She laughed so hard tears flowed from her eyes. Then her watery eyes lit on the old man, Jin. He was looking down toward the steps, his shoulders hunched forward, as if he regretted not being with the others.

As they walked downstairs together into the basement of an annex to the National Forensic Service building, Jang Mu-hyeok (male, age forty-one) listened while the detective summarized the case. The detective looked tired and downcast. He had the appearance of a man who was looking death in the face. And he was, in fact, going down to look into the face of death. The basement of the annex building housed the autopsy lab. The cadavers there would never speak again and had not left any word on the reason for their deaths. When they left that basement the only place left for them to go was the grave.

As he went down the stairs, the detective's legs moved unnaturally, like a marionette. He walked heavily, and slower than Jang, even though Jang was wearing boots. Nonetheless, he was anxious to describe the details of the case. He said the bodies had been found inside a car, but it wasn't a traffic accident. And no external wounds were found on the bodies. Jang looked at the results of the blood tests. No poison or drugs or alcohol had been detected. There was no trace of disease either. The blood taken from the two dead bodies was clean.

The summary of the case was simple: two corpses. A young man and a younger woman. Found in a car parked on the hard shoulder of a freeway. Wearing seatbelts. The detective's voice was frayed, like stiff knee joints. His threadbare murmur echoed with confusion and despair. Like the knees of a lonely man who had no one left in his life to call out to. It was as if his knees had been the source of strength he had drawn from to fight against all kinds of evil.

A simple case meant a brief autopsy, a complicated case a detailed one. Jang checked the results of the blood tests one more time. They left no room for doubt. They were beyond clean. A deceptively simple case and excessively clean blood. The simplicity of the case was itself rather suspicious. The autopsy might turn out to be a lengthy and difficult one. It might necessitate sawing open the skulls and severing every joint. Park, the only female scientist at the National Forensic Service, leafed through the blood test report. She frowned.

Jang told the detective the results of the blood tests. The confusion and despair that resonated in the detective's voice matched his face exactly. Maybe he did indeed have no one left to call out to, other than himself. He slowly pressed his temples with his fingers.

Jang's head was pounding from a hangover. He hadn't been able to get to sleep the previous night and had decided to have one glass of whisky, but in the end he'd had five. He had autopsied an eight-year-old girl. She was the same age as his daughter. The girl's buried corpse had been discovered a month after she'd been kidnapped. She had been raped and strangled. Or perhaps she was sexually assaulted after being killed. A cadaver could reveal anything—even the DNA of the criminal—but the motive for the crime. Maybe they would never know everything. Maybe they knew nothing.

On his way home after work, Jang would stare at anyone who was the same age and sex as the bodies he had autopsied that day or who bore a resemblance to the deceased. By the time he got home, the image he had of the people he had autopsied became as faint as an old smudge. But he couldn't escape the smell of death; he was tormented by the smell even in his sleep as it chased him to the depths of his dreams. It wasn't like the stench of a corpse. It was more like the smell that is given off when what was once called passion or hope withers and decays. A vile smell that is unwelcome even in hell. It clung to his hair, so he shaved his head like a monk. He would have done anything—anything at all—to shake off the vile stench of death.

The previous night, even when he got home, Jang hadn't been able to get the dead girl's image out of his head. He hadn't been able to look at similar girls on the bus or in the subway, although he had seen two or three girls who looked like her. He couldn't bring himself to look at their faces. Just the thought of looking at the girls disgusted him. Besides, he wasn't confident he could force a smile when he met their gaze. If he couldn't even manage a polite smile for an eight-year-old girl, it meant that—apart from a glimpse at the treasures of the gods—there was nothing beautiful left in this world.

A stiff drink didn't help. It was only after he had sat until dawn watching his sleeping daughter that the image of the dead girl grew dim. His daughter woke up as the sun began to rise.

"Did you have a bad dream again, Daddy?"

"Yes. But it was just a dream. No matter how bad it is, it's just a dream," he muttered, stroking his daughter's head. She offered to read him a fairy tale.

"'Let's go together to my kingdom tomorrow,' the prince said. He and his princess slept peacefully that night. The next morning, a coach drawn by eight white horses arrived at the castle. Heinrich, the prince's loyal servant, was there too. When the prince had been turned into a frog, Heinrich had been so very unhappy that he'd had three hoops fastened around his heart so that it wouldn't burst from sorrow. Heinrich took the reins and drove the coach, with the prince and princess inside it, towards the prince's kingdom. After a while, the sound of something breaking was heard three times. It was the sound the three hoops around Heinrich's heart made as they broke and fell away because he was overjoyed that his master was happy again."

Jang lay down on the floor. He didn't even have a sheet under him. He couldn't sleep in a comfortable bed when the smell of death chased him in his dreams.

The bodies of the young man and woman were laid side by side on the autopsy table. While Park set about examining the woman's body, Jang began to work on the man's. He slowly pulled on latex gloves, and glanced at the face of the dead man, as if they were greeting one another. The face, with its clear-cut features and well-defined jawline, was good-looking but not unusually so. It was not a memorable face.

Jang examined the outside of the body from head to toe. It was clean. Not a scratch on it. The detective looked down at the man's body and then the woman's. He was clearly ill at ease. It was the unease of a man lost to despair and resignation. He looked like someone who, having smoked for thirty years, hadn't had a cigarette in three days.

Using a scalpel, Jang sliced through the dead man's abdomen. He took out the stomach and collected what remained of the man's last meal. It didn't amount to much, but enough to determine what the man had eaten before his death. The liver was all right, but the heart was scorched and dark. Jang removed it carefully. He cut into the right atrium, which was the blackest part. The interior was darker than the outside surface, as if the heart had burned from the inside out.

Jang sliced the right atrium into small pieces to examine a cross section. Each part he looked at had a different degree of damage. The tissue near the entrance of the superior vena cava was the most severely burnt. This was the part called the sinuatrial node, where the electrical impulses that drive the cardiac muscles are generated. A sort of generator for the heart. The heart must have stopped when the sinuatrial node ignited for some mysterious reason. It was as if the heart's "fuse" had melted and switched off the current. That was the end of it. But Jang couldn't write it up that way in the autopsy report. He had seen so many human hearts damaged in so many different ways, but he had never seen one like this. He ran through various terms—angina, irregular pulse, atrial fibrillation, and myocardial infarction—over and over, but nothing matched up.

There, in the palm of his hand, Jang held the evidence of how the young man had died, and yet he could not specify a cause of death. He turned to look at Park, as if to ask for her help. She was holding the dead woman's heart in her hand and looking into it, frowning intensely. The right atrium of the dead woman's heart was scorched, just like the man's. Jang felt as if he had been possessed by something. If he hadn't seen it with his own eyes, he wouldn't have believed it. He looked at one of the hearts, then the other. The same part of each heart had been burnt by an unknown source, leaving the rest of the bodies untouched.

When Jang and Park left the building at lunchtime, the detective was standing under a wisteria trellis, looking vacant. Jang invited him to join them for lunch, but the detective declined, saying he had to go somewhere. When Park asked him what the relationship was between the dead man and woman, he answered abruptly that the case was still under investigation.

"What should we eat today?" Park asked.

"What would you say to ox-blood soup?" Jang responded.

"Sounds good."

Jang looked back involuntarily. The detective was sitting on a bench in the shade of the wisteria vines, his back hunched. He had shoved his hands deep into the pockets of his trousers, as if he were feeling a chill in the air. Stooped over, his head bowed, the detective looked like a gigantic question mark.

The Queen of Romance

The day the World Trade Center collapsed, I was with the Queen of Romance. I was supposed to be taking photos of her library. Her novels always went straight to the top of the best seller list the moment they came out. "Queen of Romance" was an absurdly pretentious nickname for an author.

My girlfriend explained that the nickname had come about because the writer had focused on just one genre: romance novels. When I first mentioned that I would be meeting this writer, my girlfriend kept asking if I was really being serious. It was as if I were going to interview someone like Brad Pitt. When I asked if the author was really that well known, my girlfriend just stared at me, dumbfounded. Then she said she understood now why people talked about my lack of emotion. She was referring to a remark one of my *seonbae* had come out with at a party after my first photography exhibition. He wasn't being entirely serious, but I couldn't help taking it to heart. I don't take pictures of anything except structures, and I always do my best to make my photos impersonal. Looking at my girlfriend and me, the *seonbae* added that we were both baffling types of people. I met my girlfriend in college in a photography club. She only took pictures of people from behind.

The Queen of Romance had never allowed her face to be seen in public. Not even in photos. On the covers of her books, all you can see is a laptop and her hands. All five of her novels have the same image: hands in black lace gloves barely touching the white keyboard. The fingers are small and fine, the nails painted black. The hands look as if they've never done anything as menial as changing a light bulb. Without offering any explanation, the Queen of Romance refused to appear at any official events or ceremonies.

I set about reading all five books that had reportedly sold like hotcakes. It wasn't that I planned to show my respect for the author that way, or that I had been urged to do so by my girlfriend, an avid fan of the Queen of Romance. It was purely out of curiosity. She wasn't even called the Queen of Romance Novels, but the Queen of Romance! To be honest, I had never even glanced at a romance novel before, because I hated the overblown sentimentality of the genre. If I feel like reading about other people's lives, I prefer biographies or memoirs.

I was able to finish all five books in just four days. The sentences were overladen with emotion, and the stories themselves were contrived. Once they had found true love, the protagonists generally developed a rare disease and died. In most cases, it was the female protagonist, rather than the male, who died. There was even one female protagonist who came back to life in the body of a living person, specifically the body of the man she had been forbidden to love. When a male protagonist did die it was invariably by car crash. The characters died of different things, but always in the same way: excessively tragically at the most joyful moment of their courtships. The final pages of each of the books my girlfriend lent me were smudged from her tears.

In the first novel by the Queen of Romance, the word "love" appears forty-one times. In her second novel it appears forty-seven times; in the third, fifty-two; in the fourth, fifty-six; and in the fifth, fifty-nine times. Her overuse of the word gets worse and worse. The next most frequent word after "love" is "destiny." Thirty-two times, then thirty-five, forty-one, forty-five, and fifty-one times in each novel. Despite all of this, I couldn't put the books down. To be honest, I wanted to see just how bad they were, right to the last page. And, unsurprisingly, they all turned out to be as awful as one could imagine.

In the subway on the way to and from my studio, or at a café waiting for my girlfriend, I would often spot other people reading something by the Queen of Romance. They were mostly young women, and they all looked blissfully happy, as if they had just received a long-awaited declaration of love from a boyfriend. If they caught sight of what I was reading and our eyes happened to meet, they would smile enigmatically at me. The smile was always the sort of cryptic smile exchanged by members of a secret society and understood by them only.

These people couldn't have suddenly appeared by pure chance. They must have been there, all around me in the subway or in cafés, sharing that secret smile, long before I started reading the Queen of Romance. Only now did I realize that the young women of this country could be divided into two groups: those who read the Queen of Romance, and those who didn't. Those who didn't read her books had nothing to say on the topic, but those who did were fanatical about her. They worshiped her to an absurd degree. There were a few people who read her novels critically, and their reviews were nothing short of scathing. But her ardent fans—and not just a few of them but the majority—aimed their vitriol at the critics and leapt to her defense whenever they came across any reviews or articles that were critical of her writing.

"All I'm doing is taking a few shots of her library," I said to my girlfriend, trying to sound blasé. She was deeply envious of my opportunity to meet the author, as if I had won the lottery or something.

On my way to meet the Queen of Romance, everything went wrong, right from the start. First, my car—a nine-and-a-half-year-old Hyundai—gave me trouble. I had to struggle with it for quite a while before I could get it to start. At first it gave a shudder, like a dying man breathing his last, and then finally the engine came to life. I should have paid attention when my mechanic warned me that I'd have major problems if I didn't replace a whole series of parts, including the starter and spark plugs.

I didn't have anyone with me. This was something the author had insisted on when she gave permission to have her library photographed. In fact, she had laid down three conditions: the photographer was to come alone; the photographer wasn't to take photos of anything other than her library; and she would review every photo before it was published. Although we had our magazine's standards and reputation to maintain, we had no choice. If we were going to cover this sphinxlike bestselling novelist, we had to knuckle down and agree to her demands. Given what we had poured into this project already, we couldn't afford to walk away from it, even if she had come up with another three thousand conditions. People were even saying that another project of ours—on Paul Auster and Milan Kundera and their libraries—had been launched just so that we'd be able to pull in the Queen of Romance. Maybe it was a coincidence that we were covering them, too, but she had once mentioned that they were her favorite authors. Her interview was going to be conducted in writing. By none other than the editor-in-chief. And it would be her first interview ever.

I drove upstream beside the Han River for about an hour and a half, but I couldn't find the exit shown on the hand-drawn map. The editor-in-chief had assured me that I would see the exit sign right after I passed the confluence of the two rivers at Dumul-meori, but the only sign I could see was one that showed the distance to Chuncheon. There was nothing resembling an exit off the highway. I'd be in Chuncheon in no time, unless I turned back. I must have missed the exit.

I crossed the bridge at Cheongpyeong Dam and called the editor-in-chief. I urged him to check the directions shown on the map, but he brushed aside my doubts. He sounded annoyed and told me that the map had been sent by the author herself. I asked him for the author's phone number, but he said he didn't have it. He explained that he had been communicating with her by email and fax, and that the map had been faxed to him. He said he would try to get some more information and then call me back.

I pulled over onto the hard shoulder. I was studying the map when my cell phone rang. It was the editor-in-chief. He told me to drive along the right bank of the Han River past Dumulmeori and look out for C'est La Vie. Right after it, he said, there would be an exit ramp leading up a hill to the left. I asked him what C'est La Vie was. He said he thought it was probably a café.

I backtracked towards Seoul and crossed the river near the

Dumulmeori confluence. C'est La Vie wasn't a café, it was a motel. I passed it and continued for another thirty yards or so. Then I spotted a narrow road leading up into the mountains. There was no stoplight, so I had to cut across the oncoming traffic. I slowed down, watching for a chance to cross, but there was an endless stream of cars coming from the opposite direction. The drivers behind me honked angrily. All I could do was abandon the idea of turning, and drive straight ahead. I had to keep going for another ten minutes before I could make a U-turn.

By the time I reached the road I was already an hour late for the appointment. It was a narrow, rough lane, and the car struggled up the hill. I was surrounded by dense, dark forest, and it felt like wild animals would suddenly spring out at me. There was no sign of a house. I was beginning to think I'd taken the wrong turn when I spotted a white building just barely poking out from behind a rise. At the top of the lane I saw that it was a two-story house overlooking the river. It was covered in ivy and surrounded by a large lawn.

A woman with remarkably beautiful eyes opened the door. She was extraordinarily striking. The Creator must have had the pattern of perfect beauty in mind when He made her. A black jacket, a black shirt, and black pants. She was wearing all black. As if she were mourning her beauty as it faded with every second that elapsed. When I told her the name of the magazine I worked for, she smiled faintly. It was an elegant smile. She smiled again in the same way when I apologized for being late. A delicate, graceful manner and a sensitive, reserved personality. She was not that different from what I had imagined when I read her books, but she was far better looking than I had anticipated. Was she over forty? No one in the office knew her age.

The woman invited me to sit down, offering me a chair at an antique table. I sat down and looked around. One half of the first floor was open up to the rafters, while the other half had a second floor above it. A spiral staircase in the center divided the space into a living room and a kitchen. At the bottom of the stairs stood a pot of ivy that climbed all the way up to the second floor. It was a real plant. Beyond the stairs, in the wall facing me, were three doors, side by side. An entire wall was covered in shelves from floor to ceiling. They appeared to have been custom built for the house, and they were packed with books. There was even a library ladder.

"Is this where you write?" I asked.

"The author works only upstairs," replied the woman in black. "She'll be down in a moment. She has a cup of tea every day at this time."

I had been mistaken. This woman was not the Queen of Romance.

As I waited for the Queen of Romance to appear, I scanned the bookshelves. The books were arranged neatly by subject. Many of them were on psychology, and there were some on anatomy. A moment later I heard an upstairs door open suddenly, followed by the sound of heavy footsteps coming down the spiral stairs.

"This is the photographer." The woman dressed in black introduced me to the Queen of Romance.

The author was wearing a purple cheongsam with a tiny plum-blossom pattern. She was short and lean, and her face looked very young. With her short hair cut in a bob and her square chin she almost looked like an adolescent boy. She had a small nose and thin lips, but her eyes sparkled with a steely sharpness. It was as though the Creator had endowed her with that knifelike gaze to cut through the conventions of beauty and ugliness and make up for his mistake, having made her look neither female nor male.

"Hello," I said. "How do you do?"

"Ju-yeong, would you bring some fruit for our guest?" said the Queen of Romance.

She sounded like a boy whose voice had just broken. And she was wearing braces on her teeth. I wanted to say, don't bother with the fruit, but I couldn't bring myself to speak up. Probably because she sounded so childlike.

The woman in black brought in tea and grapes. Without acknowledging me or offering any of the customary greetings, the Queen of Romance helped herself to a grape.

"I like grapes," she said picking one off the bunch and tossing it into her mouth. Though it had a tough skin, she ate it without peeling it. I looked at her hands. Her fingers were short and thin, and she was wearing black nail polish.

The Queen of Romance polished off an entire bunch of grapes by herself while the tea was infusing. When the water in the glass teapot had darkened, she poured it into the cups. She said it was pu'er tea from the Yunnan Province of China. Then she talked about the benefits of the tea, saying that it helped boost the immune system and prevented aging, explaining that this was why it had been prized by the Chinese Emperors.

"How old are you?" the Queen of Romance asked, unblushingly. It was exactly what I wanted to ask her. I told her my age, and she continued to ask me several more questions. I had answered five of her questions before I realized that she had been using a casual form of address when she spoke to me.

"D'you mind my informal way of speaking to you?" This was the seventh question she had directed at me.

"No."

She used the familiar form of address so naturally that I hadn't even noticed it. Most of her questions were personal, the sorts of questions that could well seem rude directed at someone you had just met for the first time. Yet I didn't feel offended. It seemed to me she was just being curious. I had quite a few questions I wanted to ask her, but I could barely get a word in.

Though she eagerly asked me one question after another, the Queen of Romance didn't comment on my replies. It seemed like she couldn't have cared less what my answers were. Nonetheless, I tried to respond honestly. Except, that is, for one question: Are you seeing anyone?

"Oh my, I'm talking too much! You're the first man to visit me here in this house. I'll allow you to ask me a question, just one. Any question."

Coming so suddenly, this invitation took me by surprise, and I spoke without thinking.

"Why do you write only romance novels?"

"I have never written a romance novel. I just write novels. Or to be more accurate, I just write."

The Queen of Romance stared at me. Like a teacher checking to see if a student understood something she had just explained.

"A category is defined by what is not included in it. And what's outside a given category is, in turn, part of a larger, more comprehensive category that exists outside of that. When someone is standing in front of me, I see a different aspect of that person depending on where I am standing. This holds true only when the other person and I are at the same level. If you are in an airplane in the sky and you look down at a person on the ground, that person looks like the same speck, no matter what angle you see him from. That's because he belongs now to a different category or level. Do you know why people are obsessed with categories? It's because they're afraid of what lies outside their own category. They're afraid of the fact that they are a mere speck. That's also why they simply consider everything outside their own category as alien and exclude it. Just as Procrustes did when he cut people to size in order to make them fit his bed. It is fear that drives Jack to chop down the beanstalk, isn't it? And of course his fear ends up making him unable to climb up to the world beyond the clouds, ever again. Poor fellow! When people lock themselves into the category they call 'romance novels,' they end up reading Dostoyevsky as romance. Keep this in mind. The alien doesn't exist outside you, it's inside you."

The Queen of Romance's speech was eloquent and well-reasoned. She gave the impression of having carefully prepared and reworked her words, as if she had been asked the question a thousand times before. Her answer almost sounded mathematical and formulaic. I was surprised, because I had expected something sentimental and romantic from her. I had trouble picturing her as the same person who had written five successful romance novels. I abandoned my next question—how do you like the nickname "Queen of Romance"?—and pulled my chair closer.

"Ju-yeong," said the Queen of Romance to her assistant, "another bunch of grapes."

"You've been snacking enough already today," the woman in black responded.

"Just one more bunch."

"You know you shouldn't." The woman in black sounded as if she were talking to a child.

The Queen of Romance glanced at her watch and sprang to her feet, saying that she should have gone back to work seven minutes ago.

The process of photographing the author's library went smoothly. It was bright enough, as sunlight streamed in through the large, south-facing windows. There were some nice objects I could get good shots of: the bookshelves covering an entire wall, the crowds of books that took up the shelves, and the library ladder. I lay on my back looking up at the ladder leaning against a shelf and took several shots. I liked the way the shelves of books looked like a castle wall.

I took a few final, close-up shots of books and then ran out of film. The sunlight that had been streaming through the big windows had dwindled noticeably in the meantime. I took an anatomy book off a shelf and opened it. Long, and written in English, it was the kind of book that only a medical student would read. It wasn't likely to be helpful to someone writing romance novels. There was also a book of Da Vinci's drawings of human anatomy. When I came across an English version of the Kama Sutra I whistled involuntarily. It described and illustrated various sex positions. There were hardly any sex scenes in the Queen of Romance's novels. Any time the characters did have sex, it was couched in euphemistic terms, so the Kama Sutra was just as surprising to me as the anatomy textbook. Frankly, what intrigued me most about the Queen of Romance, and what I should have asked her when I had the chance was: Do you draw upon your own experiences for your novels?

The Queen of Romance did not emerge from her private study when I went to leave. The woman in black said that the author never came downstairs when she was busy writing. What she meant was that I should just leave without saying goodbye to the author. She was so definite about this that I had no choice but to comply. Awkwardly bidding her farewell, I handed her my business card and asked her to give it to the Queen of Romance.

As I got into my car, a text message came up on my phone.

"Maybe I should register my marriage.[5] Don't you agree?"

It was from my girlfriend. I tried to figure out what it was supposed to mean, and I realized it was the third time that she had sent a text message of that nature. The first one was "Do you mind if I go on a blind date?" It took me less than a minute to reply. "Do as you please." Forty-seven seconds, to be precise. Perhaps I should have taken the question more seriously, because so much had changed since then. When she texted her second question— "Maybe I should get married. Don't you agree?"—I took about ten minutes to reply. Nine minutes and fifty-two seconds, to be exact. It was her birthday, and I texted back, "Why are you asking me?" After that, I didn't get to spend her birthday with her. She married a man she met on her second blind date.

I couldn't reply right away. I didn't know what to say. Two things were certain: that I should take more than ten minutes to reply, and that this was going to be the last question she would ask me.

I put the key into the ignition and tried to start the car. It didn't move.

"No big deal," I mumbled to myself. "Take it easy. Everything will be all right."

Not knowing what else to do, I called my regular auto shop. The owner answered. When I said that I was afraid the ignition switch needed replacing he said I should have listened to him from the outset. I asked him if he could send someone right away. Complaining that he was already shorthanded, he asked me where I was. When I told him, he sighed. Only when I promised to pay double for the service did he agree to send one of his mechanics.

I reclined my seat, leaned back, and closed my eyes. Apparently I fell asleep for a moment. Then I woke with a start when someone knocked on the car window. The woman in black was standing beside my car. I put my seat back upright and lowered the window. She asked me what the matter was. When I explained my situation she invited me to wait inside. Glancing up at the second-floor window, I asked if she was sure it would be okay. She said that it was what the author had suggested. And she added

---

5 In Korea, the registration of a marriage is often independent of the marriage itself, and by delaying registration, a couple can avoid a record of divorce if the relationship does not last. (Translators' note)

that she was preparing dinner and I could eat with them. Before I could say anything, my stomach growled.

The woman in black served veal tenderloin for dinner. The Queen of Romance was in high spirits throughout the meal. She seemed to be happy with the writing she had done before sitting down to dinner, and ate heartily. She even asked the woman in black to bring a bottle of wine. I wasn't able to enjoy the meal. The text message from my girlfriend was on my mind. An hour had passed since I had received it. An hour and four minutes, to be precise. The fact that I had not yet replied made me feel even worse.

"Do you know why there are so few women among the greatest writers throughout history?" the Queen of Romance asked me.

"Hmm, I have no idea."

"Because they had no one to cook for them. If you want to write a great book you need someone to take care of meals. Men aren't able to cook for themselves. Women do it for them. That's why many women haven't managed to write great books. My five books are all thanks to Ju-yeong. Let's drink a toast to all the cooking heroes the literary world never celebrates!"

The woman in black blushed, as if she were being complimented by her lover. She, too, was wearing black nail polish. Her fingers were small and fine. I suddenly wondered about the relationship between the two women.

The Queen of Romance offered me a glass of wine, but I declined it, saying that I had to drive home. I reckoned that if she pressed me I could drink a little, just one glass, but she didn't. Each time the Queen of Romance paused, we were silent.

Silence was my language, crying was my girlfriend's. She would often complain that I spoke too little, particularly when we ate together. She objected to the fact that I didn't talk while we were eating. I hadn't been aware of this until she pointed it out. I would finish my meal quickly, put down my chopsticks and wait in silence for my girlfriend to finish eating. Although she disliked my reticence she had never asked the reason for it. I usually just prefer not to speak unless I'm asked a question. Otherwise, I'd just babble. If I'm asked a personal question, I lie. When people dispense with lies and silly nonsense, some have nothing left but silence, and others can only cry. The truth must lie somewhere between silence and tears.

I asked the Queen of Romance what she was currently working on. She talked in the same eloquent way, and so earnestly that it was as if she had been expecting the question. She was writing an essay for a magazine. And a series of essays that she had spent over a year working on was going to be published as a collection. It was her first collection of essays. I asked her who was going to publish them. She named a well-known publisher. It was an imprint of a large publishing conglomerate. The magazine I worked for also belonged to the group. I realized why the magazine had been so keen to interview the Queen of Romance.

The Queen of Romance had not yet chosen a title for her essay collection and she harped on about it. "No Second Chances at Love." "Madly in Love." "In Love, Nothing is Unforgivable." She asked which one sounded best. I picked the first, and the woman in black chose the third. The Queen of Romance said she was leaning towards the second, and asked the two of us what we thought about it. The woman in black slowly looked down and said she was flattered that the author asked her opinion. Her cheeks reddened, perhaps because of the light, or the wine. Then she added shyly, "I like it if you like it."

"What do you think, sir?"

"Well, it seems to me a little too much . . ."

"I think it's cool," the woman in black cut in.

"The titles with the word 'no' or 'nothing' in them sound so negative. It would have a negative effect on sales, wouldn't it?" asked the Queen of Romance.

Silence fell again. One hour and fifty-four minutes had passed since I had received the text from my girlfriend. Fifty-five. Fifty-six. Fifty-seven. Fifty-eight. Fifty-nine. I poured some wine into the glass in front of me.

"Didn't you say you have to drive home?" asked the Queen of Romance.

"Just one glass of wine will be okay."

The wine tasted dull and bitter.

When the owner of the auto shop called me on my cell phone, I had had three glasses of wine. He said he was too busy to send a mechanic right away, but he could send someone the next morning. He added that he could give me the numbers of other auto shops if I wanted, but I wouldn't get any response this late in the day no matter which one I called. I told him I needed time to think about it and I hung up.

"Don't think about it," said the Queen of Romance. "Your mechanic is right. Nothing is going to be open at this hour. It sounds to me like he left it this late on purpose. If you insist on leaving tonight we could give you a ride. But Ju-yeong rarely drives at night. You're welcome to stay here tonight. Tell your mechanic to come tomorrow, and ask him for a discount since he let you down. Next time, forget that auto shop and find a different one. I'll bet that guy has overcharged you every time he's worked on your car. Don't ask for an estimate. Wait until the mechanic gets here."

We had drained a second bottle of wine when the Queen of Romance suddenly asked me to tell her a *chengyu*.[6]

"A *chengyu*?" I echoed. Having had several glasses of wine I was becoming relaxed in the company of the two women.

"Any idiom that comes to mind."

"*Sogonsogon*,"[7] said the woman in black.

"That's not Chinese."

When the author corrected her, the woman in black smiled airily and said she was joking.

I offered "*Ju-ma-gan-san*,"[8] and the woman in black suggested "*Yu-gu-mu-eon*."[9]

"You're afraid of many things, aren't you?" asked the Queen of Romance, looking at me. "You're afraid of loving someone, and far more afraid of being loved by someone. You're afraid of being hurt and even more afraid of causing pain. That's why you don't want to get off your horse and make a commitment."

---

6 *Chengyu*, or Chinese four-character idioms, are concise sayings expressed in a standardized format. (Translators' note)

7 An onomatopoeic word that describes people whispering to one another. (Translators' note)

8 Literally "sightseeing from horseback," this phrase implies looking cursorily rather than attentively. (Translators' note)

9 Literally "having a mouth but no words," this is a phrase people use when they cannot explain what they have done. (Translators' note)

The Queen of Romance studied my face intently, as if she were trying to understand some abstruse book. Is this how she would look when she was reading the English translation of the *Kama Sutra*, or the anatomy textbook? It was the kind of stare that would break through the most hardened soul. There was nothing of either mercy or evil in her stare, just a relentless determination and a look as penetrating as a bullet.

I don't remember exactly when, but my girlfriend told me that she wished she could see me cry, just once. I knew for certain that she wasn't joking. It was a habit she had—when she was uncomfortable talking about something she'd make a joke of it. Like when she asked me whether I'd mind if she went on a blind date, and when she asked whether I'd object if she got married. When she couldn't even bring herself to make a joke of her feelings, she would express herself by crying. She cried a lot. She wept like she had just been told that her world had been destroyed. She cried even if I told her she should do whatever she liked, and she cried if I asked her why she wanted my opinion. She was pathologically emotional, and crying was her first language. When she spoke this language of hers, which was inscrutable to me, I would find myself breaking out in a cold sweat. I was confused because I couldn't figure out what I had done wrong, and then I was embarrassed that I couldn't find anything particularly wrong no matter how hard I tried to think back. What was I supposed to do to stop her crying? That was all I could think about. Would it be better if I had said things in a different way? Would things have turned out differently if I had responded this way or that way? A series of meaningless what-if questions kept me awake, and I would come to the same conclusion every time: she was bound to weep, no matter what. She would have wept even if I had told her not to go on a blind date, or if I had told her not to marry the man she had met on the blind date.

"Let me think, *yu-gu-mu-eon* . . ."

I could no longer hear what the Queen of Romance was saying. Shimmering on the wine glass in front of me was an ugly old man on a horse. An old man on horseback who had been constantly hounded by fear, night and day. And his life, a life of utter isolation without so much as a dog for company, a life of monotony with no flicker of emotion ever expressed—not even to the god of hopelessly lonesome people—appeared fleetingly there on the glass.

I drained my wineglass in one gulp. The frightened old man and his horse disappeared without a trace. As for fear, I could discuss it for hours and hours. I could talk on and on about it, without having to resort to telling a joke or faking drunkenness. While truth lies somewhere between silence and crying, love lies somewhere between restlessness and fear. Crying is to restlessness as silence is to fear: the one who cries is restless; one who keeps silent is fearful.

I grew uncomfortable in the strange situation. The Queen of Romance's unfaltering, logical speeches, the enigmatic beauty of the woman in black, the mysterious atmosphere surrounding the two women who looked so incompatible. I was annoyed with myself for feeling uncomfortable about all these things. I drank more and more wine in an attempt to get over the feeling of awkwardness. In order to drink more, I proposed various toasts. Not once did either of the two women decline to drink with me. I was the one who opened the third bottle of wine. As I grew more inebriated my glass emptied faster and I spoke more slowly. So did the two women. Three hours had elapsed since my girlfriend had texted me. Three hours and twenty-seven minutes.

"Why do you read anatomy books?" I asked the Queen of Romance.

"Da Vinci studied human anatomy quite a lot. That's how he was able to delineate the human body so vividly and accurately. The same applies to writing a novel. To achieve good depictions of characters' movements, you need to know every detail of the body's muscles and organs."

"When did you start writing?"

"You know, every school has a student like this: good-looking and academically gifted; envied by their peers and loved by their teachers. There was a girl like this in my high school. She was very talented at writing, and she won almost every writing contest.

On one occasion, I happened to win the school writing contest. I hadn't even entered it. It turned out that the girl had submitted her entry under my name. She had written with a purple ballpoint pen that she had borrowed from me. When I found out about it my heart raced. I couldn't admit to the girl how excited I was, though. I just couldn't. That was when I started scribbling."

"What happened to the other girl? What's she doing now?"

The Queen of Romance reached for the wine bottle, but the woman in black stepped in.

"You've had enough for today."

"Just one more glass."

"No, you mustn't."

"Just one last glass, please."

"Don't you remember that you drank a whole bottle of wine last night? Because you said you couldn't get to sleep without drinking."

"Just one more glass. I promise."

"That was what you said before you started drinking yesterday, and the day before."

"But we have a guest today, so will you . . ."

The woman in black snatched the bottle away from the author. The Queen of Romance suddenly looked downcast, like a child who has been scolded.

"Oh wait! Switch on the TV!"

The woman in black picked up a remote and turned on the TV that hung on the kitchen wall. She was clearly excited, and said that the hero and heroine were finally going to kiss in today's episode. All of the Queen of Romance's novels had been made into TV dramas. This one was an adaptation of her fifth novel.

"It said in the newspaper that the lead actor and actress are dating," said the woman in black.

"That's just a made-up story. To promote the show," the Queen of Romance said nonchalantly.

Four hours and forty-eight minutes had elapsed since I'd received the text message from my girlfriend. I hadn't replied yet. Four hours and forty-nine minutes. And I still hadn't replied.

"Oh!" the woman in black cried.

There was a breaking news bulletin on the TV. Two skyscrapers that stood side by side were engulfed in flames. Beyond the flames lay an abyss of darkness that seemed about to devour every living thing. The abyss was spewing out dark smoke and black ashes. In its impersonal way, the TV camera caught the misery and chaos. Like the detached gaze of a god looking down into hell.

"Oh my god!" murmured the Queen of Romance.

"It can't be true!" said the woman in black.

The three of us watched, speechless. Time itself seemed to have stood still. I don't know how long we sat there, watching in silence.

"By the way, the twin towers, aren't they 110 stories high?" the Queen of Romance asked.

"One hundred and six, I think."

"The restaurant where we watched the millennium celebrations was on the 107th floor."

"Oh, yes, the French restaurant. The chef there is a descendant of a royal cook, right?"

"I think it's 110 stories."

"I seem to remember it was 109."

"Was it?"

"I think so, but I'm not sure."

"I'm really curious to know."

"Do you want me to look it up?"

"No, don't. I'd rather remember for myself. Or my brain will just turn to mush."

"Really?"

"Do you happen to know?" the Queen of Romance asked me, her eyes still fixed on the TV.

I said nothing. A heavy silence fell over us.

The Queen of Romance turned and looked at me.

"Do you?"

I still said nothing. The Queen of Romance stared at me, her eyes wide open, as if she wondered what was wrong with me. It was exactly how my girlfriend had reacted when I told her I'd never heard of the Queen of Romance. Frankly, it was also how I had responded when she wept in front of me. How many hours had passed since I'd received her text message? None of us seemed to want to break the silence. It was as if we were competing to see who could stay silent the longest.

The Queen of Romance showed me to a room beside the downstairs bathroom. I brushed my teeth using a toothbrush and toothpaste that the woman in black had provided, and washed my face. I noticed that my business card had been tossed into a wastebasket. I took it out and put it back in my wallet. The bed was already made. The sheets seemed new, as if no one had slept in them before.

I flipped open my cell phone and pulled up my girlfriend's phone number several times only to cancel it each time. I typed a text message, but I couldn't bring myself to press "send." I composed several more text messages, but then deleted them all: Are you all right?; Are you still up?; Will you call it off if I'm against it?; Tell me a Chinese four-character idiom, the first one that comes into your head. Now it was as if I were deliberately writing them in order to delete them. The messages evaporated in a flash, without being sent, let alone being planted in someone's heart as a seed of hope. They disappeared just as all words do, as if to show that the real obstacle to truth is the word "truth," and the real obstacle to love is the word "love."

I'M SORRY. This was the text message that my clumsy fingers clung to until the last moment. And then my fingers slipped and sent the message instead of deleting it. The envelope icon on the screen sprouted wings. I wished I could break its wings off.

I switched off the light and lay on the bed, but I couldn't sleep. The premonition swept over me that, when I woke up, I would find myself alone in the world. Every time I tossed and turned, the darkness rustled as if it were a shroud that the Earth had put on.

I opened my eyes in the dark, feeling thirsty. I stared into the darkness. It glared back at me. It even frowned. I switched the light on and looked at my cell phone. It was just after five in the morning. For a moment I couldn't remember where I was until I noticed my camera case which I had thrown carelessly aside.

I went into the kitchen and drank a glass of water. Empty bottles, glasses, plates: a vivid reminder of the previous night. The house was completely quiet. There was no noise to be heard, not even the sound of breathing. Through the all-encompassing silence I could just detect the darkness growing thinner. I sat down on a chair and looked around. I could not help looking toward the spiral staircase. The door of the downstairs bedroom was firmly shut. I crept stealthily up the stairs.

There were two rooms on the second floor. One of them had to be the Queen of Romance's private study, which she refused to show to the public. I opened the door of the room to my right. I was startled. Two figures were standing in the darkness. But as my eyes adjusted, they turned into two sets of clothing—a purple cheongsam and a black jacket, hanging along with a pair of black trousers and a black shirt.

I fumbled for the switch and turned on the light. What had been veiled in darkness was now revealed. Clothes were hanging on two crowded rails that stood side by side. Hanging behind the purple cheongsam were numerous others of the same color, and an endless series of black jackets hung behind the first black jacket. They were like two lovers cursed by a dark spell that prevented them from looking one another in the face.

I heard someone moving downstairs and hurriedly switched off the light. I stood still, holding my breath. I heard someone open and close a door, the sound of dragging feet in slippers, and then a door opened and closed again. Apparently someone had just gone to the bathroom. I left the room and crept gingerly back down the stairs.

The darkness had begun to disperse. Across the river, a mountaintop came into view. It looked tranquil, like a mound of wax that had dripped from a candle during the night. The top of the mound glowed deep orange.

I got into my car and tried turning the key in the ignition. It started right away. Leaving the engine running, I got out of the car and went into the house. I was on my way back out with my camera when the bathroom door opened.

"Are you leaving?" It was the woman in black. She was wearing a nightdress now. It was black too.

"Yes. May I see . . . to say goodbye?"

"The author isn't up yet. She'll wake in an hour," said the woman in the black nightdress, closing the bathroom door behind her.

"Is your car fixed?"

I said hurriedly that it was working again, to my relief, and then I practically ran out of the house and jumped into the car.

I had almost reached Seoul when I sensed that I was missing something. I figured out what it was, but I still hesitated. I knew I didn't really have to, but I turned around all the same. I just felt like it.

Once again, it was the woman in black who came to the door. I saw her eyes narrow. She asked if I had left something behind, and I said I had a favor to ask of the author. The woman asked me what it was, and I replied that I wanted to ask the author in person.

"Who is it?"

It was the voice of the Queen of Romance. She was drinking tea in the living room. She looked exactly the same as she had when she'd descended the spiral stairs the previous day.

I sat across from the Queen of Romance, a table between us. She was expressionless and silent. She was being so aloof that I felt I must have dreamt that we had been drinking together the previous night, and I felt obliged to hand her my business card again. I took a book out of a pocket in my camera bag. It was her fifth novel.

"Can I get your autograph?"

"Did you come back just for that?"

I scratched my head.

The woman in black was standing with a fountain pen at the ready.

"What's your name again?" asked the Queen of Romance.

"It's for an acquaintance of mine . . . a big fan of yours."

"The name of your acquaintance?"

I told the Queen of Romance my girlfriend's name. My voice trembled.

The Country Where the Sun Never Rises

On my way home I stopped by the 24-hour corner market, where, in the early morning, night shift workers often cross paths with the day shift. A young woman was standing in front of the store. She was wearing heavy makeup. She kept looking around, and seemed to be waiting for someone. The serial killer, who had murdered twenty-one women, would call hookers and get them to stand outside a 24-hour convenience store. Cloaked in darkness he would watch the women and take them if he liked them or leave them if he didn't. It was clear that he had lured the women to the brightest spot in the dark street, so that he could see what they looked like. Just standing outside a store at night, people put their lives on the line.

The part-timer at the cashier's counter was drinking coffee. She was young, and she had just started the job the previous day. Her eyelids were heavy with sleep. I set down on the counter a bottle of *soju*, a packet of cigarettes and a scratch-off lottery ticket. Exactly the items I needed, nothing more and nothing less. *Soju* for Grandfather, cigarettes for Father. The lottery ticket was for me.

As I left the store, the heavily made up woman was getting into a white Sonata. I looked carefully at the license plate. The sedan headed off between the gray buildings, where the ghostly light of dawn was beginning to appear. Feeling lightheaded, I quickened my pace.

A parrot welcomed me when I walked into the house. Flapping its wings and kicking against its perch, the bird set his whole cage shaking. Since Mom had left us, I had never been welcomed by anything or anyone. Father, standing at the kitchen counter where he was chopping scallions, turned and looked at me and the parrot in turn. He started to say something, but gave up and went back to chopping the scallions.

"Where did the bird come from?" I asked, locking the front door behind me.

"Someone left it behind, I guess," Father answered nonchalantly, dropping a handful of chopped scallions into a pot.

Father worked as a janitor in an apartment building, and often brought discarded items home. Frankly, almost all of the appliances—including the TV and the washing machine—that filled our tiny house had come from the apartment building. They may have been discarded, but they had belonged to the residents of a wealthy neighborhood, and they were mostly still quite serviceable. I had never seen a Large Item Pick-Up sticker—which you're supposed to buy from the district office—on any of them, not even any sign that a sticker had been pulled off. Which meant that these people had surreptitiously thrown the items away at night. Once something was left behind like that, it became a windfall for Father, who could help himself to whatever he wanted. I shouldn't say "windfall," because Father hates that word more than anything. His motto in life is "There's no such thing as a free lunch."

It would be fairer to say that the appliances in our house are not so much a free gift as the fruit of Father's conscientiousness and hard work. He and the other janitors were supposed to take turns working nights, but Father had been taking all the night shifts. It was his own choice. And none of the others had objected. Father thought he was lucky to have to work only at night. He was not at all sociable, and what was worse, cataracts had affected his vision. This often led to misunderstandings and complaints from the residents. They automatically assumed that Father was being impolite when he didn't respond to their greetings. In this apartment complex, where even the preschool kids chatted to one another in English, nothing but the darkness extended any kindness to Father, with his poor eyesight and meager education.

I looked at the stranger who had welcomed me home, and I wondered how I could repay the creature for its kind greeting. I ought to find a way to do so, if I agreed with Father that nothing in this world is free. And I believed most of what Father said. Because, clearly, what fathers say to their sons in a public bath house while they scrub their backs cannot be hogwash.

I opened the refrigerator, took out a stack of bowls containing side dishes, and spread them out on the table.

"Go wake up the old man," said Father, tasting the stew to see if it was salted enough.

At a certain point in time, Father had started calling Grandpa "the old man." I'm not sure whether it was before or after Mom left us. As far back as I can remember, Grandpa was already an old man. He was born in 1916 and was approaching 70 the year I was born. It was only natural that I should see him as an old man, but it was a different story for Father. I'm not trying to make an ethical point here. I'm just describing Father's attitude towards Grandpa. I mean, the cold tone of voice he used when he insisted on calling Grandpa "the old man." The old grudge that he clung to and the anger that pervaded his soul had not mellowed with age.

I once asked Father why he called Grandpa the old man. He said nothing, and the cigarette between his lips burned its way to the filter. The ash dropped noiselessly, as though it could no longer bear the weight of Father's silence. Silence was his way of responding to a question he found hard to answer.

Father was born the year the Allies landed in Normandy, and he is an old man now. He'll have to retire from his job as a janitor sometime next year. I have an old man for a father now, as well as for a grandfather. Mom had abandoned two old men and a young lad to go and serve her god. Once Mom had left us, Father grew old unbelievably fast. I even had trouble telling him and Grandpa apart when I saw them from behind, sitting side by side watching TV, their shoulders drooping forwards. Still, I've finally worked out which is which, because one always has a bottle of *soju* in his hand, while the other has a cigarette.

Next year, when Father retires, I will probably have to ask my boss for a raise. Or I might have to find a job at a different gas station, given how stingy my boss is. Instead of hiring a part-time worker, he has been getting all the work he can out of his nephew, who recently applied for a leave of absence from school to do his military service.

"Mackerel pike again?"

"Can you smell it?"

"You should wash the empty can and let it dry before you throw it in the trash."

I picked up the can that was wedged in the drain of the sink, washed it thoroughly and set it upside down to dry. Then I went into the bathroom, filled the washbasin with lukewarm water, and washed my hands. The grease stayed stubbornly under my fingernails. Since starting work at the gas station, I no longer bite my nails. Mackerel pike is Grandpa's favorite fish.

I came out of the bathroom. Father was scooping rice into a bowl. I opened the door of the big bedroom. The room was dark, and the TV was booming, but no one was watching it. I shook Grandpa awake.

"Son?"

Grandpa's eyes had gotten so bad that he couldn't even tell Father and me apart. When we asked about surgery, the eye doctor said brusquely that Grandpa's eyes were no better than a dog's and he had no choice but to manage with the vision he had for the rest of his life. What an asshole! Couldn't he have been polite about it? I would have punched him in the face if he hadn't been wearing glasses.

I have no interest in how the world must look through the eyes of a dog. Dogs get excited and bounce around ecstatically when snowflakes begin to flutter down, while people just hurry along, burying their necks between their shoulders. I couldn't tell you whether the world looks more beautiful through a dog's eyes or through the eyes of a human. It probably wouldn't be that unsatisfying for Grandpa to spend the rest of his life seeing through the eyes of a dog, given that the world he saw with his own eyes was never kind to him.

"It's me: your grandson. It's time to eat."

I helped Grandpa walk to the table and sit down. He leaned close to see what was on the table, then frowned and tightened his twitching lips.

"Oops, I nearly forgot!"

I put into his hand a bottle of *soju*—already open and with a straw sticking out of it. Only then did Grandpa smile.

The mackerel pike stew was too salty. Since his sight had deteriorated, Father would often mistake salt for sugar and add too much of one or the other. I boiled some water in a tea kettle and poured it into the stew.

I ate, and from time to time I put a piece of fish on Grandpa's spoon, first removing the bones. We sat in silence at the table; the noise of chewing was the only sound to be heard. According to Grandpa, only the lowest class of people talk with their mouths full. Whether he's right or wrong, our family has always been very taciturn. When I think about this, I begin to understand why Mom left us. Her god would surely respond from time to time, if she prayed to him earnestly enough.

"I'm gonna bury you all!" the parrot cried, all of a sudden.

Grandpa and Father looked at one another, their eyes wide open. It was the first time in ages that they had made eye contact. But the glance didn't last. The two old men looked away quickly, as though they'd just seen something embarrassing.

As soon as I woke up I checked the alarm clock that I'd placed beside my pillow. It would go off in five minutes. I pressed the button to cancel it—I had set it for sundown. I had never been woken by the alarm. My body always woke spontaneously when the daylight started to fade. Father had already gotten up; his bed was rolled up and put away. I drew aside the thick velvet curtain and opened the window. The scent of darkness immediately thrust its way into my nostrils. I poked my nose out the window and sucked in the musty, sweetish smell of the dark. My head cleared. The streetlights had been lit early, and they shed their light on the people bustling up and down the steep alley, making it look as if their bodies ended at their ankles. This bedroom, which was partially below ground level and faced west, was the last to grow dark and the last to get bright. That was why I chose to sleep in this room, even though it was small and we had a larger bedroom.

"Was it you who did that?" Father asked me, rinsing rice and nodding towards the birdcage, when I walked out of the bathroom after washing my face. The cage was covered with newspaper. I shook my head and removed the paper. The parrot fluttered its wings and shrieked. It must have been floundering around desperately in the darkness. Feathers lay in a heap at the bottom of the cage. It thrashed its wings frantically, bumping against the top of the cage, as though protesting the mistreatment of having been covered up. I tried making a cooing sound and whistling to it, but to no avail. Only when Father filled the feeder with sunflower seeds did it finally calm down.

"That old man is just helpless," Father clucked, looking at the bird.

I made soybean-paste soup and went into the big bedroom. I turned off the TV and shook Grandpa gently to wake him.

"Leave the TV on," Grandpa said, his eyes still shut.

"I thought you were asleep. It's time to eat."

"Asleep? You shouldn't sleep while the sun's still up."

Grandpa spent most of his time, day and night, lying on his mat on the floor, with the TV turned up to full volume. His vision was so bad that the TV was nothing more than a radio to him. But he liked watching it anyhow, in fact he loved it. He particularly liked watching movies. Any time a movie was on, he would sit close to the TV and wouldn't budge.

When he was young, Grandpa had had a reputation for being a big spender. He would sit around all day at home, and then, when the sun went down, rush out to a gambling house. But small strokes fell great oaks. The wealth of Grandpa's family—which had been so great that no one could leave the village without crossing the family's land—had gradually dwindled. It wasn't just because of Grandpa's gambling. He had also poured a not inconsiderable sum of money into moving pictures. He finally left, taking the family's money and land registration documents with him, and saying only that he was going to Seoul. But when he returned just a few months later, he was penniless. There was some talk about the moving picture that Grandpa was said to have bankrolled, but no one ever claimed to have seen it. Some women in the village whispered that Grandpa had started a family with another woman in the city. Grandpa's father—that is, my great grandfather—pretended to know nothing about his only son's reckless extravagance. He did almost nothing to intervene, which was hard for me to understand, though not totally incomprehensible given that he had had a stroke and was bedridden. Even on his deathbed he admonished the family not to say anything against Grandpa. So Mom told me, and I assume she heard it from someone else in the family. Because by the time Mom had married Father, Father's family was far from rich and living from hand to mouth. Father avoided any mention whatsoever of Grandpa.

As soon as he had finished eating, Father sat down in front of the TV and watched the news. He normally went for a walk in the hills behind our neighborhood at that time of day, but he didn't seem to be planning to leave the house. He just stared at the TV, as if he was waiting for something specific to come on. A middle-school girl who had been missing was found dead and dismembered; descendants of some collaborators during the Japanese occupation had filed a lawsuit against the government to get back their confiscated land; a fire, the cause of which was unknown, had broken out in a residential area in Manridong; a three-car collision had occurred on Gyeongbu Highway; a moving truck that was being loaded with household items had turned over. Scarcely had the news ended when Father stood up, changed his clothes, and hurried out. He had plenty of time before his shift began, but he dashed away.

Father probably blamed Grandpa for Mom's having left us. She had to see to as many as twelve ancestral ceremonies every year—Grandpa was very devout and insisted on that. Mom had also taken on the rites for a distant relative, because he had no direct descendants to perform the ceremonies. If Father hadn't objected, Mom would probably have had to take on even more. Father had never raised his voice to Grandpa in his life, except for just one time. It happened when we'd set the ancestral ceremonial table for the first time after Mom left. I can't recall exactly for whom we had prepared the ritual table. It was certainly not for Grandma—that much I remember clearly. Father's eyes were blazing with anger when he yelled that Grandpa alone had made the once well-off family destitute, and all he had to bequeath to his blameless child was the burden of the ancestral rites.

"You should understand," Grandpa said, his voice shaking. "It was all for the sake of our country. We even had to lie to our own family because we had to be on the lookout for spies. It was a secret between your grandfather and me. Everything was done according to your grandfather's will."

"You're starting that nonsense again. Aren't you ashamed of yourself?"

Father couldn't take it. We weren't able to finish the rites that day.

When I'd finished washing the dishes I changed the parrot's water. As I was putting the water feeder back into the cage, the bird pecked at the back of my hand. It didn't hurt me, though. I looked it straight in the eyes and spoke to it.

"I love you."

The bird made no sound and just nodded its head. Like everyone else in our house, the bird was sparing with its words.

I went into the big bedroom and turned on the TV. I switched to a movie channel, and Grandpa sat close to the TV, his eyes open wide. I took the jigsaw puzzle from the table and placed it carefully on the floor. It was a thousand-piece puzzle. A shop window reflecting the darkness outside; a deserted, greenish sidewalk; a yellowish wall inside the shop, and two stainless-steel boilers; brown tables and stools; a waiter in a white uniform and two men with fedoras pulled down low over their brows; a fair-haired woman in a red dress.

My eyes were drawn to the expressionless woman and the man sitting beside her with his back to the darkness that had devoured the street. They looked as though they had either just met for the first time or had known each other for centuries. I was also drawn to the second man, who appeared to be watching them. I wondered more about the expression on the second man's face than about the relationship between the first man and the woman. The two men sitting at the counter—one with his back to the viewer and the other sitting next to the fair-haired woman—were wearing identical clothes. A blue suit and a dove-colored fedora. I had almost finished doing the jigsaw puzzle, and most of the picture was complete.

When he saw the picture on the top of the box, Father had asked me if it was a movie poster. He used to paint film posters. Although he worked for the Daehan Theater for a period of time, most of the posters he painted had hung outside back-alley cinemas that showed re-runs. Like the figures in the jigsaw puzzle, the people in Father's movie posters had impassive expressions.

I couldn't find the puzzle piece to complete the head of the man sitting with his back to me, so I tried putting together the pieces of dark background surrounding him. Although the sidewalk was dark too, the shading varied slightly, suggesting where the pieces belonged. But when it came to the man's head, I only had the shapes of the pieces to go on. After several unsuccessful attempts, I sighed and laid the puzzle back on the table. Grandpa was still there, rooted to the spot right in front of the TV, sipping *soju* through a straw.

I took the scratch-off lottery ticket and a coin out of my pocket. It was a five-hundred-won coin minted in 1986, the year I was born. The day she walked out, Mom had slipped it into my hand and said I could buy an ice cream for myself. Five hundred won. That was apparently how much guilt she felt when she left the family. I doubt she noticed that the coin was issued the year I was born. She probably just gave me the first one that came to hand. The coin had a hole in it. I had pierced it. I'd even put it on a key chain so that I wouldn't lose it. I was nine at the time.

I scratched the lottery ticket with the coin. Nothing. That meant I would have to go to work at the gas station again today, as usual.

I was about to leave the bedroom when Grandpa spoke in a gravelly voice.

"If you bump into a cop, you should always pretend to be deaf and dumb, no matter what."

Grandpa's mind had regularly begun to wander some time ago.

And it had gotten worse recently. He even asked how long Japan had been ruling the country. Grandpa had taken Father out of school because, he said, being successful in a world where collaborators had prevailed and prospered was a sin in itself. That was why Father had no education beyond elementary school. And Father had beaten me with a baseball bat when I was in my second year of middle school because I didn't want to go to school. "You want a life like mine, do you?" he snarled, seething anger gleaming in his eyes. He beat me so savagely that the bones in my legs were laid bare. He might have been less harsh if I had cried out in pain or had pretended to, at least, but I didn't even whimper. It wasn't a matter of courage on my part. Father, believing I was simply defying him, battered me all the more harshly. We were both shocked to see through to the bone. I felt no pain, though. Grandpa fainted when he saw my legs all torn and bleeding, and Father's hands shook uncontrollably when he lit a cigarette. Seriously, I didn't feel any pain. And that was the real problem. That I felt no pain at all.

Someone once said that if you really want to hurt your parents but you don't have the guts to be a homosexual, then you should be an artist. Father might have become an artist if he had been able to continue in school. To get even with Grandpa. And certainly Father didn't have the guts to be deliberately gay. Was that why he had chosen to design movie posters? His posters always exuded an air of anger that made me feel inexplicably numb.

The night air was charged with the deeply rooted rage of those who had neither the guts to be homosexual nor the talent to be artists. Their anger, mixed with the murky night air, made my bare skin shiver. Unable to vent their fury, they roamed the nighttime streets in search of their prey. I could feel the very core of their rage.

It was early morning, when even the last drinkers have fallen into a deep sleep. The boss's nephew, who would fly into a rage for no reason, was banging on a vending machine as if trying to break it. He hadn't put any coins into it. Spewing curses at the "stupid" machine, he struck it again and again. And eventually, as if the machine couldn't stand any more banging, it vomited a can with a clatter. It was a cola this time.

"That cheap asshole! He owns five gas stations and four apartments, but he never fills the staff refrigerator. You want a drink too?"

The boss's nephew was two years younger than me, but he spoke to me as if I were younger than him. I shook my head. He flopped down next to me, opened the can of cola and gulped it down. He often wore a T-shirt with a Marine Corps logo on it. I wondered where he had gotten it. He had applied to the Marine Corps to do his national service, but he hadn't started yet.

"Have you ever heard of the Cheolli March?"

I shook my head.

"It's a military fitness test where you have to cover 240 miles in a week carrying twenty pounds. Two hundred forty miles! It's like walking from Seoul to Busan. Here's a quiz for you: Which of the following is not included in your military backpack for the march? One, an entrenching shovel. Two, a toothbrush. Three, a magazine for your gun. Four, a blanket. Five, a sleeping bag."

The boss's nephew belched in my face. His breath reeked of the fried chicken he had had for a late night snack. I held my nose.

"You say number three? Huh, you're pretty good. But the next question isn't so easy. Which of the following poses the greatest difficulty during the Cheolli March? One, a soldier's full gear. Two, the cold. Three, the heat. Four, the dark. Five, sleepiness."

I shook my head.

"I knew you wouldn't get this one. The answer is sleepiness. One of my *seonbae* served at a GP in the DMZ. GP is short for guard post. It's like a bunker that's set up near the barbed-wired fence. You know the fence—it's always being shown on TV— and how soldiers go on patrol with German shepherds? There are land mines buried all through the area, and the North Korean soldiers are so close you can sometimes see the glow of their cigarettes. My *seonbae* said he managed to get over his fear and anxiety and so on, but he was never able to beat the sleepiness. He figured that ten or more North Korean spies could have snuck in while he was dozing. Do you know why I work the night shift at this gas station, even though I don't get paid? It's because I want to train myself to resist sleepiness. Because Marine Corps operations usually take place at night. Because they do covert ops. The old man will never understand . . ."

The phone rang in the office, interrupting the boss's nephew. He dashed to answer it. "The old man" was what he called his uncle. Sometimes he called his father that, too, but I almost always knew who he was talking about, because although he chatted a lot about almost everything, he was reticent when he talked about his father. I got the impression that his father managed one of the gas stations that the boss owned.

Sleepiness was the reason I had dropped out of school. Ever since I was small, I've tended to be awake at night and asleep during day. Apparently, even when I was in my mother's womb I would kick only at night. This sleep pattern of mine had gotten out of control in middle school when I had a growth spurt. I was just overwhelmed by the sleepiness that would invariably sweep over me only during the day. I would doze off through an entire class. Nothing helped: not the various punishments my teachers thought up, nor the powerful stimulants that I took. On more than one occasion I was almost hit by a car when I nodded off as I was crossing a road. I eventually went to a doctor and had an MRI and a test of my brain activity. But the doctor just tilted his head to one side and kept saying unhelpfully that it was really odd.

We had handed in the forms for dropping out of school. Father was walking ahead of me on the way back home. His shadow was blurry. I didn't want to admit to myself that my eyes were clouded with tears. At home Father knocked back several drinks one after the other—it had been a long time since he had even touched any alcohol—and told me to sit across from him. He spoke a lot, which was unusual for him, but I don't remember what he said. Because I had drifted off to sleep.

When I told Grandpa I had dropped out of school he said "Good for you!" and patted me on the head.

"The only education the patriot Kim Gu got was from the village teacher when he was a child," Grandpa added, "and yet he taught himself and then became the leader of our nation."

When he went on to argue that the most egregious villains in the world were people who had a high level of education and used it to manipulate others, I wasn't sure whether or not his mind was wandering again. But it soon became clear.

"The Korean Liberation Army in Chongqing, China, has declared war on both Japan and Germany," said Grandpa, looking grave. "The young men of this nation who were conscripted into the Japanese army are deserting. Risking their lives, they are rushing to join the Korean Liberation Army. Soon the Korean Liberation Army will defeat the Kwantung Army of Japan in Manchuria and cross the Amnok River. The day we regain our independence is not far off. And when that day comes it will be time for you to resume your studies."

Father urged me to enroll in night school and at least get a high school diploma but I wouldn't listen to him. I argued that I could sit the exam for the diploma any time my education was a concern. I was sure that even at night school I would stick out like a sore thumb. Just imagine the weird kid who was wide awake, his eyes sparkling, while the rest of the class was nodding off.

"Don't worry about it, Uncle. Trust me."

The boss's nephew was practically bowing to the phone. The boss called him "the Oil Scholarship Student" in front of the other employees. So that it wouldn't go unnoticed that he was paying his nephew's tuition. The nephew gulped down the rest of the Coke. A gang of motorcyclists was speeding down the road, honking and cursing.

"Those jerks should all be made to go into the army," said the boss's nephew, spitting noisily.

I stopped at the corner market on my way home from work. The woman was standing outside. The woman with heavy makeup. A white Sonata pulled up right in front of her and she got in. I didn't look at the license plate this time. The girl at the checkout was blowing a bubble with her gum. It burst when I pushed the door open. I bought a bottle of *soju*, a packet of cigarettes, and a scratch-off lottery ticket. I remembered everything on my shopping list.

I found the bird cage covered with newspaper again. The parrot, sensing that I was approaching, shrieked and fluttered. The minute I removed the newspaper the bird shot off its perch and banged its head against the cage. I didn't know how to calm it down. It pecked at the latch and lifted the door, holding it up quite high. It seemed to be trying to stick its head out of the cage, but every time it let go of the latch the door would slip down and the bird would be locked in again. It was clearly angry, and it kept squawking and pecking at its feathers. The feathers drifted down into a heap at the bottom of the cage. The bird's plumage had become very sparse.

I washed my hands and put some rice on to steam. I was about to open a can of tuna for *gimchi* stew when Father opened the door and walked in. He was holding a newspaper. It was today's edition. He was appalled when he saw the bird. I told him the cage had been covered with newspaper, and his face grew rigid. I set the table and went into the big bedroom. I switched on the light and turned the TV off. I gently nudged Grandpa awake.

"Why did you cover up the bird cage?" Father demanded an answer from Grandpa.

"Because it said it's gonna rat on us all," Grandpa answered, sucking some *soju* through a straw.

"It said it's going to bury you all," I said, shouting into his ear, but Grandpa just shook his head.

Father opened the newspaper on the floor and read it as he sat and ate at the low table. Even with his glasses on, he had to hold his face close to the page. It was unlike Father to read a newspaper, especially during a meal. If I had done so, Grandpa would certainly have told me off and said that when I was sitting at the table I should focus on eating. Otherwise, he used to say, my luck would soon run out. Grandpa didn't look at the parrot, not even once, during the entire meal. Even when it shrieked it didn't catch his attention. Father didn't pay any attention to it either.

When we had finished eating, the bird made a rasping sound and shouted, "I'm gonna bury you all."

In one motion, the two old men turned toward the bird.

"I told you," said Grandpa.

Father lit a cigarette, held it between his lips, gathered up the newspaper, and went into the small bedroom, while Grandpa walked into the big bedroom carrying a bottle of *soju*. Since I was neither a smoker nor a drinker, I just washed the dishes. The bird had gone quiet. I changed its water. It pecked wildly at the back of my hand. But it didn't hurt.

I went into the large bedroom, laid out all the puzzle pieces, and started to put the jigsaw puzzle together. The TV was blaring as usual, and Grandpa was lying down with his eyes closed. After an hour I had barely put together six pieces. I couldn't focus, because my eyelids kept drooping. I set the puzzle down on the table and looked at Grandpa. He seemed to be asleep. I turned off the TV.

"I'm not asleep," said Grandpa in a gravelly voice. I turned the TV back on and left the room. I brushed my teeth and went into the small bedroom. Father was asleep and snoring loudly. I checked the newspaper to see what time sunset would be and set the alarm. I closed the curtains and I lay down. I fell asleep right away.

I woke up and saw the alarm clock was going to go off in five minutes. Father was nowhere to be seen, and his bed was rolled up and put away. I pressed the button on the alarm clock, got out of bed, drew aside the curtains and slid the window open. The earthy smell of the darkness wafted into the room. I breathed in and my head cleared immediately. Father was in the kitchen preparing food.

"Mackerel pike again?" I asked.

"Can you smell it?" Father replied

"You should wipe the oil out of the empty can and then wash it and let it dry."

I picked up the empty can, washed it and stood it upside down to dry.

"Go wake up the old man," said Father, scooping rice into a bowl.

Pushing the door open, I stepped into the big bedroom. I switched on the light and turned off the TV. I shook Grandpa gently and woke him up.

We had scarcely finished eating, when Father, lighting a cigarette, hurried to watch the news on TV, while Grandpa sipped *soju* and lay down. I took out the puzzle and started where I had left off.

As I assembled the pieces darkness formed around the man whose back was to the viewer. I had only a few puzzle pieces left, and I couldn't find the piece for the back of the man's head. I was fitting each of the remaining pieces in here and there, when Father let out a moan. A mother and her two daughters had been found dead in a house in Bangbae-dong after having been beaten with a blunt instrument. The killer was a man named Kang, forty-three years old, the husband of the woman and father of the two girls. After murdering his family, the man had taken poison in an attempt to kill himself. But he was found in time and taken to an ER where they saved his life. The police investigation, the report said, had come to a standstill without discovering the motive for the crime, because the man wouldn't speak but just kept mumbling to himself. The man's neighbors couldn't believe what he had done, and said he was such a family guy that a weekend never went by when he didn't take the family out somewhere for fun. The two murdered girls, aged five and seven, had been adopted by the couple.

When the news was over, Father stood up, got dressed and left for work. I had put five more pieces into the puzzle. There were four empty spaces and only three puzzle pieces left. I looked in the box and searched the room, but I couldn't find the missing piece anywhere. The spot where the piece was missing was where two parts of the picture met. Where the shadow of the brim of the man's hat met the darkness of the street seen through the store window. Coincidentally, the empty space was in the middle of the picture. I couldn't tell whether the puzzle had been defective from the start, or if I had dropped the piece somewhere.

I put the remaining three pieces into the puzzle. Now that I had nine-hundred-ninety-nine pieces assembled, the space where the piece was missing bothered me more. Disappointed, I set the puzzle board and empty box on the table and took the lottery ticket and the coin out of my pocket. I scratched the ticket with the coin, and saw that I had won nothing. I would have to go to work at the gas station again today, as usual. And I would have to stay up all night with the boss's nephew.

I stopped at a toy store on the way to the gas station and bought a jigsaw puzzle, the same one that I had at home.

"Damn slow today," the boss's nephew muttered with a wide yawn. By midnight only three cars had come in. They were all diesel cars, and only one customer asked for a full tank.

Standing up and stretching, the boss's nephew walked to the vending machine and started punching it. After three blows the machine gave in and dropped a can. It was cola again.

"You want a drink too?" asked the boss's nephew, holding up the can of cola. I shook my head.

"You know, this world is like a vending machine. You put in money and get what you want out of it. Just fine and dandy. It's a trick, though, that fools people into believing money turns into a product—that there's no such thing as a freebie from this vending machine, and it doesn't rip you off either. Do you know why people get so pissed off when they don't get what they expect when they've put their money into it? It's because they feel ignored, deceived, betrayed. A mere vending machine ignores me, deceives me, and betrays me, huh? You know how upset they get and how they complain that the machine's just swallowed up their money? What idiots! That's what the machine is always supposed to do, swallow coins! Try opening up the machine. You'll see that the slot where they put in their coins isn't connected to where they take out their drinks. All the money gathers in one spot, and someone rakes it all in. Fuck them! My point is, just a few people have all the fun!"

The boss's nephew drank from the can of cola and walked into the office. He opened his cell phone, touched a few keys and, leaving the phone open, set it down on the table next to the can of cola. Then he picked up the office phone, and dialed a number.

"Hi! It's Dong-cheol. Did you see Choi Hong-man getting knocked out? Wow! That giant collapsing and making the whole ring shake! What? In the middle of a game? All right."

A moment later the boss's nephew was tapping on his cell phone again, and making another call on the office phone.

"Seriously? You're fucking asking who this is? It's me, Dong-cheol. The most loyal friend in the world. Did you see Hong-man get knocked out? Wow! When that giant of a guy fell down, even the camera shook . . . I see. I'll call you later."

The boss's nephew stole a glance at me as he put down the phone. I turned away quickly. A few seconds later I heard him again.

"Who the fuck do you think it is? It's me, Dong-cheol. You don't recognize your best friend from high school? Did you see Choi Hong-man getting knocked out? Wow! It was like a mountain was collapsing. What? Didn't you go to Wooseong High School? I'm sorry."

The boss's nephew put the receiver down and went to the bathroom. He emerged after quite some time, and came over and sat next to me. Clearing his throat several times, he prattled on.

"One of my *seonbae* was assigned to GP in the DMZ. GP is short for guard post. You know—the barbed-wired fence that they patrol with German shepherds. You often see it on TV. A GP is like a bunker that's set up near the fence. Land mines are buried all over the place, and the North Korean soldiers are so close that you walk across the streams of piss where they've taken a leak. My *seonbae* said that fear or anxiety weren't a problem. He managed to get over them, but he could never beat boredom. He said he even ended up talking to a squirrel. He reckoned more than ten North Korean spies could have sneaked in without him noticing because he was talking to a squirrel. Do you know why I work nights at this gas station for no pay? It's because I want to train myself to get used to boredom. Because the Marine Corps does a lot of stake outs. By the way, even those bikers—sons of bitch-es—are quiet today."

Just as he stopped talking a BMW glided up to the gas pumps

and the driver's window slid noiselessly down. The man behind the wheel was wearing sunglasses and looked no older than the boss's nephew. The girl sitting next to him seemed younger. She took a compact out of her purse and, looking into the mirror, began to fix her makeup.

"Put in thirty thousand won," said Sunglasses, speaking rapidly and quietly, and sticking his head out of the car window.

"That son of a bitch smells of his mother's milk and he dares to talk down to me as if I was just a kid!" murmured the boss's nephew under his breath. "He's driving a BMW and he wants just thirty thousand won of gas? What a loser! And why the hell wear sunglasses at night? That trust-fund baby is having all the fun— driving around in a BMW and flirting with the chick beside him. And I have nothing better to do than pump fucking gas for them all night. What lousy goddamn luck I have!"

I unscrewed the gas cap and poked the nozzle into the opening. Pressing the keys on the fuel pump, I entered thirty thousand. Then I took a credit card from Sunglasses and walked into the office. It was a platinum credit card. I ran it through the card reader. Then I tore off the receipt and went back to Sunglasses.

"So what are you giving away? Don't tell me there are no free gifts," said Sunglasses as I handed him a pen and the receipt. The girl next to him was fixing her lipstick.

"No, we don't have anything."

"So this is how you rake in all the money, huh?" said Sunglasses, scribbling his signature on the receipt. I handed him his card and his copy of the receipt, and the car window immediately slid up.

The boss's nephew had already finished fueling the BMW and was pulling out the nozzle. It was a diesel pump. Our eyes met. He held up his hand and showed me his thumb and forefinger almost touching one another, as if to say "just a little." He flashed a smile and winked at me.

At the last gas station where I worked before getting this job, a guy, a part-timer, accidentally pumped gasoline into a diesel car. He had his whole month's wages docked, since the car's gas tank had to be cleaned out and parts of the fuel system had to be replaced. He was lucky the engine wasn't completely destroyed. I wondered how much diesel the boss's nephew had put into the BMW, but I didn't ask him.

I stopped at the 24-hour corner market on my way home. The woman with the heavy makeup wasn't there. As I pushed the door open and walked inside I was confronted by a robber in a stocking mask. He was holding a knife. He threatened me with it and I staggered backward. He glanced sideways at the door and then forced me away from it, inch by inch. I was between him and his escape route. He just wanted to get out through the door, and I just wanted a bottle of *soju*, a packet of cigarettes, and a scratch-off lottery ticket. He seemed to be trying to shove the door open with his shoulder and make his escape, but it wasn't as easy as he thought. He was pushing at the hinge side. As he edged toward the center of the door, the knife came toward me. There wasn't much space between the knife and me, and I was backed right up to a magazine rack.

The robber and I both needed a cool head and some space. I had a cool head but no space, while the robber had some space but he wasn't cool. I could see his throat twitch as he swallowed. I could feel his anxiety racing through his blood vessels and spreading throughout his body. To show that I had no intention of fighting, I went to put my hands up and stupidly pulled my hand out of my pocket. That was my mistake. The knife flew towards my belly, and I reflexively stuck out my hand to block it. There was a sudden shriek from the direction of the checkout counter, and it was that cry, rather than the knife or the cut in my palm, that startled both the robber and me and brought us back to reality. We separated, like two boxers fighting fiercely and then abruptly turning away from each other at the bell. He ran out through the door, and I picked up a bottle of *soju*, a packet of cigarettes and a scratch-off lottery ticket, walked to the cashier and put them down on the counter.

The girl at the checkout, bug-eyed, asked me if I was injured. I didn't think so, I replied. She thanked me, saying I had prevented the robber from taking anything from the till. Then she said that as a token of thanks, she wouldn't charge me for the items. I tried to decline the offer, but to no avail. She was determined not to let me have the items unless I took them for free. She was giving me a harder time than the armed robber. I had never talked that much with a girl my age before. After arguing for a while we ended up agreeing that I would just pay for the *soju* and cigarettes, but not for the lottery ticket. It was her idea. And I didn't think it was a bad one, since I wanted to pay for the *soju* and cigarettes with my own money, no matter what. And I imagined that a scratch-off lottery ticket that someone bought for me would probably bring the good luck, or a hint of it at least, that had never yet come my way.

I was about to leave the store when the girl stopped me and asked for my phone number. I didn't have a cell phone. I had never owned one or wanted to. My home phone number? Its cord was almost always pulled out of the wall by Father when we slept or by Grandpa when we were awake. Because Father said phone calls interrupted his sleep, and Grandpa said that the Japs had bugged the phone. In any case, we rarely received any phone calls. If we had decided to cut off the phone service we would have gotten our deposit back, but Father wouldn't do so. He didn't care how many times we had to move because of rent hikes. The only thing he cared about was keeping the same phone number.

In the past we often used to get a mysterious call. The second we picked up, the person at the other end would hang up without saying anything. I had a feeling it was Mom. She seemed to be using a public phone, because there was always quite a lot of background noise. Once I heard a faint sound as if she was sobbing. I waited without saying anything. Clenching my teeth. Until I heard her hang up. Over time, the mysterious phone calls came less and less often, and by now they had stopped completely. They usually happened on Sunday evenings. Sunday. The day of the god Mom believed in.

"But I come here every day," I said, instead of giving the girl my number. .

"Every day?"

"Yes. I stopped by yesterday and the day before. And the day before that too."

"You did?"

"Yes. Yesterday you were blowing a bubble with your chewing gum. And the day before, you were stretching. And the day before that, you were drinking coffee, am I right?"

"Was ... was I?"

The girl's face stiffened. I couldn't tell if it was because she realized a stranger had been watching her without her noticing or because she couldn't recall that I stopped by the store every day. One thing was certain, though: I had just said too much. I hurried out of the store. Reaching up to scratch my head, I felt something odd, opened my hand, and found a long cut on my palm. The blood that had oozed from the deep cut had dried dark red. The cut looked like a large rusted nail. I felt no pain.

I was almost home when I realized I had left the new jigsaw puzzle at the gas station. I looked at my watch and hesitated. It would soon be daybreak. I had stayed too long at the corner market. There wasn't enough time to go back to the gas station and get home before sunrise. Still, the empty space for the last, missing piece kept nagging at my mind. I raced down the hill, almost tripping in my haste.

By the time I reached the main road, an intense pain was searing through my head. I could barely breathe. I stood still for a while, and the pain gradually eased. But I still felt lightheaded and nauseous. Not knowing what else to do, I turned back.

Half way back up the hill, the alarm on my watch went off. Everything around me turned bright all of a sudden, as if it had been waiting for the alarm. I felt like my heart was about to explode and my muscles were being torn. The cut in my palm burned with intense pain. I pulled my hand out of my pocket, uncurled it, and looked at my palm. The congealed, dark red cut had developed some bluish spots. They looked like mold. I folded my hand into a fist and thrust it back into my pocket. Sweat was trickling down my face making everything in front of me a blur. Struggling to pull myself together, I walked slowly, one step at a time. People heading to work were rushing down the hill in waves. I was the only one going uphill. The ground beneath my feet seemed to be spinning. I suddenly felt queasy and my stomach heaved. I bent over and threw up. The pale, liquid vomit smelled of mackerel pike. Father didn't like mackerel pike.

Turning to go into the house, I ran into Grandpa at the front gate. He was wearing a *durumagi*[10] and a bowler hat. In his hand he had a bundle wrapped in cloth. He was almost unrecognizable. He looked hale and hearty and full of spirits. He was standing up straight, his eyes sparkling. Grandpa was already an old man when I was born. But the Grandpa who stood in front of me now was no old man. His face was bright with supreme dignity. It was blinding. I collapsed, as helpless as a wind-up toy soldier whose spring had wound down completely.

"Get up. There's no time to lose. The Japs will catch you any minute. We must hurry to Incheon and take a ferry for Shanghai. I must meet Mr. Kim Gu without fail."

The moment Grandpa stopped shouting, my body was lifted up with a sudden jerk. Grandpa was holding me in his arms.

I was woken by the alarm clock. I couldn't see Father anywhere. His bedding had been put away neatly in the corner. My headache was gone and my hand didn't hurt anymore. The cut had healed, and the bluish spots had disappeared. I got up, drew aside the curtains, opened the windows, and breathed in the scent of the darkness. I immediately felt refreshed. When I walked out of the bedroom, Father stopped chopping scallions and stood at the kitchen counter staring at me. He started to say something but stopped.

"You're cooking mackerel pike again?"

"Can you smell it?"

"Have you ever had mold grow in a cut?"

"Were you dreaming? Just go wash and wake up the old man."

"You should wipe the oil out of the empty can and wash and dry it before throwing it away."

I took the empty can from the sink, washed it with detergent, and left it upside down.

---

10 A traditional Korean coat. (Translators' note)

"Take a day off today. You were sleeping so soundly you missed breakfast. You must be burned out."

Father didn't seem to know anything about my fainting and Grandfather's attempt to leave the house. I went into the big bedroom, switched on the light and turned off the TV. Grandpa's *durumagi* was hanging from the doorknob. Holding the coat, I opened the closet. Inside, on the floor, lay a bundle wrapped in cloth. It was the one Grandpa had been carrying. I hung up his coat and then untied the bundle. In it was a box made of light cardboard; it bore the logo of an underwear manufacturer. It was very old and battered, and the sides of the lid were almost torn off. I opened the box and found a large quantity of bank notes inside. It was mostly one-thousand-won bills, and some of them were very old and grimy. At the bottom of the box lay a number of coins. I closed the lid, wrapped the box in the cloth and put it back into the wardrobe. I looked over at Grandpa. He was just a gaunt, shriveled old man. I shook him awake gently.

As he ate, Father kept looking at a newspaper. It was an evening newspaper. He must have gone out to buy it when he got up. The lines and wrinkles on his forehead showed as he read. He had become noticeably older in just a few days. Grandpa, with his pallor, looked no better. I could tell he was a bundle of nerves, like a hunted man.

As soon as they left the table, Father sat in front of the TV watching the news, and Grandpa took his *durumagi* out of the closet, hung it on the doorknob, and lay down on the floor. When the news ended, Father got dressed and left the house. I switched to a movie channel, but Grandpa didn't stir.

The phone rang. At first I thought the sound was coming from the TV. I let it ring for a while. It had been a long time since we'd heard the sound of the phone. I picked up the receiver but there was no voice at the other end. Just a cacophony of noises: cars honking, street vendors shouting, music, a young woman trolling for business, children giggling, someone swallowing dryly. The sounds of people who were barely getting by. I neither put the receiver down nor spoke. After some time—I couldn't say how long—the person at the other end hung up. My hand, gripping the receiver tight, had become sweaty. I put the phone down slowly.

The birdcage was enveloped in newspaper again. The parrot, which had been shrieking madly at the slightest sound, was quiet. I removed the newspaper and saw that the bird had fallen off its perch and was lying at the bottom of the cage. It was smeared with blood and had lost all its feathers. It was barely breathing. I opened the cage and took the parrot out. Dipping my little finger in water, I held it out to the bird, but it didn't react. I could feel the bird's pain. There was no hope. I looked into its eyes. They were desperately trying to tell me something. And I could tell what that was.

I put my hand around the parrot's neck and tightened it. My fingers trembled. Or maybe it was the parrot. The bird gave in serenely. It went limp. I shrouded it with newspaper. Taking the bird and a trowel, I left the house and headed up the hill. I walked up the trail until I found the first sign indicating the distance to the summit. At the sign I took nine paces to the west and dug a hole. But then I filled the hole again and went back to the sign. This time I took nine paces to the east and dug another hole. I unrolled the bundle of newspaper. The parrot had shrunken to half its size. It was as if something had escaped from its body. I buried the bird. And alongside it I buried the coin with the hole in it. The one Mom had given me when she left.

Today wasn't Sunday. I checked the date and found it was my birthday. I wasn't concerned about how many birthdays I had had so far. I had a very long life ahead of me, as long as Father's and Grandpa's. People who have a mission to complete, or have something or someone they're desperately waiting for, don't give up the ghost easily. I wasn't sure who would live longer, Father or Grandpa, but I was willing to bet both would live far longer than I expected. And I would have to live for countless more days after they had passed on. Still listening to someone hitting the vending machine, still glancing furtively at someone struggling not to fall asleep, still watching with concern a woman standing at night in front of a 24-hour store and risking her life. I would still be doing all this until I grew very old, so old that I couldn't figure out my age. I would dig up the coin and look at it if I became curious about my age.

The next day, Father asked me about the parrot. I told him I had buried it because I'd found it dead. Father glanced in turn at the empty cage and at me and tried to speak but said nothing. I set the table, went into the big bedroom, switched on the light, turned off the TV, and gently shook Grandpa awake. His *durumagi* was hanging in the closet, where it belonged. Grandpa ate a bowl of rice and sipped his *soju*. Father didn't even look at the newspaper he had bought.

After doing the dishes I went into the big bedroom. Grandpa was sitting close to the TV, which was showing a movie. Slowly and carefully I took the jigsaw puzzle board down from the table. I took the lid off the new puzzle, tore open the plastic wrapping, and shook out the puzzle pieces. All one thousand pieces rattled onto the floor. My hands groped around in the heap of puzzle pieces. To find the one piece I needed to complete the abyss of darkness.

Oh, I almost forgot. I had stopped by the convenience store after work. The woman with heavy makeup was standing in front of the store and a young man with an acne-covered face was working at the checkout. He was new. Holding open a comic book, Acne Face was giggling. I set a bottle of *soju* and a packet of cigarettes down on the counter. I didn't buy a lottery ticket.

Bastille Day

In the course of a life, one day sometimes stands out and seems interminable. For Yeong-sin, this was one of those days. She didn't know it was going to be an unusually long day when, early that morning, she found that her period had started. It had come a week earlier than usual. She had felt bloated when she got into the train in Berne, but she had simply put it down to being tired from all the travel she was doing. She woke up from a weird dream to find a stain on the sheets. She felt as if she had been attacked. She would have been in trouble if it hadn't been for the maxi pads she had packed just in case.

Her periods had become more and more irregular. Yeong-sin could hear her mother's voice nagging her.

"You stubborn fool! It's because you still haven't given birth, and here you are pushing forty. Look around you. Every woman your age is a mother, but not you."

"One step at a time, Mother. I'm not even married. Don't talk to me about giving birth!"

"You stubborn fool! Always dashing around in foreign countries. That's why you don't have a boyfriend yet."

"Don't worry. I'll find a guy soon, a handsome white guy."

This was how conversations between Yeong-sin and her mother always went.

It was not in fact the case that Yeong-sin didn't have a boyfriend. She was seeing a man she'd met in grade school, and who now worked as a pilot for a foreign airline. Every time he flew overseas, he sent Yeong-sin a postcard of a famous landmark. On the backs of the postcards he would write something affectionate, beginning with "My dear Yeong-sin" and ending with "I really miss you." But when they met in person he was distant. When he gazed at her, he had a faraway look in his eyes. It seemed to say that he would never see her again and was trying to fix her image in his mind. Perhaps it was because of that look that Yeong-sin had never mentioned her boyfriend to her mother.

"You stubborn fool! I'll never get a good night's sleep until you're married."

Yeong-sin's mother had made up her mind to divorce as soon as Yeong-sin—the only one of her three daughters who was still single—got married.

"What happened this time? Did Dad put his money on the horses again?"

When Yeong-sin urged her mother to explain why she had once again left home, her mother remained silent, as if that was the only way she could defend her already wounded pride. For some time now, Yeong-sin's mother would turn up at her daughter's apartment carrying a suitcase.

When she came out of the bathroom Yeong-sin looked at her watch. It was just after six. Her watch was always set to European time. Even when she was back in Korea she didn't change it. She had long since wanted to be transferred to the European team, and she applied several times before she eventually made it. She hadn't been able to sleep a wink the night before her first European tour guide assignment.

Yeong-sin had always felt at home near airports. Any time she felt despondent she would go and sit at a café near an airport and watch the planes taking off and landing. It soothed her, as if by magic. One of her friends had once derided this aspect of Yeong-sin's personality as bourgeois. He was a *seonbae* of Yeong-sin's at college, whom she met at a meeting of a college singing group, and he was her first love. One spring day in college when she was weary and run down after having had an abortion, and again some years later, when she finally decided to end her five-year career at the real estate investment agency, she wound up at an airport. What consoled Yeong-sin was not the sight of a plane landing, but watching one take off. This was her third European tour.

The previous night Yeong-sin had asked the person at the

front desk to let her tour group into the breakfast buffet at six. It normally opened at six-thirty. In Rome she had learned the hard way that they would have a better sightseeing experience if they started earlier than other groups. Her tour group had had to wait in line for three hours in the scorching sun to get into the Vatican, while another of her company's groups had only had to wait an hour because they had started their day a little earlier than the schedule stated.

Yeong-sin had other reasons, too, to get her group started early. They had only one day to cover Paris, and they had to do it all before sunset. Four countries in ten days meant a grueling schedule. On the tour operator's website there was a series of comments by dissatisfied customers: "I felt like I was on a military exercise" and "It couldn't all be done in the time allowed—it was Mission Impossible." This group had a "select" itinerary, so at least it wasn't as bad as the regular ones. Yeong-sin hurriedly dried her hair and went down to the lobby.

Some of her group were sitting in chairs around the lobby, and the rest were hanging around outside. They were supposed to be eating breakfast. Yeong-sin went to the front desk and demanded an explanation. The agent spoke a mixture of English and French that was incomprehensible to Yeong-sin. She struggled to communicate using gestures, and it eventually emerged that the person in charge of the front desk the previous night had failed to leave a message for the next shift.

"Oh, my god!" Yeong-sin let out a big sigh, but the agent just shrugged his shoulders and did nothing to help. It was Yeong-sin herself who had to insist on the urgency of the situation. She asked him to see to it that her group had breakfast as quickly as possible. "*Bari bari*," the agent muttered mockingly, imitating the Korean for "quickly, quickly." Yeong-sin pretended not to hear him.

The local tour guide showed up on time. She had originally come to Paris to study European art, and had stayed. She was two years older than Yeong-sin and the people in Yeong-sin's office called her Madame Lee.

Madame Lee had a discriminating palate and never considered eating street food no matter how short of cash she was. She often described her dining experiences, and always in melodramatic terms. She had once fasted for three days because she wanted to eat at a particular restaurant that she had spotted. When she got there she ordered a dish of foie gras, but as soon as she finished it she had to dash to the restroom to throw up. She said her stomach had shrunk to the size of a duck liver and couldn't hold the food. Even her vomit tasted so out of this world, she added, that it brought tears to her eyes. She had been living in Paris so long that she dressed and spoke like a Parisian. Today she was wearing a black, sleeveless Chanel-style dress and a white cardigan.

"*Merde!*" she cursed, when she heard that they were delayed.

The tour bus started and Yeong-sin picked up her mike. She began by explaining why breakfast had been delayed. She repeated that it had been the hotel's fault and not hers, but her group just looked apathetic. Hardly anyone was paying any attention to what she was saying.

"The weather in Paris has been very gloomy for the past couple of days," said Yeong-sin, changing the subject, "but we're in luck today. It's bright and sunny."

"It's hot in here. The air conditioning isn't working," complained the kids sitting in the front seats. There were more kids in this tour group than usual. It was the middle of the school year, but their schools regarded the tour as a field trip and allowed them a leave of absence. Yeong-sin was more anxious than usual because of the number of children in her group. Madame Lee asked the driver about the air conditioning, and he said he was low on gas and wouldn't be able to fill up until lunch time. When she passed this information along to the tour group, Yeong-sin rolled up her sleeves. She would never have considered wearing a short-sleeved shirt, because her skin would break out in rash after just a few hours of exposure to the sun.

"We've struck it lucky today," Yeong-sin said, and then tried to catch the group's attention by throwing out a question. "Does anyone know what day it is today? Yes, that's right. It's Bastille Day. A question now for the students sitting up front: Do you know when the French Revolution occurred and why it happened?" No one answered. It had been the same way since the beginning of the tour. In her previous job she had often been in the same situation—she had had to keep talking without getting any response—but on the phone. *Ma'am, we have a very nice piece of real estate in Gangwon Province that we would like you to consider. Sir, we've just received word of some land with excellent potential for redevelopment* . . . Some of her clients would react by swearing at her and some by playing nasty jokes on her. Worst of all was when they said nothing. She would be overcome by mortification every time she realized that she might as well be talking to the wall.

Yeong-sin tried to swallow, but her throat was dry. She had memorized some facts about the French Revolution before setting out on this tour. It had been a long time since she had worked so hard to commit something to memory. She had read *The History of the French Revolution* when she was in college and had joined a discussion group about it, but the only thing that stayed with her was the term *Ancien Régime*. How could she have forgotten so much? She had been the laughing stock of the group when she asked who this person named Ancien Régime was.

"As you know, it happened in 1789," Yeong-sin continued. "In order to defy England, France joined America in the War of Independence. And because of all the money spent on the war, France went bankrupt and the common people were reduced to dire poverty. To replenish the public purse, France tried to tax the clergy and the aristocracy, but the attempt was unsuccessful. The failure of these reforms enraged the common people and an armed mob stormed a prison known as the Bastille. This incident lit the fuse of the French Revolution. And today is the anniversary of the storming of the Bastille. Louis XVI and Marie Antoinette were guillotined, as you all know. To escape the havoc, the couple had sought refuge in Austria. On their way to safety they took a break at a farmhouse near the border, believing they were far enough ahead of their pursuers. They dined there and paid with a silver coin. The head of Louis XVI was engraved on the coin, and the farmer's wife recognized him. She raised the alarm and thereby brought about the fall of the Bourbons. Versailles Palace, which we'll be visiting this afternoon, is where the couple lived."

The atmosphere in the bus had grown even quieter and more apathetic. Yeong-sin introduced Madame Lee and quickly handed her the mike.

"Please call me Madame Lee. Mademoiselle Lee is too much of a mouthful. But whatever you do, don't call me Miss Lee, because I'm certainly not going to mislead you. I'll pretend not to hear you if you call me that, even if you shout yourself hoarse."

Here and there, some of the group laughed.

There was already a long line of people waiting to get into the Eiffel Tower. And there were soldiers with M16s standing around. They had apparently been placed on alert following the terror attack in London a few days before. The soldiers' eyes were constantly watchful, and the security guards were checking the tourists and their belongings very thoroughly. They were not only searching handbags and backpacks, but also asking people to empty their pockets. The elevator was moving up and down incessantly, but it couldn't accommodate the ever increasing flood of people. A number of tourists left the queue for the elevator and took the stairs instead. Yeong-sin's heart sank when she saw how long the line was. It was moving very slowly because of the tight security.

An hour and a half later Yeong-sin's group finally reached the front of the line. Madame Lee held up a little Mickey Mouse flag so that the group wouldn't lose sight of her. When Madame Lee raised her arm, Yeong-sin noticed a hole the size of a quarter in her cardigan. Yeong-sin hesitated, uncertain whether she should tell Madame Lee about the hole, but she was already quite far ahead. Above the sea of people, Yeong-sin could see Mickey Mouse smiling sweetly at her.

Yeong-sin decided not to go up the Eiffel Tower. She was having some cramps, and she remembered how disappointed she had been when she climbed it for the first time. There was nothing particularly impressive about it, other than the view of Paris. She thought that the tower was fairly dramatic, at least when seen from a river boat cruising along the Seine. She had had the same sense of anticlimax when she stood in front of Leonardo da Vinci's *Mona Lisa*. The painting was dark and small, quite unlike what she had imagined. Even so, the room had been jammed with people eager to take a picture of the little painting. The surface of the painting was covered with cracks that reminded her of a jigsaw puzzle, and that alone caught her attention. They marked the passage of time in a way that even the most high-tech color printer can't reproduce, and, at the same time, they demonstrated that even a masterpiece by a genius can't defeat the inexorable march of time. Yeong-sin thought she could understand how Hemingway must have felt when he had said he wasn't able to write about Paris until he left it. Nonetheless, she liked the city. Paris was like a cat: free-spirited, smug, and elegant. As the morning clouds dispersed, it grew hotter. Yeong-sin shook her head briskly to fight off sleepiness.

"Did you nod off?" Madame Lee asked, nudging Yeong-sin on the shoulder.

"No." Yeong-sin answered faintly, getting up from the bench where she had been sitting. She felt a stiffness in her abdomen.

"Are you all right?" asked Madame Lee, looking worried. "You look pale."

"I'm fine," Yeong-sin murmured, looking at her watch. It was well past eleven. They'd been out for two hours already and all they'd seen was the Eiffel Tower. If they went on like this they'd have a hard time keeping to their schedule for the day.

"Why did they build this iron tower in the first place, and create so much hassle for tour guides?" Madame Lee said, looking up at the structure.

The tour bus was waiting. Yeong-sin asked if everyone in the group had come back down from the tower. Madame Lee nodded. Yeong-sin turned toward the group standing beside the bus. Fifteen, sixteen. Two people were missing. It was the late-middle-aged couple. The hat team. Yeong-sin didn't memorize the names of the people in her tour groups. She didn't think it was really necessary, and she made it a rule not to look into the personal details about her clients. Otherwise, she would have preconceived notions about them. She mentally categorized her clients into smaller teams, instead. The husband and wife team, the mother-daughter team ... If there were two families with children she identified them by the sex of the children: the girls family, for example, or the boy-and-girl family. If two families had the same number of children of the same sex, as was the case in this tour group, Yeong-sin noted the sex of the eldest child in each family: the girl family or the boy family. There were two elderly couples in this group. One of these couples always wore hats, and Yeong-sin thought of them as Mr. and Mrs. Hat. The husband wore a sun visor and the wife a straw hat with a narrow brim.

Yeong-sin decided that she couldn't wait any longer for the Hats, and she had the rest of the group board the bus and leave for their next destination. There were now even more people waiting to climb the Eiffel Tower, and the line looked endless. She held up the red triangular flag with her tour operator's logo. As she did so, she felt her armpit in spite of herself.

It wasn't until forty minutes after the bus left that Yeong-sin found Mr. and Mrs. Hat. Mr. Hat explained grumpily that he had happened to lose sight of the tour guide while they were waiting for the elevator. When Yeong-sin told him that their tour bus had left, he grew angry. Yeong-sin pleaded with him to understand that they had no choice but to stick to the tour schedule.

"What's her name? Miss Lead, is it? I mean the local tour guide. Why did she have to dash away like that? Was there a bomb scare or something? Isn't she supposed to make sure we're all with her all of the time? She didn't even give us any information about what we've been seeing around here. I can't believe how irresponsible she is. Do you think we paid for this premium package to be treated like luggage? Don't you think that as premium clients we deserve the best service?" The man's anger continued unabated, and there was nothing Yeong-sin could do but bow her head apologetically, while beads of sweat formed on her brow. The man's wife caught Yeong-sin's eye and, smiling slightly, said, "It isn't this lady's fault." Yeong-sin didn't dare return her smile.

They weren't able to find a taxi, because there was a police roadblock nearby. It was too late for them to catch up with the rest of the group for lunch and too early to go to the Louvre, which was the next item on the schedule. Speaking diffidently, Yeong-sin explained the situation to the couple.

"What about our escargot lunch?" Mr. Hat demanded.

"I'm sorry about that," Yeong-sin apologized again.

"Well, that's just our bad luck," said Mrs. Hat.

"We're in Paris and we don't get to eat escargots. What a letdown!" said the man, disappointed.

Yeong-sin and the Hats decided to walk along the Seine towards the Louvre. It was unpleasantly humid, as it had rained off and on during the last few days. But at least the tall trees along the river were in full leaf and threw a wide shadow, and Yeong-sin felt that the walk wouldn't be that bad.

Whenever she had severe cramps, Yeong-sin would always go out for a walk. As she wandered along with no destination in mind, dusk would begin to fall and the changing color of the sky would take her mind off the menstrual pains shooting through her body. She comforted herself by imagining that each star in the sky represented all the suffering that one person had endured that day, and that the harsher the suffering the brighter the star, just as a rare gem shines more brightly the more it is polished.

When Yeong-sin and the Hats reached the Palais Bourbon, Mr. Hat suggested that they stop for lunch, and they walked into the first restaurant they came to. Mr. Hat ordered escargots and veal steak. He also asked for a bottle of red wine, though Yeong-sin and his wife tried to dissuade him. Yeong-sin made a phone call to Madame Lee and arranged to meet the group at the entrance to the Louvre Pyramid.

"These escargots look really fucking weird."

"They're as big as your boyfriend's wiener."

"Bitch! You're talking like you've seen it."

Two Korean girls at the next table giggled, their digital cameras flashing. Mr. Hat frowned deeply. Yeong-sin hesitated as she took her camera out of her purse. She thought it might be best not to take photos of escargots for her blog just now. She would wait until the next time she was in Paris.

"Please, Honey," Mrs. Hat implored, grabbing her husband's hand.

Yeong-sin had a bitter taste in her mouth, but thinking of what lay ahead that afternoon, she forced herself to eat. The man offered her wine. She knew that even one glass would make her face turn red, but she held out her glass nonetheless. She didn't know what else to do, because he looked stern and said that one should never turn down any offer from one's elders.

"You shouldn't hold a wine glass when someone is filling it. You should just leave it on the table. Are you still single?"

"Eh, yeah ... yes," Yeong-sin answered, taking a quick drink of water.

"You look more than old enough to get married. Aren't you going to marry? Don't you have a boyfriend?"

"Well ..."

Yeong-sin had barely opened her mouth to speak when Mr. Hat interrupted.

"How old are you?"

"Honey!" Mrs. Hat snapped, looking askance at her husband.

"What's wrong with you, woman? I'm asking her these questions because she reminds me of our daughter."

He drained his wine in one gulp and poured himself another.

"I'm thirty-seven," Yeong-sin said, unable to bear the oppressive silence.

"See? She's as old as our Ji-hye. My daughter's eldest will be starting grade school next year. And she has two more kids— that's how patriotic she is. She studies psychology and she's writing her PhD dissertation. What people say is true: having a daughter guarantees you a luxury overseas vacation. This package tour, it's our son-in-law's gift to us. My son-in-law is now ..."

"I'm sorry to interrupt, but I need to go to the bathroom."

Yeong-sin stood up awkwardly.

In the six years that they had been dating, Yeong-sin had never brought up the topic of marriage with her boyfriend. Neither had he. There had even been times when she doubted whether they were in a romantic relationship. When she lay naked beside him, she felt no particular excitement. She figured it might be because she had known him for a long time before they had any passionate moments together. She imagined that if she did ask him what he thought about getting married, he would say that it would be like marrying a member of the family.

On one occasion, Yeong-sin had asked her boyfriend why he was dating her. Without the slightest hesitation he answered, "Because I can relax with you." He was being honest, more honest than if he had said it was because he loved her. Yet she couldn't help feeling forlorn. He was no expert in empty flattery. If she complained that she was getting more wrinkles, he would just murmur that time doesn't play favorites. Given the nature of his personality, Yeong-sin had to believe that when he wrote "I'm missing you" on his postcards to her, he really meant it.

A friend who had divorced her husband because he had cheated on her, had surprised Yeong-sin by confiding that she had felt liberated when she found out about her husband's affair. It stunned Yeong-sin, because she knew that her friend was being completely truthful. And Yeong-sin shuddered to realize how the unvarnished truth could make a mockery of the reassuring platitude that people marry because they're in love and separate because they are no longer in love. It was a platitude that most people, including herself, wanted to believe. Once the truth is revealed, it is impossible to go back to the world as it had been before. That's because we have changed in light of the truth, but the world has not. If the truth is discomfiting or cruel, that's because only we are changed by it. Before we know the truth we tremble in fear of it; after we know the truth we shiver with regret. Platitudes are the lies that we tell in order to escape fear or regret. On the one hand Yeong-sin hoped her boyfriend would propose to her, but on the other hand she was afraid he would.

When Yeong-sin went into the restroom, the stall was occupied. There were some clothes hanging over the top of the door. A young woman was fixing her makeup in front of the mirror. She was one of the two Korean girls who had been sitting at the next table. A few minutes later the door was flung open. The second Korean girl came out wearing a red dress.

"What do you think?"

"It's fucking cool."

"Are you shitting me? If you are I'll kill you."

Red Dress checked herself out in the mirror, turning her body this way and that.

"Excuse me, but I'm in a hurry."

Yeong-sin's voice was barely audible. Red Dress didn't respond.

"It's weird. It looked so slim on the mannequin, but it doesn't on me. Don't you think I look gross?"

"Of course, you idiot. Because the mannequin is a different size than you!"

"That's not why. It just feels different than when I tried it on in the store. It's driving me nuts. Why the hell do I look different!"

"Different how? You look just the same to me."

Yeong-sin couldn't wait any longer and went into the stall, locking the door behind her.

"You should know better. This is not a fitting room!" Yeong-sin bellowed.

It wasn't like her to raise her voice, and she trembled, startled to hear her own voice bursting out from deep inside of her. The room was quiet all of a sudden. The silence was tense. But it didn't last long. Hardly had the clothes been snatched out of sight when the door began to rattle from being kicked repeatedly.

"You're welcome to the fucking toilet, and I hope you shit blood, you fucking bitch!"

Yeong-sin flinched at the sound of the restroom door being slammed shut. When she returned to her table she noticed that the table beside theirs was now empty. And not only that. The bottle of wine was also empty. Mr. Hat's face had grown red, while his wife's complexion had turned pale.

Yeong-sin and the hat couple said nothing until they reached the Louvre after crossing the Alexander III Bridge and walking through the Place de la Concorde and the Tuileries Garden. The weather had grown hotter and more humid, but there was a chilly air between the man and his wife. Yeong-sin was uneasy, feeling that she was responsible for the strained atmosphere. The museum had seemed impossibly far away. And when she finally saw the top of the pyramid she was so relieved she could have wept for joy.

"We took this vacation to celebrate our thirtieth anniversary. Thirtieth! The proverb says that you should never boast about your youth to a river or brag to the sun about how fiery red a flower is. Now I realize it's true. How fleeting my life is! I used to think it would last forever," lamented Mr. Hat. Yeong-sin thought she should respond, but she couldn't speak. The man started to hum a song.

"Life is a road a vagabond takes. Where he comes from and where he goes, no one knows . . ."

The last time she saw her boyfriend, he had talked about a site that he had come across on the Internet. It had a collection of recordings from people who had died. Their voices had been recorded by the black boxes of airplanes during crashes. These people, up in the sky, tens of thousands of feet above ground level, had bequeathed their voices, right before death, to someone on the ground. These last words must have engraved themselves in the heart of someone, someone who might have been fixing himself a snack, or someone waking up after a night of drinking, someone honking angrily at a car trying to cut in, or someone anxiously waiting to hear the results of staff reassignments.

"Do you know what someone who knows they're about to die is most likely to say?"

"This is why you needed to see me?" Yeong-sin snapped at her boyfriend. "I'm taking a plane in two days and you keep talking about death. You're jinxing my trip. Didn't you say you had something to tell me? What is it?"

Her boyfriend didn't speak until he had lit a cigarette, something he rarely did. "The truth is, I used to be married. But we broke up after just one year."

Without knowing what she was doing, Yeong-sin kept dropping sugar cubes into her coffee.

"That's the fourth sugar you've put in," her boyfriend said cautiously.

Only then did Yeong-sin take her hand away from the sugar jar. The coffee didn't taste sweet.

Yeong-sin was waiting with Madame Lee in the Louvre Pyramid, when she saw a team rushing toward them and knew instinctively that they had a problem. It was the mother-and-son team: a mother who wore Bulgari sunglasses and her grade-school-aged son who always carried a camcorder.

"I got pickpocketed," said Mrs. Bulgari breathlessly. "I was just leaving the Apollo Gallery when I noticed that my purse was open. I checked it and found that my wallet was gone."

The Apollo Gallery was where the treasures of the Bourbon dynasty were displayed, including the Louis XV's diamond-studded crown.

"Oh, my goodness! Oh, my goodness!" Yeong-sin shifted from foot to foot nervously.

"How much cash did you have in the wallet?" Madame Lee asked.

"About one thousand euro," replied Mrs. Bulgari, matter-of-factly.

"Oh my! That's more than one million won!" Yeong-sin's voice rose.

"I bought the wallet at the flagship Burberry store in London. Can I borrow your cell phone? I need to stop my credit card right away." Mrs. Bulgari said, and now she sounded really annoyed.

"Do you know your card number?" Yeong-sin asked, holding out her phone. Fortunately she had signed up for international roaming.

"I know what to do."

Mrs. Bulgari rummaged in her purse and took out a receipt. She then called her husband, gave him her card number and pin, and asked him to take care of the problem. She sounded business-like as she spoke to her husband.

"The problem is my passport," Mrs. Bulgari said, frowning. "Today is a holiday. I'm not sure they'll reissue it."

"Your passport was stolen too? But we're leaving for England tomorrow . . ."

Yeong-sin's voice trailed off, and her expression became grim. "Why don't we try checking in the restrooms? You know, pickpockets often throw bags and passports into the trash as soon as they've grabbed the cash."

Madame Lee was doubtful about Yeong-sin's idea. She said there were too many public bathrooms, and it would be better to get the woman and her son temporary passports.

Yeong-sin got into a taxi with the mother-and-son team and headed towards the Korean Embassy. Desperately hoping this mishap would be the last one for the day.

They had almost reached the embassy when Yeong-sin remembered that they had to bring a police report showing that the passports had been stolen. She asked the taxi driver to stop at Les Invalides, and the three of them got out. Then, stopping people and asking directions to the nearest police station, Yeong-sin made slow headway. At every step stifling heat rose from the sidewalk.

Yeong-sin and her clients made their police report and received a confirmation letter without a hitch. It was all thanks to Mrs. Bulgari's excellent French. She and her son would need photos for temporary passports. Photo studios would certainly be closed for the national holiday. A police officer told them there was an instant photo booth in the Invalides metro station. It was only a fifteen-minute walk away, but it was a very hot and humid day for walking. If everything had gone according to plan, Yeong-sin would now be doing some leisurely shopping in the duty-free store. Her mother had asked her to get her a new style of Louis Vuitton purse. But the money she had given her was not going to be nearly enough. Yeong-sin felt a cramp in her lower belly. She wanted so badly to change her pad. To her relief, Mrs. Bulgari's son began to complain that he was hungry, so they headed for a nearby McDonald's. Yeong-sin went straight to the restroom. The old pad was stained reddish brown, the color of rust.

Mrs. Bulgari handed Yeong-sin a Coke. The boy was licking ketchup off his fingers, having already gobbled up a hamburger and fries.

"That's enough," said Mrs. Bulgari, watching the boy out of the corner of her eye. He didn't stop noisily licking his fingers.

Only when she slapped him on the back did he take his hands away from his mouth.

For some reason, Yeong-sin couldn't help studying the mother and son. Mrs. Bulgari was slim, while her son was fat. It was hard to believe they were related. But the same expression — the shadow of a blind longing for something they were lacking — fell across both their faces when they stared into space.

"What is the rest of the group doing now?" Mrs. Bulgari asked.

"They've probably finished shopping and left for the Palace of Versailles," Yeong-sin answered, checking the time. "I'm sorry you missed the palace tour," she added, feeling sincerely apologetic.

"No worries. I've been there before. What time does the duty-free shop close?"

"Six o'clock."

Mrs. Bulgari looked at her watch. "What's scheduled after the palace tour?"

"We're going to eat at a Korean restaurant, take a cruise on the river, and then go to the Arc de Triomphe, the Champs Élysées, and the Place de la Concorde."

Mrs. Bulgari seemed to be trying to figure something out.

"Do you think we could go shopping?" Mrs. Bulgari asked as they were leaving the embassy. Time was tight, but Yeong-sin nodded remembering the things her mother had asked her to buy. She also needed some cosmetics. Mrs. Bulgari asked Yeong-sin to pay for her shopping and promised to pay her back as soon as they got back to Incheon Airport. The duty-free shop that Yeong-sin's company had an account with was close to the Opera and not far from the embassy. Yeong-sin hailed a taxi. The road block at the Place de la Concorde had been lifted, so they were able to go straight to the Madeleine.

In the duty-free shop, the cashier at the check-out recognized Yeong-sin and greeted her. Apparently, Madame Lee had mentioned that Yeong-sin had been delayed, because the cashier didn't ask her why she wasn't with her group. Everything the group bought there was calculated into Yeong-sin's achievement points. She was curious to know how much the group with Madame Lee had spent, but with Mrs. Bulgari standing next to her she felt too inhibited to ask.

Yeong-sin went up to the second floor where the purses were and picked out the one her mother had asked her to buy. When she got back downstairs, Mrs. Bulgari was looking at skin care products and cosmetics, and chatting with the store manager. Yeong-sin took her shopping list out of her pocket. The list had grown quite long, as she had added gifts for her sisters.

"Chanel is the best brand of cosmetics. But if you need skin lotion you should go with Sisley." Mrs. Bulgari scanned the shopping list in Yeong-sin's hand before starting to choose her own items: Lancôme Galatée Confort cleanser and Chanel Les Ombres Quadra eyeshadow. The names were unfamiliar to Yeong-sin.

"You have exquisite taste, Ma'am," said the manager. Mrs. Bulgari didn't hide how flattered she was by the compliment. She completed her shopping by adding Chanel Coco Mademoiselle, the newest Chanel fragrance, according to the store manager.

Yeong-sin was paying for her shopping, when a TV on the wall behind the counter caught her eye. It was tuned to CNN. A breaking news report was saying that a German airliner had been hijacked by a group of unidentified armed men. The plane was heading toward Istanbul having departed from Frankfurt. It belonged to the airline Yeong-sin's boyfriend worked for. She suddenly thought she remembered him saying he was scheduled to fly to Turkey. Her eyes narrowed as she stared at the TV. The aircraft had made an emergency landing at Antalya Airport, where the hijackers were in a stand-off with the police and were holding the passengers and crew hostage. There were one hundred twenty-eight passengers and eight crew members on board, but their identities had not yet been released. Yeong-sin's face turned white. She felt as if a swarm of bees were buzzing inside her brain. She hurriedly took out her cell phone. Her boyfriend's phone was turned off.

In a taxi on the way to rejoin the group at the Korean restaurant, Yeong-sin could think of nothing but the hijacked airplane.

The taxi driver kept glancing at the piece of paper where Yeong-sin had noted down the address of the restaurant. She didn't know exactly where it was, because it was one of her company's new accounts. Some streets in the center of the city were still cordoned off. To get around them, the taxi driver kept swerving into unfamiliar alleys. At one moment they glimpsed a sign that read Place André Malraux, and then the Opera came into view in the distance. Whenever he had to stop, the taxi driver murmured incomprehensibly. Mrs. Bulgari's son whined and kept asking when they would get to the restaurant.

It was a phone call from Madame Lee that made Yeong-sin aware that they had been driving around in the taxi for half an hour already. Madame Lee said she and her group had eaten and were leaving for the quays. Yeong-sin told the taxi driver to go straight to the quays. The sun was beating down on the car, and her boyfriend's cell phone was still not responding. The taxi was at a dead stop on the street leading to the Madeleine. Yeong-sin and her clients got out.

"We're back at the same spot!" the boy shouted, looking around. He was not mistaken. They were indeed back at the du-ty-free shop. Yeong-sin's legs were trembling.

Yeong-sin stopped abruptly at the Franklin Roosevelt metro station. She had intended to head towards the River Seine, but she had been walking in the opposite direction. She saw the Champs-Élysées stretching out in front of her. It was pandemonium, with an endless stream of traffic moving very slowly and a sea of pedestrians in every direction. Similar-looking, baroque-style buildings stood elbow-to-elbow all around her. She was flummoxed, not knowing which direction to go. She paused at every intersection and looked around repeatedly. Even after she had decided which way to go, she kept looking back.

Mrs. Bulgari asked a passer-by for directions and then led the way. They headed down a street lined with luxury stores. Yeong-sin was anxious and jumpy. She thought it would be less distressing to know what had happened to her boyfriend, even if it turned out that he was among the hostages. She kept imagining one catastrophe after another, making herself crazy. Her phone rang. It was Madame Lee. She said her group would arrive later than expected because of the traffic. Yeong-sin ended the call with barely a word. The shopping bags kept slipping off her shoulders.

The boy, who had been trailing along with his eyes fixed on the ground, suddenly spotted some food carts at the end of Avenue Montaigne. He devoured a fat baguette sandwich filled with sausage and lettuce and ordered a hotdog too. Yeong-sin asked Mrs. Bulgari if she'd like something to eat, but the woman replied that she never touched food after seven in the evening. Yeong-sin bought a bottle of Evian water to quench her thirst. *The baguette was an invention that Napoleon Bonaparte had ordered his men to come up with before they embarked on their invasion of Russia. It was hard because they wanted to use it as a pillow in the battlefield during the campaign.* Yeong-sin would normally have told an interesting story about the origin of the baguette. But now she couldn't even utter a word. It was as if she had been gagged.

Reaching the crossroads at Alma-Marceau metro station, Yeong-sin and her companions turned left. There was a bridge ahead, the Pont de l'Alma.

"That sculpture of a flame over there, that's where Princess Diana was killed in a car accident," Mrs. Bulgari said, pointing to the Pont de l'Alma tunnel. "It was ten years ago already." She sounded quite emotional. "I can still vividly remember her wedding in Saint Paul's Cathedral. Paris is where the Princess of Austria had been killed. And the Princess of Wales lost her life in Paris too. It's a weird coincidence."

Yeong-sin remembered how she had been fit to burst with excitement about watching the Princess of Wales's wedding. She was in the fourth grade at the time. Every day at school she and her friends talked incessantly about the wedding. About how Diana, a preschool teacher, had met the Prince of Wales for the first time, about her wedding dress and where the couple was going on their honeymoon, about why Korea had no royal family. Yeong-sin couldn't remember the faces of the friends she had had these discussions with—all of whom, she was sure, must have grieved over Diana's death.

The moment they reached the river cruise waiting area, Yeong-sin sank down into a chair.

Dusk had already fallen when Yeong-sin returned to her hotel. As soon as she got to her room, she turned on the TV. The hijackers were still holding the airplane. There was no word yet of who they were or what their motive was, but an unknown source cautiously speculated that the hijackers might be linked to Al-Qaeda. They were demanding that the airliner be refueled, but the Turkish authorities seemed to be playing for time. The news coverage switched to various local events celebrating Bastille Day. The festivities on the Champ de Mars were reaching their climax, while in the center of the city there were numerous protests against the government. There was no further news of the hijacked airplane. Yeong-sin changed her maxi pad and went down to the hotel lobby.

In one corner of the lobby there was a computer where guests could get onto the Internet. Yeong-sin pulled up the CNN website. It had quite detailed coverage of the hijacking. An expert was analyzing the situation and saying that the demand for refueling suggested that the hijackers seemed to be planning to take the plane to their base, somewhere in the Middle East. Various Middle Eastern countries that had a hostile relationship with the US were mentioned as possibilities. Yeong-sin went to the website of the airline her boyfriend worked for, got the customer service number, and tried to call. It was apparently swamped with people looking for information, and the line was busy. She trembled with a sense of utter helplessness. She tried to rid her mind of bad thoughts. But each time she tried, an even more catastrophic image washed over her. Her own uncontrollable thoughts scared her more than the hijackers did.

She was haunted by the image of her boyfriend's face from when she'd last seen him. She hated herself for having refused to respond when he had finally confessed to her that he had been married before. Finding herself trembling with bitter regret, she realized that she couldn't escape the naked truth that had come to her unannounced, and she knew that her world would never be the same again.

Yeong-sin found herself typing in another web address. It took her to the website her boyfriend had been so excited about, where you could replay the black box voice recordings of people. *Memento Mori*—"remember that you will die." Below the heading was a list of air crashes, including a Korean airliner that had been shot down by a Soviet fighter jet, and an American airplane that had hit the World Trade Center. And there were the messages people left when they were dying, trying to say something for the last time to someone they knew. Yeong-sin put on a headset and clicked play. Some voices were desperate, others were calm. Some people groaned and others sobbed. These people's last words, while they primarily conveyed the message that they were about to die, usually ended in a tremulous voice, like a first declaration of love. *Ouhibouka; Ya vas lyublyu; Te quiero; S'agapo; Aishiteru; Ik hou van jou; Saranghae; Ich liebe dich; Je t'aime; I love you ...* Yeong-sin remembered the question her boyfriend had asked her: Do you know what someone who knows they're about to die is most likely to say? She felt her eyes fill with tears.

Her boyfriend's phone still wasn't on two hours after the news broke that the hijackers had been overpowered and the passengers and crew were all safe. Perhaps he hadn't been involved in the hijacking at all. Still, the anxiety and dread that had been weighing on Yeong-sin's heart wouldn't abate. There were no other guests around, and a heavy silence hung in the lobby. She sat quietly in the corner, like a ghost. She ought to go to bed now if she was going to catch the Eurostar train early next morning. The man behind the front desk kept glancing at her, as if watching a piece of luggage that he had grudgingly undertaken to keep an eye on. Yeong-sin looked down vacantly at the cell phone she was clutching in her hand. She pressed a key and heard a dial tone. She swallowed. She wasn't sure how to describe the day that had seemed interminable, what she would go through the following day, or how she would feel if she were high up in the air and about to die. But she was sure of one thing: what she wanted to say to her boyfriend at that moment. She was determined to pronounce the familiar phrase that she had never said to anyone but had wanted to hear from someone else—a phrase that was, banal though it may be, the first spark of the flame of truth in her mind. Yeong-sin looked out the window. Barely impinging on the darkness, a street lamp shed a dim light, like the embodiment of a regret that kept someone from sleeping, watching over his bed as he lay awake. Finally, Yeong-sin heard her boyfriend's voice through the phone. Hesitatingly, she opened her mouth to speak.

"Where are you?"

Keeping vigil over those who had long gone to sleep and those who were unable to fall asleep, Bastille Day silently came to a close.

Father's Kitchen

I had completely forgotten about the Mimi's Kitchen set that I had longed for as a little boy. But memories are not expunged, they are just sealed up. It can take a month to unseal them, or it can take a half century. In my case, it took as long as it takes to reach adulthood, plus one phone call.

I swallowed and instinctively braced myself when I received the call from a high school classmate of mine. We had been out of touch for a long time, and I knew that when someone calls for the first time in ages it's often because they have a favor, big or small, to ask. He sounded quite upbeat. After we exchanged the usual platitudes—"How have you been?" and "It's been ages!"—a silence fell between us. The sort of tense silence that descends before someone gets to the point. I swallowed again.

Still sounding cheerful, my old classmate asked if I would have time to meet him that evening.

"Why?" I responded, and my voice sounded stilted to me. I immediately regretted having said it. I remembered a passage that I had learned by heart. *A refusal should be done pleasantly, even if you hope never again to see the person making the request. Remember that it's a small world, and you could easily run into this person again, at any time and in any place. So, if you have to refuse, do so, but without making an enemy. And do so as naturally as water flows. Remember—as naturally as water flows.*

"Let's go out for *soju* and roast pork belly and catch up," he said, laughing heartily.

Having already said "Why?" I couldn't even pretend that I already had an appointment. He sounded as if he really meant that he had suddenly missed me and decided to get in touch. I finally agreed to meet up with him. Still, I felt uneasy, particularly since

I had only ever gone out with him as part of a group. When he offered to come and meet me at my office, I couldn't help bracing myself again. He wasn't the type to go out of his way for other people's convenience. I was pretty sure something was up. I ran through the how-to-say-no skills I had learned. *Create a situation where you can say no comfortably. Let the other party decide on the date and place. The real enemy is not the other person's manipulative behavior but our own unwarranted feelings of guilt. Try to create a situation where you can refuse without feeling apologetic. Keep in mind this Sudanese proverb: The truly deadly enemy lies in ambush nowhere but in the shadow of your own house.*

Although I told him not to bother, my former classmate insisted on coming to my office. This time I was determined not to give in. Two weeks earlier I had ended up signing a contract to buy a car because I was unable to say no to an old friend from college. When she saw the contract that I'd brought home, my wife stopped speaking to me. If she had something urgent to say to me, she used our son as a messenger. In fact, we couldn't afford to keep two cars and we had to sell our other one, which was only four-years old. I would have felt better if she had snapped at me the way she usually did. To begin with, the silent treatment scared me. But as one week went by, and then another, I became more afraid that she would start to speak to me again. She would probably want to talk about getting a divorce.

To be honest, my innate inability to say no was the reason I had gotten married in the first place. I had been her private tutor. A hundred days before the university entrance exam, she badgered me into buying her a drink, since it was a tradition among the exam candidates to go out drinking a hundred days before the exam. So I took her to a bar where I, unable to say no when she offered me drinks, wound up drunk, kissing her, and starting to date her because she argued that I had no choice but to date her after having kissed her, and eventually marrying her since I was unable to end the relationship.

I didn't feel bitter, though. I consoled myself with the knowledge that I would have ended up married anyway because my inability to say no would have led me into marriage eventually. Yet a cloud still hung over me. It wasn't a question of regretting what might have been. Rather, it was that I was plagued by my pathological pattern of behavior: being incapable of saying no on the spot, bitterly regretting it immediately afterwards, and wanting desperately to punish myself.

A month ago I took the subway to work for the first time in a long while. My wife had said she wanted the car so that she could go for a drive with her friends. The train was just pulling out of Anguk Station when I heard a familiar pop song—"Holiday" by the Bee Gees. My mind instantly recalled a girl who had loved the song. We'd met at prep school after I'd failed the university entrance exam. That was years ago, but I could still vividly picture her captivating eyes against a bleak wilderness of dark soil.

The day before one of our monthly practice tests, I'd snuck out with the girl after lunch. Despite our determination to cut class, we had no particular adventure planned, so we just walked along until we came to a bus stop, where we got on a random bus. The bus drove for a long time, well past the outskirts of the city. We were the only remaining passengers when we got off at the last stop. And there, spread in front of us, was nothing but the black wasteland of a bare mountainside. Rusting train tracks meandered haphazardly across the empty landscape like the tracks of disoriented animals. The rails led into a tunnel at the foot of the mountain. The abandoned mine looked so bleak and dreary that even the most fearless adventurer wouldn't have had the nerve to explore it.

Nearby, under a large elm tree, there stood a small snack bar. It listed to one side like a boxer whose legs had gone limp, and its signboard was so beat-up that the words on it were barely discernible. Sitting on a low bamboo bench in front of the store, the girl and I each took one earbud and listened to music as we ate an ice cream. Warm breezes came sweeping across the black wasteland. I breathed in a burnt smell that was wafting in the air. It was the scent of the approaching summer. I quietly held the girl's hand. Right then, the Bee Gees's "Holiday" started to play.

Beauty never lasts as long as one hopes. The more you expect from it, the faster it fades. So it was with my first love, my love for that girl. One Sunday, early that summer, I was reading when I heard the phone ring. I dashed to pick it up only to find that Father, who had been roused from his nap, had gotten there before me. His eyes narrowed and his voice grew louder. He asked who the caller was and where they lived. Then, slamming down the receiver, he pulled on his clothes.

"Get dressed," he said to me.

"What for?" I asked.

"We're going out."

"Where?"

"You'll see."

His eyes were cold and I stopped asking questions.

We went out to the main road and, to my amazement, Father hailed a taxi. Normally he would carefully count out the coins for bus fare. I looked nervously at the back of his head as he sat next to the cab driver. I had no idea what was happening until Father pressed the doorbell of a house in an unfamiliar neighborhood. I was certain that whatever this was about it wasn't going to be any fun. Standing hidden behind Father, I stared at the blue metal gate with the name plate that I didn't recognize. I pictured the face of my grim fate beyond the gate, willing it to remain firmly closed. But it soon swung open with a squeal.

"Who is it?"

The deity of my grim fate was clearly a goddess rather than a god. The voice was that of a young girl. And it sounded familiar.

"You know Yeong-ho, don't you? I'm his father."

I peered around Father to see the girl. Apparently she had been watering the flowers in the yard, as she was holding a hose. Seeing me, she instantly dropped the hose, and her eyes grew wide. We both froze simultaneously.

"Are your parents in?" Father asked, speaking so loudly that anyone inside the house was bound to hear him.

"This is really your father?" the girl's wide-eyed expression seemed to ask. I shook my head. As vigorously as I could.

When the girl's mother showed up carrying a basket of dirty

laundry, Father launched into his harangue.

"My son can't afford to fail again. He has to get into law school this year, no matter what. He has no time to date girls. You'd better watch that girl and stop her from calling a boy who needs to focus on his studies."

I just wished I could disappear. I wanted to die. By opening that blue gate, Father had opened the gates of hell.

The sound of the pop song came nearer as a man in a navy suit appeared carrying a suitcase. The music was coming from a CD player attached to the suitcase. The man turned the volume down and, looking around him, began to speak.

"Good morning to you all, my fellow passengers. Please forgive the interruption. But may I have your attention for a moment please? I'd like to show you a product that will never disappoint you. This special edition CD collection contains a selection of golden oldies. I guarantee that the recordings are all original. A rare, superb collection of seventy of the most beautiful songs ever recorded all on these seven CDs, and all for an unbelievably low price, just 25,000 won."

The man turned the volume up again and looked around. None of the passengers appeared interested. He began to hand out a booklet, pressing it on the seated passengers who had a hand free to take a copy from him. I skimmed it. Most of the songs were ones that I used to listen to a lot in middle and high school.

The song was reaching its climax. I could once again feel the girl's hand in mine as we listened to the song. Her soft, silky, warm skin. It felt as though a small bird was nestling in my hand. I was still savoring the lingering memory when the salesman came up to me.

"I guarantee top quality sound. You'll never regret it. If you find anything wrong with the product, you can contact me at any time and I'll get you a new one right away."

The man must have read something in my face. He worked especially hard on me and even gave me his business card. It didn't look like he was going to give up easily. I awkwardly accepted his business card—how could I not when I'd never even refused to take a flyer handed to me on the street?

"Thank you so much for your purchase," the man said in a loud voice. "You, sir, deserve this special offer: just 25,000 won."

Now that I had accepted his business card, it was impossible for me to ignore him. To make things worse, I felt all the other passengers' eyes on me. I hastily took out my wallet.

I heard the Bee Gees's "Holiday" once again that day, in the subway on my way home. It was the same situation all over again, except that the man in the navy suit was replaced by a woman in a black suit, and the price was different. The woman showed up with a suitcase, turned the volume down, took a look around, and started to speak.

"Please forgive the interruption. But may I have your attention for a moment please? I'd like to show you a product that will never disappoint you. This special edition CD collection contains a selection of golden oldies. I guarantee that the recordings are all original. A rare, superb collection of seventy of the most beautiful songs ever recorded all on these seven CDs, and all for an unbelievably low price: just 23,000 won."

The woman turned the volume back up again and looked around. None of the passengers appeared interested. The woman began to hand out a booklet, urging each seated passenger to take a look. And yet no one was interested.

My mouth became dry and my heart started beating faster as the woman approached me. I steeled myself, determined to say no this time, but I was anxious about how things would turn out. My fear that I would end up giving in grew as the woman came closer to me. Cold sweat stood out from every pore of my body. I just wanted to make a dash for the next car, and I envied the passengers who hadn't been given a booklet. I felt as though my heart was about to explode.

The saleswoman finally came right up to me. Clenching my jaw, I tried to hand the booklet back to her, but she wouldn't take it from me, and simply stood there. I looked up in spite of myself. Our eyes met. She looked at me imploringly. Her eyes were unusually big. Like those of the girl I'd listened to the music with. Not knowing what to do, I fidgeted with the booklet, and the woman began to speak.

"Thank you so much for your purchase. You, sir, deserve this special offer, just 23,000 won."

I felt everyone's gaze directed at me. I froze, as if I had just been caught misbehaving. I desperately wished for the situation to end. I felt rather relieved once I had given her the money.

When the woman disappeared into another train car and the passengers shifted their attention away from me, I compared the two booklets, clinging to the vague hope that they might be different. But they were identical. I wanted to bite my tongue until it bled, and die. I felt as if all the passengers—indeed the whole world—were laughing at me. Suffocated by self-loathing, I couldn't even breathe. I stood up impulsively and walked toward the door. Outside the window, the darkness was deep and abysmal. I felt as if I were standing on the edge of a cliff. When the subway stopped, a man's head came into view. His face looked young, but his hair was white. His broad smile beamed from a poster on a concrete column. It was advertising a book. The words of the title were printed across his face. *Learn to Say No and Be a Winner*. This book might have been written specifically for me.

I eventually met up with my old high school classmate. I was less anxious than when we had spoken on the phone. As I watched pork belly sizzling on the cast-iron skillet I found I was able to relax. It felt good to eat a piece of tender pork and a slice of lightly cooked *gimchi* wrapped in lettuce, and to reminisce about high school.

My classmate remembered a lot. He recalled what was in the love letter that I had written on his behalf, and he even recited the poem I had written for him for the student exhibition. He wasn't the only student who had asked me to ghostwrite for them. They had all had different excuses but the same motivation: they said they needed to save face when their girlfriends came to see their poems. The only time I had ever written poetry was when other people asked me to.

"Our Korean teacher was smart. You remember what he said after he read through all the poems? 'Well, it looks like the poems were all written by one guy.' My heart fell when he said that, but what he said next was a huge relief. 'You guys are all bad imitators of Jun-seok!'"

He laughed as he mimicked the Korean language teacher. Throughout the year, Jun-seok had gotten the best grades in our class.

"I wrote a poem for him too," I said.

"I knew it! That asshole was always so smug. Now I know he was just an arrogant snob!"

My former classmate took a sip of *soju* and went on talking.

"It's a crying shame no one cut him down to size by beating him out for first in our class. If only you'd made that free throw!"

"What free throw?"

"In mid-terms. Remember? You narrowly missed being first in the class because you screwed up the PE test. Don't you remember? I still can't believe you missed all ten shots, even if you were nervous."

He sounded regretful, as if he were talking about himself.

What he was recalling was true, but it was far from the whole truth. I had been nervous during the PE test, not because I was afraid I'd miss the shot but because I was afraid I'd make it. I deliberately tried to miss, all ten times. The entire episode that he had been recounting had happened by sheer luck. I had gotten surprisingly good grades, while Jun-seok had messed up his midterms because he had been devoting all his time to a girl. I felt rather relieved when Jun-seok broke up with her.

"Well, at least you always had the best grades in Korean. I thought you would be making a living as a writer. Never thought you'd end up working with a calculator. Do you still do any writing?"

He poured *soju* into my glass. I felt my heart ache, as if I had suddenly heard what had become of a former lover. I had first become fascinated by poetry when I read "Annabel Lee" by Edgar Allan Poe in middle school.

It was many and many a year ago,
In a kingdom by the sea,
That a maiden there lived whom you may know
By the name of Annabel Lee;
And this maiden she lived with no other thought
Than to love and be loved by me.

. . .

But our love it was stronger by far than the love
Of those who were older than we—
Of many far wiser than we—
And neither the angels in Heaven above
Nor the demons down under the sea
Can ever dissever my soul from the soul
Of the beautiful Annabel Lee.

I had been overcome by what stirred inside me when I encountered the poem. It felt as though I had lived ten thousand years in a fleeting moment. My peers, whose facial hair was starting to grow, boasted and bragged, but to my eyes they were like apes. Surrounded day in, day out by those animals, I grew terribly lonely. Every night, to comfort my wildly lonely heart, I devoured poetry: Rilke, Keats, Proust, Rimbaud, Lorca. The more I nourished my lonely heart, the more my body became gaunt. Father had black goat tonic made up for me.

"What about me?" my younger sister complained, pouting.

"Your brother is staying up all night studying, you know," Father explained.

"Huh! I don't believe burying his head in poetry every night amounts to studying."

Father's face froze and went pale, like pork fat in winter. After that, every time Father spotted me holding a thin book, he switched off the light. When the light went out, a world died away.

"I thought you'd be the first in our class to get married," I said, pouring *soju* into my old classmate's glass. "I'm really surprised that here you are, pushing forty, and you're still single and just dating girls. When are you going to get hitched?"

"Oh God, I'm such an airhead!"

He rummaged in his pocket and pulled something out. It was a wedding invitation.

Here we go, finally, I said to myself.

His wedding was going to be in our hometown. I frowned inquisitively. The bride's name wasn't unfamiliar to me. Woo-ju. Hwang Woo-ju.

"Do you remember her?" he asked, grinning.

"Oh!" I exclaimed, and he nodded.

"I ran into her at a rest stop on the highway last *Chuseok*.[11] I was on my way back home to see my parents. Like me, she was still single. She said she had broken up with her boyfriend just three days previously. A guy she had been dating for six years. She said she had been burning her ex's letters when she remembered a letter that I had sent her, and suddenly decided to go back home. She had kept the letter somewhere in her parents' house but had forgotten about it in the meantime. Now I have to agree that destiny exists. And I think you played the role of matchmaker for us. So . . ."

He lowered his voice. Here he goes, just as expected, I thought. He wouldn't have needed to see me alone unless he had something else in mind besides giving me his wedding invitation. I swallowed nervously.

"I don't know what I was thinking. I lied to her and told her I own a small apartment. I could probably cobble together loans from here and there, but it's still . . . The thing is, I need to apply for a bank loan of fifty million won and they want me to get someone to co-sign the loan agreement . . . Is there any way you could . . ."

The atmosphere had become heavy and oppressive.

"I'm not asking you to answer me right now," my classmate said in a barely audible voice.

I looked down. Beads of sweat formed on my forehead, as my wife's angry face passed before my eyes. The same expression she wore when she threw out the CDs of old pop songs, crumpled up the life insurance contract, and tore up the payment plan for the water purifier. Then some phrases from the how-to-say-no book

---

11 Korean autumn holiday. (Translators' note)

came into my mind. *The sooner you say no the better. Decline right away. Do not avert your eyes when you say no, or people won't believe you really mean it.* Biting my lip, I looked my old classmate straight in the eyes. He had the same look on his face that he'd had a long time ago when he asked me to write a love letter for him. It was the look that the world's unluckiest man would wear when he realized that his one chance at happiness had been ruined by some minor mishap. The desperate look of a man whose ultimate fate depends on whether someone else says yes or no. How differently would my classmate's life have turned out if I had refused to write a love letter for him back then? I was frightened and embarrassed to think that someone's future depended on whether I said yes or no.

"Well, all right." The words slipped out in spite of me. I scratched my head like a student who, caught daydreaming, had blurted out a stupid answer to an unexpected question. My old classmate was delighted. He grabbed my hands and said I was his only true friend. After fervently expressing his gratitude, he added, "You won't mind officiating at my wedding, will you?" He now sounded as if he were asking a trivial favor. I sweated like an animal caught in a trap. A trap I had laid for myself.

"Are you all right?" he asked, staring at me with a puzzled look.

Our son sat in the front passenger seat and sulked the whole way to my hometown.

"Don't you like visiting Grandpa?" I asked.

"I need to watch the final episode of Starcraft!"

"You can watch it at Grandpa's."

"Grandpa doesn't have cable," the kid whined, on the verge of tears.

"That's just like the old man! Cable costs peanuts," said my wife scathingly.

This spontaneous family trip was her idea. And she made no secret of the fact that she planned this visit so that she could get out of attending the family New Year's gathering in two weeks' time. Of course, that's what my kid had told me.

"Honey, tell your dad to drop you off at a movie theater near the wedding reception hall," said my wife as we took the highway exit toward my hometown. "And tell him that after the movie you'll call and ask him to come pick you up."

"Dad, did you hear what Mom said? What movie are we going to see?" the boy asked, craning his neck and turning to speak to his mother.

"Whatever you want, Honey," said my wife, in an irritatingly nasal tone of voice.

My father often used to bring home free movie tickets. People would give him these tickets in exchange for allowing them to put up movie posters in his snack bar. It was always one pair of tickets, and they were always movies that had been released some time ago. He didn't always bring the tickets home. I could see why, if the movie was R-rated, but I had no clue why this was always the case when they were box office hits but not R-rated. My sister asked Father about it a couple of times, but he never gave her a clear answer.

My sister and I would play rock-paper-scissors for the movie tickets. The winner got both tickets. She wasn't willing to split the tickets, since she didn't want to sit by herself in a movie theater. So I suggested playing rock-paper-scissors. I wasn't willing to let the type of movie determine which of us got the tickets, because I didn't want to have to admit to my sister that I liked melodramas.

The winter of the year I sat the university entrance exam for the second time, a movie of a type I liked was released. It was a love story where the male protagonist died suddenly in an accident but his ghost stayed close to his girlfriend to protect her. It was a huge success, and its heartrending theme music could be heard on every street corner. Like me, my sister waited eagerly for Father to bring home tickets for this movie. She even declared that this time the tickets were going to be hers — period! I objected and said we should play rock-paper-scissors, same as always, but in fact I didn't expect Father to give us any tickets this time. Since the movie had done so well, the odds were that he wouldn't have any tickets for us. My sister was impatient and nagged him about it, but, as I anticipated, it did no good. Father explained that he had given the tickets away to someone who had asked for them.

When I went by myself to see the movie, there was already a long line at the box office. I waited over half an hour to buy a ticket. I was fidgeting with the ticket and trying to decide how to kill the two hours until the next screening, when I saw something that left me completely floored. Some distance away, Father, his hat pulled down low on his head, exchanged a few words with a young man, and then exchanged something for cash. The young woman who was standing arm in arm with the man jumped for joy when her boyfriend took two tickets from Father. Then Father, licking the thumb of his right hand, counted the cash, folded it in half, stuck it into his trouser pocket, and started to walk in my direction toward the main road. I quickly turned away. After a little while, I turned back around and spotted him in the distance. I couldn't take my eyes off him until he limped around a corner and out of sight. He had fallen off a ladder when he worked as a carpenter. The accident had damaged his hip and caused him to limp. That was when I was three. In cold weather his limp was more pronounced.

I had to sneak out of the wedding reception when my son called. I pretended I had to go to the restroom. Otherwise I was afraid someone would insist that I stayed, and I wouldn't be able to say no.

We ate dinner at a restaurant near Father's house. The boy said he wanted to eat sashimi. His mother must have put him up to it. Looking at the menu, Father was astonished at how expensive the food was, and yet he ate it all up. When he chewed, he made a noise like two blocks of wood hitting one another. His new dentures didn't seem to fit well. Clearly he had once again had them made by an unlicensed technician. Every time Father's teeth clacked my son's eyes grew big and round. The kid imitated his grandfather, clicking his teeth and opening his mouth as wide as he could.

"Naughty boy!" said my wife.

Father ordered *soju*. My wife frowned when he poured it into a water glass. The boy ordered a soda, half-filled his glass and clinked it against his grandfather's glass. My wife frowned again. Father poured *soju* into my glass this time, but I didn't drink any of it. After drinking two bottles of *soju* all by himself, he cleared his throat several times and began to speak.

"You know Mrs. Park, the fruit seller next to my snack bar, don't you? Would you be free to come and have lunch with me and her tomorrow? I'll pay."

A sudden silence fell over us. My wife stared at me, her chopsticks motionless in midair. I couldn't believe my ears. Partly because this invitation to lunch came completely out of the blue, but mainly because the way he had just spoken to me was so uncharacteristic. He had never — not even once — asked me to do something, but had always given me orders. I felt as if, up until this moment, I had been deceived.

"No way!" I shouted, as if a terrifying nightmare had caused me to scream in my sleep. The boy, who was now leaning against a wall and engrossed in his Nintendo game, looked up at me with a startled look on his face. Father's ears turned fiery red and he idly fumbled with his glass, not saying a word.

"You're not going to leave right after breakfast, are you?" Father asked the next morning. I hesitated, not knowing how to answer.

"How about going to the zoo a little later?" Father looked at his grandson.

"It's boring," the boy replied with a vacant expression.

"There are monkeys, tigers, and even elephants," Father said, looking serious.

"What else do they have?"

"There are pandas too."

"Are you certain?"

"I sure am," Father replied, stroking the child's head.

My wife shook her head and gave me a disapproving look, but I ignored her.

The rice felt like sand in my mouth. I hadn't slept well. I had been kicked out of the guest room where I had gone to bed. I had taken my pillow and comforter to the living room, since my wife complained that she couldn't get a wink of sleep because of my snoring.

"Snorgk-phbuph, snorgk-phbuph." The boy had been awake too, and he imitated my snores.

The living room was cold and drafty, but I couldn't move into the main bedroom, because Father was sleeping there. I curled up and was just beginning to fall asleep when I was woken by the sound of the door being flung open. It was Father. He went into the bathroom and relieved himself, without closing the door. I could hear him clicking in the darkness. His stomach seemed to be upset, because he went back and forth to the bathroom repeatedly. I was kept awake all night by the noise of the door opening, his dentures clicking, the toilet flushing, and the door being closed again.

When Father went out to buy cigarettes, my wife finally lost her temper. "You never even set foot in the kitchen when you're here! And yet you're willing to cook at home. What's your problem? You must realize how ghastly it is for me, cooking in this tiny, dirty kitchen. I'm not doing the dishes. You can do them!"

I was relieved that she had started to speak to me again. Even if it was thanks to Father's cramped, nasty kitchen. Father never used to let me near it. He would yell at me and tell me to get out and go memorize another English word if I had time to spend in the kitchen. He would often tell my sister to work in the kitchen, but she would run to her room and lock herself in, saying that she had to study. So Father always had the kitchen to himself.

I stacked up the empty plates and bowls and carried them into the kitchen, which was too small for more than one person at a time. It had originally been a utility room. Two years earlier, Father had remodeled by combining the existing kitchen with the living room, because he had said that as it was, the living room was too small when the whole family was there. This was right after my sister had had her first child. In fact, the whole family hadn't gotten together even once since. My sister left the baby with her in-laws and was spending all her time studying for the bar exam. She didn't even show up on Father's birthday or for the anniversary of Mother's death. For nine years she had done nothing but study for the bar exam.

The pots and pans and all the kitchen utensils were in terrible condition, as if they had been picked out of the trash. A ladle was missing its handle, and the inside of a pot was scorched. Besides being shabby, they were all unbelievably dirty. Each and every item in the kitchen, from the cups to the iron pots, was covered in so much caked-on dirt that there was no way of telling what color it was supposed to be. A sticky substance, the residue of hundreds of soup spills, coated the gas stove. There were greasy rings around the sink, and the knobs on all the drawers were stained from having been touched countless times by dirty hands. Nothing had changed. From the outset, the word "cleanliness" had never been part of Father's vocabulary. He would use a dirty rag and then go right ahead and rinse rice without stopping to wash his hands, and he often left bowls and spoons to dry with specks of food still on them. I would wash them again when he wasn't around. I stayed away from the kitchen when Father was cooking, primarily because he wouldn't allow me in, but also because I didn't want to know how he cooked.

I scoured the filth off the dishes using a pad of steel wool and plenty of dish soap. By the time I'd finished, my arms were aching. I covered the bowls of leftovers with plastic wrap and put them in the refrigerator. I noticed there were only a few jars of *gimchi* left. Then I found bottles of *soju* in the door of the fridge, and some fruit—apples, pears, persimmons, and oranges—on the bottom shelf. They all looked fresh. I tried to remember what Mrs. Park, the fruit seller, looked like, but I couldn't recall her face.

In the end, our son didn't see any pandas. He saw only a few animals: a couple of penguins, a sleepy tiger, three monkeys that had gotten away from their group, a peacock that seemed to have forgotten how to display its tail, and five turkeys. Most of the zoo animals were curled up indoors because of the cold weather. The boy kept whining to his grandfather that there was no panda, and Father could only say that he had seen one the last time. Exhausted by trying to find the panda enclosure, Father kept having to stop and sit on a bench or hunker down on the ground to catch his breath. There were more animals in the cages than visitors walking around looking at them. By the time we left the zoo, not one of us—Father, my wife, the boy, or me—had a word to say. And it wasn't just because the harsh, icy wind had numbed our faces.

My wife suggested stopping by the gallery next to the zoo. She was keen on all kinds of exhibitions and went to a lot of them. Apparently she wanted to do something to make up for what had so far been a boring day. The child was unhappy and kept complaining about the cold, but my wife coaxed him by saying it would be warm inside, and she led the way.

The gallery was showing the work of a young artist. The theme was "Space." Most of what was on display was installation art. And many of the works were highly unusual, such as an hourglass as tall as a man but without any sand in it, and a room lined with innumerable hand mirrors.

In keeping with the theme, the exhibition space—shaped like an angular letter C—had been divided up in such a way as to create various curves and corners. Moving between the artworks, all differing in size and shape, viewers had to go around one corner after another. I kept losing sight of Father, because he was stopping all the time to rest. Every time I went round a corner, I had to wait a long time for him to catch up. The boy also kept disappearing out of sight, dashing ahead like a disobedient puppy. Although my wife called after him and stopped him several times, there was nothing she could do to keep him from getting bored.

"Wait behind and take care of your father," my wife said. Then she hurried off in the direction the child had disappeared.

As I came around the next corner, I froze to the spot. A pink kitchen stood before my eyes. Everything in it was pink and made of plastic: the sink, the table, and the forks on the table. The title of the work was Mimi's Kitchen. It was a life-sized version of a toy kitchen. A life-sized Barbie doll was sitting at the table. Mimi's Kitchen was what I had wanted more than anything else in the world when I was eight years old.

The day before my first exam in elementary school, Father promised me that he would buy anything I wanted if I came top in my class, and I could think of nothing but Mimi's Kitchen. The maxim Father had drilled into us was "Be the head of a snake rather than the tail of a dragon." Whenever drowsiness would sweep over me, I would shake it off by conjuring up the image of Mimi's Kitchen, and I would drive myself even harder to study for the exams. And in the end, my longing for Mimi's Kitchen won me the glory of being top of the class. Father was overcome with joy when he read my report card.

"Well done, my son," he said. And then he asked, "What do you want me to buy for you?"

"Mimi's Kitchen," I answered without a second's hesitation.

Father looked perplexed, and my sister burst out laughing.

"Whose kitchen?" he asked again, still looking puzzled.

"That's a girl's toy! Girly, girly, girly!" my sister jeered.

A cloud fell over Father's face.

The next day, when Father came home drunk, what I saw in his hand was not Mimi's Kitchen but a toy machine gun.

Every time I passed the toy store I would stop. Mimi's Kitchen was in the center of the window display. Tapping me on the shoulder a boy in my class asked, "Do you want it too?"

Looking around furtively I said, "You too?"

The boy nodded and said, "I've got the Tiger Tank and the Mustang Plane, but not that one."

My eyes alighted on a kit for a model aircraft carrier next to the Mimi's Kitchen set.

"I want the new machine gun too," he murmured. "Damn it, why do we only have one birthday a year?"

"Have you saved up any pocket money?" I asked.

I sold him my toy machine gun for half its original price. To be precise, he agreed to give me all the money he had saved, and that was how much it turned out to be. My heart was heavy. It was not that I regretted having sold an item that was almost brand new for just half what it was worth, but that I realized it would be very hard to raise enough money to buy Mimi's Kitchen.

Though it took the Creator six days to make His world, it took me only five to decide to raid my sister's plastic piggy bank. I had never before touched anything that wasn't mine. My hands shook as I tried to widen the slot of the piggy bank with a knife, and my heart stopped every time a coin fell to the floor. The man who owned the toy store gave a strange smirk as he handed me the Mimi's Kitchen set.

I set up Mimi's Kitchen in the attic and in the beam of a flashlight, the pink kitchen looked superb. I had so much fun playing with it in my perfect world. An elegant pink paradise. I imagined that if only I had a real kitchen as perfect as this one, I could make the sort of magical dishes that exist only in fairy tales. At the beginning of the semester we had been given our student profile cards, and in the space for "dream job," I had written "the world's greatest chef."

My paradise didn't last long. My sister finally noticed that her piggy bank had become lighter. Clutching it to her chest, she burst out crying. I couldn't stay silent forever and confessed. And the result was simply merciless. My Mimi's Kitchen was shoved into a trash can, and I was tied to a telephone pole on the street outside my house. Father's eyes were burning when he threw out the toy kitchen, but when he tied me to the pole they were dark with sorrow and concern.

An occasional passer-by laughed at me. I blushed with shame. Maybe it would have been less shameful if I'd been tied with a rope or cord. Father probably chose a plastic hose on purpose. At least the alley was not busy, to my relief.

The plastic hose was not designed for tying someone up. After a while, it loosened and slipped off. When it fell to the ground it coiled, like a snake. And I stared at it, like a slow-witted kid contemplating the meaning of what he realized too late was a joke. My instinct was to run off, but I struggled to stay put. I was stubbornly determined not to move an inch until Father came to take me home.

Stars had come out. The sky had become as black as if it had been plastered with shoe polish. The stars looked to me like white pebbles that someone had dropped along a path to help find the way back home. The smell of fried fish wafted from a neighbor's kitchen. My stomach gurgled, and tears welled up in my eyes. I didn't deny that I had misbehaved when I'd raided my sister's piggy bank, but I still felt I'd been wronged. It was Father who had broken his promise at the outset. It felt like I was up against the entire world, not just against the utility pole. A pigsty of a world. A middle-aged man stopped and asked what I was doing. I didn't reply.

"Your father is Mr. Kim, the owner of the snack bar, isn't he?" the man asked, looking me up and down.

"No!" I answered, shouting with all my might. I wished that my voice would reach the distant stars and break their spell, transforming into a golden coach to come pick me up and drive me to my real father. I clenched my teeth to stop my tears. I swore I would never make a deal with Father ever again, and I would never again come top of the class to make him happy.

As it grew darker more stars came out. Numerous constellations spread across the sky. One looked like a sink, another like a table. Mimi's Kitchen which I had seen dumped into a trash can had actually risen up into the sky. There it shone brightly, even without a flashlight. Never again would I put down "the world's greatest chef" as my dream job on my student profile card.

When I left the gallery my wife and son were at a convenience store across the street. My wife was drinking coffee and the boy was eating cup noodles.

"After we drop your father off at his house, let's go straight home," my wife said.

I bought some snacks for us to eat in the car. Father hadn't shown up by the time the child was finished eating his noodles. I left the store and went back into the art gallery. I retraced my footsteps for some distance before I found the old man.

He was sitting on a chair in the Mimi's Kitchen set, facing the Barbie doll. Some people shook their heads disdainfully as they passed by, while others burst out laughing. I went up to Father and saw that he was dozing off and murmuring in his sleep. His face looked older than usual, probably because of the lighting. His head kept nodding, and his hands lay between his knees. He looked like a person begging for something. He snored. "Snorgk-phbuph, snorgk-phbuph." The sound of an old locomotive laboring along. I reached into the shopping bag and took out the tangerines, the packets of hard-boiled eggs and bottles of water, and placed them on the table. For the first time in my life, I set the table for Father. Then I carefully laid my hand on his shoulder and shook him gently.

Love — It Always Involves Hatred

Critical Afterword by Gwon Hee-cheol

From a Free Agent . . .

After breaking off his engagement to Regine Olsen, Søren Kierke-gaard wrote:

> Marry, and you will regret it; don't marry, you will also re-gret it; marry or don't marry, you will regret it either way . . . you will regret both. This, gentlemen, is the essence of all philosophy. (*Either/Or: A Fragment of Life*)

The lesson is that we should put off making any decision for as long as we can. Once we decide, the cogs start moving, and as soon as they catch us, we are doomed. We are doomed to the conse-quences of our decision, the consequences of those consequences, the whirlwind of subsequent consequences, a turmoil of regret and confusion and commotion. Marry your beautiful girlfriend, and you will watch her waist grow thicker and thicker as you lis-ten to incessant nagging from those sweet smiling lips of hers. You will find not only that she becomes a bore, but also discover how she and her family interfere with your life plans, whatever they may be. Then you will rue your hasty decision. Refuse to marry your girl, and you will end up a cruel man who, pursuing only his own happiness, has sucked his woman dry. Or you will become a pathetic individual incapable of shaking off his regret at having destroyed the happiness that could have been his if he had not blown his chance at marriage, and who, at every mishap, small or great, will feel guilty for having left his girlfriend. Whether or not you marry, you are doomed to regret.

In order to avoid being trapped in a turmoil of regret, confusion and commotion, we should guard against getting caught in a situation where we have to decide between two courses of action. As soon as you find yourself relishing sweet, beautiful moments, and before you are burdened with the responsibilities that arise from a decision, you must flee. Love only as long as you're free to go, and aren't forced to decide whether or not you'll commit yourself to your woman.

Wait a second. Doesn't this sound like the advice of a shamelessly self-indulgent commitment-phobe? A clever, selfish person who avoids trouble by refusing to engage in the significant events of life? But the truth is that, satisfied only with fleeting pleasures and believing that they are all that life amounts to, this self-indulgent freewheeler negates his own life. He lacks passion, the kind of passion that, according to existentialism, an individual is supposed to have, and he shirks engagement and responsibility.

In his debut novella *An Outsider* (1993) Kim Kyung-uk delved into the devastated inner self of a young character. His meticulous exploration of the inner self of this character is similar to the way the lonely drifters examine their own lives in his early short stories. Although they have options beyond seeking pleasure or embracing a cause for the sake of society, they limit their choice to one or the other and always hesitate when faced with the fate they impose upon themselves. In this way they defer their decisions as long as possible to postpone taking part in life in any meaningful way. Paradoxically, however, they are eager to study the feelings of distress and anxiety they experience in this state of hesitancy and indecision.

These disengaged characters could, in some ways, be considered recluses who live entirely in their own emotional world. Instead of engaging fully in life, they acknowledge the moments of anxiety and agitation they experience, and derive satisfaction from believing that they are serious about life because they fully appreciate the depth of their anxiety and agitation.

... *To a Warrior*

Kim Kyung-uk's uncommitted characters reach a different stage of development in *God Has No Grandchildren*, the author's sixth collection of short stories. His despairing drifters no longer simply equivocate, but decide to act, even if only by small degrees.

In "The Queen of Romance," the aimless central character doesn't look so much like a freewheeling procrastinator. When this male protagonist, a photographer, is asked to visit a bestselling novelist known as the Queen of Romance, and to take pictures of her library, he reads all five of her romance novels and decides that they are merely overblown, contrived love stories. He has, it seems, no great hopes of his meeting with the author.

However, during his visit, the main character experiences two critical moments. After taking photos of the author's library, he gets into his car to return to Seoul when he receives a text message from his girlfriend. "Maybe I should register my marriage. Don't you agree?" What is this text supposed to suggest? As a carefree individual, the photographer had previously declined to make any commitment to his girlfriend. And she, hoping to make her boyfriend clarify the nature of their relationship, asked him "Do you mind if I go on a blind date?" And the commitment-phobic free agent answered, "Do as you please." So his girlfriend met a man on a blind date and the man seemed promising. Later, the girlfriend asked the protagonist a second question "Maybe I should get married. Don't you agree?" The freewheeler replied simply, "Why are you asking me?" His girlfriend then married the man, but, as many couples do nowadays, she postponed registering the marriage.

The free agent's girlfriend asks him a third question, the one he receives the day he visits the Queen of Romance: "Maybe I should register my marriage. Don't you agree?" Will you now make up your mind, because once I record this marriage everything will be over between you and me? The free agent replies, "I'm sorry." This almost amounts to Do as you please or Why are you asking me? and seems to mean, I will stop being part of your life from now on, and I won't let myself get sucked into the vortex of consequences and the turmoil of regret.

The second critical event occurs when the free agent can't get his car to start. After calling his mechanic, he goes back into the Queen of Romance's house to wait. At dinner, the author asks him to think of a *chengyu*, and he comes up with *"Ju-ma-gan-san."* Then he listens as the author interprets the Chinese four-character idiom in light of his mindset, particularly his love life. "You're afraid of many things, aren't you? You're afraid of loving someone, and far more afraid of being loved by someone. You're afraid of being hurt and even more afraid of causing pain. That's why you don't want to get off your horse and make a commitment." The author sees into the unattached narrator's mind. Having been so accurately analyzed by the author, he likely can't sleep a wink all night, haunted by the vision of "[a]n old man on horseback who had been constantly hounded by fear, night and day." Early next morning he hurriedly leaves the Queen of Romance's house. However, when he gets to Seoul he suddenly turns his car around. He returns just to get the Queen of Romance's autograph for his girlfriend. As he tells the author his girlfriend's name, his voice trembles. And here we can glimpse a small but critical moment of change in his noncommittal attitude. For our focus is not on whether he will get his girlfriend back, but on how he finally leaves his position of safety and resolves to throw himself into his girlfriend's life and thus into his own. By the time we read what he says near the end of the story — "I knew I didn't really have to, but I turned around all the same. I just felt like it" — aren't we supposed to conclude that the freewheeling narrator has finally regained his long-lost appetite for living and will shortly take his seat again at the table of life?

The metaphor of the recovered appetite for life or sitting down again at the table of life recalls the closing scene of "Father's Kitchen"—the last of the nine stories in *God Has No Grandchildren*. At the end of this story, the detached protagonist, who hasn't had a good relationship with his father, happens to go with his father to an art gallery. After seeing an exhibition on the theme of Space, the protagonist leaves the gallery and waits outside for his father to come out. When he thinks he has been waiting long enough he goes back inside to find his father dozing off in an installation piece — a life-size Mimi's Kitchen set. At that moment, something stirs within the protagonist, prompting him to set the table for his father for the first time in his life. But, what does this closing scene — where the unengaged narrator sets the table for his father for the first time — have to do with the topic of recovered appetite and re-taking one's seat at the table of life? To see the connection, we need to look at what happened between the disconnected narrator and his father in the past and how they became estranged.

When he was a first grader, the young narrator brought home his report card which showed that he had come first in his class. Delighted by the boy's achievement, his father promises to buy him anything he wants. When the young protagonist says he wants a Mimi's Kitchen, the father cannot accept that his little boy wants such a girlish toy. Disillusioned by his father's broken promise, the boy renounces his dream of being the world's best chef and resolves never again in his entire life to be first in his class or give his father any reason for happiness.

Believing that he has had his life's dream taken from him, the young protagonist resists taking responsibility for his own future, as if to say that whoever destroys a person's dream should take responsibility for that person's life. He in fact relinquishes his life to others.

But when as an adult the narrator visits his father and stands in his father's small, dirty kitchen again, he is no longer unengaged. He recalls how his father used to drive him out of the kitchen into his room, shouting that he was to focus on his studies, and how his father, as a single parent, took charge of all the household chores and sacrificed his life to bring up his family. As he reflects on his childhood, he realizes how tough his father's life must have been and how selfless his commitment to his family was. He finally decides to take his seat again at the table of life.

The protagonist's recognition of the true nature of his father's life culminates in the last scene of the story when the narrator finds his father nodding off in the installation piece. "His head kept nodding, and his hands lay between his knees. He looked like a person begging for something." Then the protagonist "reached into the shopping bag and took out the tangerines, the packets of hard-boiled eggs, and bottles of water, and placed them on the table." The pink fairy-tale-like table, part of the Mimi's Kitchen set, represents the disconnected protagonist's recovered appetite for life and his setting the table for his father for the first time symbolizes what, in his state of isolation, has long been missing: sincere commitment to the people around him.

To return to "The Queen of Romance," when we read the last two sentences of the story—"I told the Queen of Romance my girlfriend's name. My voice trembled."—it is clear that this passive protagonist has undergone something significant during his stay at the author's house, and has ended up modifying his initial opinion of the romance writer. His initial dismissal of the author's novels as merely overblown, sentimental love stories gives way to the realization that something has been lacking in his life and that he now needs that something.

Before his transformation at the end of the story, the noncommittal protagonist of "The Queen of Romance" finds the "overblown" and "superfluous" sentiment of her novels distasteful. Yet it is that kind of sentiment that self-indulgent freewheelers usually lack, and that very sentiment is what they need in order to become responsible, ethical individuals. Only by indulging in what they previously considered to be excessive can they fully engage in life and find the true meaning of existence.

In "The Ups and Downs of Hurricane Joe," the implication is that Hurricane Joe, a former boxer who'd had a promising career, steals the cremation urn and eats the ashes of the former world boxing champion who he believes caused him to be eliminated at the weigh-in for their fight. This represents the extremism of Hurricane Joe who desperately wants his life back, and at the same time seems to declare that this innate excessiveness has determined the ups and downs of Hurricane Joe's life. It is perhaps for this reason that the narrator, who only ghostwrites for a living and can't write "an authentic story," is drawn to Hurricane Joe.

"[The] ugly old man on a horse" in "The Queen of Romance," who has spent his whole life fleeing from responsibilities and commitments, transforms into a warrior in the story "God Has No Grandchildren." In an extreme situation the central character of this story chooses not to remain passive, but to become a warrior for the sake of love. This transformation reminds us of another scene in a different story, "Bastille Day," where Yeong-sin—the female protagonist who is chronically uncommitted—suddenly realizes how much she loves her boyfriend and decides to declare her love to him. Insofar as the warrior's initiation into a war for the sake of love means putting his life at stake and fully engaging in and affecting other people's lives, it can be seen as a revolution. And this sort of revolution—symbolized in "Heinrich's Heart" by the hearts that self-immolate—is, metaphorically speaking, something like an eruption of excessive energy and an impulse toward social change. For this reason, the day that Yeong-sin in "Bastille Day" finally decides to declare her love to her boyfriend falls on Bastille Day, the anniversary of the start of the French Revolution. Since Kim Kyung-uk compares the theme of love with various forms of social upheaval, it is not surprising that we find stories like "The Runner," "Ninety-Nine Percent," and "God Has No Grandchildren" together with "The Queen of Romance" and "Bastille Day" in the same collection.

Your Neighbor's Cheek

A prominent element in "The Runner," and the one that first catches the reader's attention, is the anxiety and jumpiness that the main character and his student show as they ride together on a bicycle alongside the Han River. If we explore what underlies their feelings of anxiety, we realize they are rooted in the reality of the social structure, as symbolically represented in the following scene:

Across the river stood a series of identical apartment blocks that looked as if they had been made in a mold. They were like the walls of an impenetrable fortress, with the river as a moat. On the other side of the deep, wide moat and beyond the tall, strong wall stood Eun-jae's apartment. Inside the fortress were the school Eun-jae attended, the private tutoring centers she went to, and the department stores and restaurants she frequented.

The apartment blocks of the rich neighborhoods of Apgujeong-dong and Cheongdam-dong in Gangnam are like a fortress that excludes outsiders. We see how true this is when the protagonist goes to give his student a private lesson and is interrogated by the security guard before finally being allowed up to her apartment. Until he can provide a satisfactory answer to each of the security guard's questions—"Which apartment are you visiting? What is the purpose of your visit? What is the name of your student?"—he is insistently treated "with suspicion." The security guard's obvious suspicion represents the wealthy residents' belief that people from outside their impenetrable fortress are a threat to the social structure that protects and guarantees their private property. Given that the haves' private property is based on their monopoly of the means of production and their constant efforts to perpetuate the current socio-economic order, it could be said that their ownership of private property verges on crime. The haves' misgivings about their ill-gotten gains, plus their hostility toward the have-nots, makes them wary of those who are not affluent. That being the case, the haves attempt to subsume their criminality into a new order and subsequently scrutinize and suspect anyone who appears to threaten that order. Thus the wealthy residents of the impenetrable fortress are constantly anxious and suspicious of people from the outside. The episodes and scenes depicted in "The Runner" all emblematically reflect the paranoia of the wealthy.

In this social context, it is somewhat predictable that the protagonist's date with a teenage girl from the stronghold of the wealthy will involve anxiety and restlessness from the outset. It's not that they are actually at risk of attack by criminals that roam around outside the fortress, but that they are possessed by the delusion—a delusion promulgated by the haves—that anyone they encounter outside the fortress is a potential criminal. While they are constantly haunted by "a suspect in the kidnapping and murder of a series of women in upscale villas and apartment complexes throughout Gangnam"—particularly because the latest victim lived near the female protagonist—the series of events that they experience seem ominous. At one point they are shocked to see a motorcycle pass by dragging a dog behind it. Then a man with a snake tattoo runs right behind them—to their alarm because earlier this same man kept looking at Eun-jae's legs. Even when they get off the bike to have a snack, they are disturbed by a gang of delinquent boys throwing stones at people for fun.

Anyone who looks enviously in the direction of the wealthy enclave can be reduced to a criminal by the prosperous but suspicious residents inside. The protagonist is no exception. Therefore, as he tries to escape what he pessimistically imagines will happen due to the failure of his date with his student from the fortress— that he will end up being accused of kidnapping a teenage girl and stealing a bicycle and a paddle boat—the protagonist, pursued by his delusion that the tattooed man is chasing him to kill him, should not have headed toward the Gangnam towers. For he will not be admitted by the inhabitants of the fortress, because have-nots like him cannot penetrate the stronghold. The last sentence of the story seems to point to his fate: "The other side of the river was still very far away."

While "The Runner" depicts a psychologically and morally murky urban reality, "Ninety-Nine Percent" reflects the subconscious of urban people who are hounded by their own twisted desires. Choi, the protagonist of this story, is crushed by groundless jealousy and his inferiority complex when Steve Kim, a new recruit to the advertising agency where Choi works, usurps everything that Choi has formerly enjoyed. As Kim becomes more and more influential because of his social skills and eloquence, Choi develops the delusional notion that Kim is someone he knew in high school and who was far less successful than him. He traces everything that he notices about Steve Kim back to what he recalls about his high school classmate, Kim Tae-man, and he tries to identify one with the other. In Choi's mind, the two men have more in common than coincidence can explain. They are both left-handed, and both have a bigger left foot than right. Besides, Steve Kim's real name, Kim Hyeon-bin, is the name Kim Tae-man used to use when he wrote to his pen pal. Is Steve Kim really the Kim Tae-man whom Choi remembers beating out of the position of top student, and whose father no one in the town knew about and whose mother ran a bar? Is Steve Kim really Kim Tae-man, who has now whitewashed his troubled past and concealed his true identity?

If we read these episodes only in terms of whether or not Steve Kim is really Kim Tae-man, we end up reading the story as a mystery. The significance of "Ninety-Nine Percent" lies elsewhere. The way Choi incessantly questions Steve Kim's identity and his past is pathological, regardless of whether or not Steve Kim is really Kim Tae-man. The obsessive nature of Choi's suspicion is what the reader is supposed to focus on. While Choi agrees that Steve Kim looks totally different from Kim Tae-man, he cannot shake off his hunch and assumes that Steve Kim has had plastic surgery to change his appearance. Choi's suspicions will never go away, even if he finds that Steve Kim does not have the same anchor tattoo that he is sure Kim Tae-man must have had. He will continue to harbor doubts about Steve Kim, wrongly believing that he must have had the tattoo removed. Recollecting how he was more successful than Kim Tae-man, he subconsciously hopes his narcissistic fantasy will replace the unbearably hurtful reality—that Steve Kim is the most competent and important person in the agency—because he desperately needs to believe he is still number one. Choi is unable to accept the fact that he isn't the center of "the look of envy and esteem" that always used to follow him.

Envy and esteem are the underlying agents of Choi's pathological suspicion and ironically, envy and esteem are the driving forces that impel those who aspire to be envied and esteemed. But the admiration of others cannot fix the absurd system that limits the limelight to just the very few; rather, the system feeds off it. The "complicated envy" of the "ninety-nine percent who despise the one percent but at the same time want to belong to it" is the driving force of this absurd system. This idea is what the title of the story "Ninety-Nine Percent" suggests.

The protagonist of "God Has No Grandchildren," the title story of the collection, seems ready to topple this absurd system. When he finds out that his grade-school-aged granddaughter has been molested by three male classmates and realizes that the authorities don't "hold offenders under age thirteen or their parents criminally liable for assault," his sincerely-held religious and moral beliefs constitute a temptation for him. The proposal by the school principal, who intends to hush up the incident, challenges the protagonist's religious belief.

> Brother, remember what our Lord Jesus says: love your enemy. Isn't it true that the little boys did what they did without really knowing what they were doing? What did Jesus say when he was nailed to the cross and died? Father, forgive them; they know not what they do. Brother, please forgive them all, and let the glorious will of God shine brightly on this world. Hallelujah.

If the man "forgives" the boys, he will fulfill the teachings of Jesus, as the principal's biblical citations assert. What can be more tempting for the man, as a faithful Christian, than fulfilling the teachings of Jesus by extending his forgiveness? In addition, he is offered a compensation of six million won by the boys' parents. Given that his gas has been disconnected and his water and electricity are also soon going to be cut off, and that he and his granddaughter are seriously ill, he desperately needs the money, which is a significant amount. For the sake of his injured granddaughter at least, he should forgive the boys and take the money. This is the moral challenge that he faces. By doing what he ought to according

to what his religion and society demand, he will be able to acknowledge that he has done his best to be just and right. However,
the man does not obey these shallow dictates.

> "What do you want me to do, Father? . . . I'm going to roll the
> dice. If my lucky number comes up, I'll keep the money."
> The man took the dice out of his pocket. There were two
> of them; their edges were worn and shiny. One die had one
> dot on each of the six sides, and the other had six dots on
> all six sides . . .
> The man tossed the dice high into the air . . . He frowned
> as he looked at the dice. One die was a six, but the other
> nothing; the dot had worn off . . .
> "Father, have mercy on this little lamb. Satan tempted
> me. I'll do your bidding."

Throwing the dice and interpreting the number that comes up,
the old man concludes that he should not accept the offer from
the boys' parents. By deciding to roll the dice and interpret the result himself, he seems to be determined to follow his ultimate free
will, rather that the religious or moral code that has been imposed
upon him. In this situation, which he himself has brought about,
he faces God directly and determines his own course of action.
And what he concludes is what the enigmatic title, "God Has
No Grandchildren," suggests: there cannot and should not be a
mediator between man and God. Even the priest of the Catholic Church can't intercede for us. If the father in the Catholic
Church is our father, then are we God's grandchildren? Are we,
because we are sure we have lived like innocent lambs guided by
the Catholic Father, therefore exempt from God's last judgment
since He is our grandfather? If we want to be true followers of
Jesus Christ or to be true Christians, we shouldn't remain the
grandchildren of God, we should be His children. In an absolute
or exclusive relationship with God—even if it means we have to
endure being social outcasts—we try to transcend our socially
constructed ego, and listen to the ultimate intention of God and

His furious call for justice. This is what the molested girl's grandfather hears from deep within himself, and this is what he concludes. Obeying what he hears directly, he gives the six-million-won payoff back to the principal and sets out for revenge.

What does it mean to hear God's furious call for justice? Does it suggest "God Has No Grandchildren" is a story about a man's vengeance? No, it does not. As the molested girl's grandfather sets about punishing her offenders, he in fact practices love, in the true sense of the word, which fulfills the calling of Christianity. Let's take an example. If someone we love doesn't understand and therefore cannot follow the ultimate message of Christianity, we should challenge that which hinders their understanding. We must uncover the reason for their ignorance, break it down, and finally purge them of it. In this sense, *agape* love, the love decreed by Christianity, is hard to understand from the secular perspective (Kierkegaard's *Works of Love*). Jesus even says "Do you think I came to bring peace on earth? No, I tell you, but division" (Luke 12:51). So we must attempt to understand what Jesus really means by the command, "Love your enemies." It shouldn't mean you have to leave your neighbor alone no matter what they do, and forgive them for whatever they do to you. If your neighbor is your enemy because you believe he or she is ignorant of the ultimate message of Christianity and lives far from it, you should slap them on the left cheek and then on the right as well, to help them to grasp the message and live up to it. This is the only way for us to love our neighbors and enemies. Thus, "God Has No Grandchildren" is a story about love, not revenge, paradoxical though that may seem.

At the beginning of "God Has No Grandchildren" there are four different scenes that start with the same phrase. Three of the four scenes share the common image of penetration: "There was a hole beside the doorknob and the deadbolt was unlocked"; "the lock had been torn off the classroom door"; "The keyhole had been reamed out." If we connect the image of penetration with how the protagonist prepares himself before he goes to the boys' apartments to take action and how he feels about his upcoming mission, what it represents becomes clear. By the time we learn why the deadbolt was unlocked and the holes were drilled, we also realize the man has infiltrated the apartment building management office and the other locations not just to get information about the boys' apartments. By penetrating the defenses of his enemies' camps, he not only symbolically penetrates the closed individual worlds of detached people, but also the hidden lairs of egos and twisted desires, the refuges of people whose religious beliefs and ideas of social morality have ossified. In general, the man is forcing a way into the dark hideouts where those people imprison themselves.

In *God Has No Grandchildren*, hesitant and indecisive free agents develop until they finally decide to engage in their own lives and the lives of the people around them. Some eventually encounter their authentic selves, some are ready to embark on a true love that borders on revolutionary. As we readers trace their psychological journey into maturity, we sympathize with them, and we feel the shock of being slapped on the cheek by someone who does not hesitate to engage in his neighbors' lives.

About the Author

KIM KYUNG-UK was born in Gwangju, South Jella Province, South Korea, and is a professor of creative writing at the Korea National University of Arts. His novella Outsider received the Jak Ga Se Gey Best New Writer Award.

About the Translators

KANG SUNOK earned her MA in English and is currently studying for an MA (honors) in Macquarie University, Sydney, Australia.

MELISSA THOMSON earned her PhD in English from Trinity College, Dublin, and is the co-author of four books.

KIM JOO-YOUNG
STINGRAY
Translated by Inrae You Vinciguerra
and Louis Vinciguerra

"Stingray should be savored, read slowly ... the author has managed a perfect reproduction of the way people spoke in the late pre-modern era, relying on circumlocution rather than direct statement ... the beauty of silence and metaphor both are presented wonderfully due to the author's exquisite craftsmanship." —*Donga Ilbo*

Hailed by critics, *Stingray* has been described by its author as "a critical biography of my loving mother." With his father having abandoned his family for another woman, little Se-young and his mother are forced to subsist on their own in the harsh environment of a small Korean farming village in the 1950s. Determined to wait for her husband's return, Se-young's mother hangs a dried stingray on the kitchen doorjamb; to her, it's a reminder of the fact that she still has a husband, and that she must behave as a married woman would, despite all. Also, she claims, when the family is reunited, the fish will be their first, celebratory meal together. But when a beggar girl, Sam-rae, sneaks into their house during a blizzard, the first thing she does is eat the stingray, and what follows is a struggle, at once sentimental and ideological, for the soul of the household.

Available at **www.dalkeyarchive.com**

HYUN KI-YOUNG
ONE SPOON ON THIS EARTH
Translated by Jennifer M. Lee

"This novel is one of the most outstanding bildungsromans in the history of Korean literature, showing us the ways in which a human being interacts with history ..." —*Hankook Ilbo*

An autobiographical novel that takes a life to pieces, putting forward not a coherent, straightforward narrative, but a series of dazzling images ranging from the ordinary to the unbelievable, fished from the depths of the author's memory as well as from the stream of his day-to-day life as an adult author. Interweaving flashes of the horrific Jeju Uprising and the Korean War with pleasant family anecdotes, stories of schoolroom cruelty, and bizarre digressions into his personal mythology, *One Spoon on this Earth* stands a sort of digest of contemporary Korean history as it might be seen through the lens of one man's life and opinions.

Available at **www.dalkeyarchive.com**

LIBRARY OF KOREAN LITERATURE, VOL. 3

JANG JUNG-IL
WHEN ADAM OPENS HIS EYES
Translated by Hwang Sun-ae and Horace Jeffery Hodges

"Jang Jung-il's debut in the early 1990s was a literary and social 'event.'" —*SisaIN*

First published in 1990, this is a sensational and highly controversial novel by one of Korea's most electrifying contemporary authors. A preposterous coming-of-age story, melding sex, death, and high school in a manner reminiscent of some perverse collision between Georges Bataille and Beverly Cleary, the narrator of this book plows through contemporaneous Korean mores with aplomb, bound for destruction, or maturity—whichever comes first.

Available at **www.dalkeyarchive.com**

LIBRARY OF KOREAN LITERATURE, VOL. 4

JUNG MI-KYUNG
MY SON'S GIRLFRIEND
Translated by Yu Young-nan

"Characterized by delicate and detailed portrayals, along with psychological details reminiscent of the classic Victorian novels … [Jung Mi-kyung's] work has a feverish intensity, rejecting comfortable paternalism and systematized compromise."

— *Hankook Ilbo*

"The greatest beauty of Jung Mi-kyung's works is that they deal with our lives, happening in this place, in this time …"

— *Kukmin Ilbo*

At once an ironic portrayal of contemporary Korea and an intimate exploration of heartache, alienation, and nostalgia, this collection of seven short stories has earned the author widespread critical acclaim. With empathy and an overarching melancholy that is at times tinged with sarcasm but always deeply meaningful, Jung explores the ambition and chaos of urban life, the lives of the lost and damaged souls it creates, and the subtle shades of love found between them.

Available at **www.dalkeyarchive.com**

KIM WON-IL
THE HOUSE WITH A SUNKEN COURTYARD
Translated by Suh Ji-moon

"Through the vivid and detailed description of . . . folk cultures in the aftermath of the Korean war, *The House with a Sunken Courtyard* is considered the representative work of contemporary Korean literature." —Maeil Shinmun

An occasionally terrifying and always vivid portrayal of what it was like to live as a refugee immediately after the end of the Korean War. This novel is based on the author's own experience in his early teens in Daegu, in 1954, and depicts six families that survive the hard times together in the same house, weathering the tiny conflicts of interest and rivalries that spring up in such close quarters, but nonetheless offering one another sympathy and encouragement as fellow sufferers of the same national misfortune: brothers and sisters in privation.

Available at **www.dalkeyarchive.com**

LIBRARY OF KOREAN LITERATURE, VOL. 7

LEE KI-HO
AT LEAST WE CAN APOLOGIZE
Translated by Christopher Joseph Dykas

"Do you want to laugh? do you want to cry? Read Lee Ki-ho
... He is the weathervane of Korean fiction in the 2000s."
—Park Bum-shin

This story focuses on an agency whose only purpose is to offer
apologies—for a fee—on behalf of its clients. This seemingly
insignificant service leads us into an examination of sin, guilt,
and the often irrational demands of society. A kaleidoscope
of minor nuisances and major grievances, this novel heralds a
new comic voice in Korean letters.

Available at **www.dalkeyarchive.com**

Library of Korean Literature, vol. 8

Yi Kwang-su
The Soil
Translated by Hwang Sun-ae and Horace Jeffery Hodges

"Matching the fame of its author, who is perhaps the most studied fiction writer in the history of modern Korean literature, *The Soil* is in the center of numerous academic and critical discussions, debates about nationalism, philosophical literature, agrarian literature, pro-Japanese literature ... literary theory and the history of literature itself." —Moonji Publishing

A major, never before translated novel by the author of *Mujông/ The Heartless*—often called the first modern Korean novel— *The Soil* tells the story of an idealist dedicating his life to helping the inhabitants of the rural community in which he was raised. Striving to influence the poor farmers of the time to improve their lots, become self-reliant, and thus indirectly change the reality of colonial life on the Korean peninsula, *The Soil* was vitally important to the social movements of the time, echoing the effects and reception of such English-language novels as Upton Sinclair's *The Jungle*.

Available at **www.dalkeyarchive.com**

PARK WAN-SUH
LONESOME YOU
Translated by Elizabeth Haejin Yoon

"These nine short stories are about the loneliness and compassion of the unavoidable and unattractive. But they are also about the flavor of living …" —*Hankook Ilbo*

Well before her death in 2011, Park Wan-Suh had established herself as a canonical figure in Korean literature. Her work—often based upon her own personal experiences, and showing keen insight into divisive social issues from the Korean partition to the position of women in Korean society—has touched readers for over forty years. In this collection, meditations upon life in old age come to the fore—at its best, accompanied by great beauty and compassion; at its worst by a cynicism that nonetheless turns a bitter smile upon the changing world.

Available at **www.dalkeyarchive.com**

JANG EUN-JIN
NO ONE WRITES BACK
Translated by Jung Yewon

"Like a fairy tale, a picaresque story whose imagery will linger ... even without any sensational plot points, this novel grabs you and forces you to read till the end." — *Donga Ilbo*

"This novel resembles a strange letter, a letter that takes its time traveling from sender to receiver ... and winds up breaking your heart." — *Cine 21*

Communication — or the lack thereof — is the subject of this sly update of the picaresque. *No One Writes Back* is the story of a young man who leaves home with only his blind dog, an MP3 player, and a book, traveling aimlessly for three years, from motel to motel, meeting people on the road. Rather than learn the names of his fellow travelers — or invent nicknames for them — he assigns them numbers. There's 239, for example, who once dreamed of being a poet, but who now only reads her poems to a friend in a coma; there's 109, who rides trains endlessly because of a broken heart; and 32, who's already decided to commit suicide. The narrator writes letters to these men and women in the hope that he can console them in their various miseries, as well as keep a record of his own experiences: "A letter is like a journal entry for me, except that it gets sent to other people." No one writes back, of course, but that doesn't mean that there isn't some hope that one of them will, some-day ...

Available at **www.dalkeyarchive.com**